THE MAN WITHOUT A COUNTRY
& other stories

THE MAN WITHOUT A COUNTRY

& other tales

Edward E. Hale

WORDSWORTH AMERICAN LIBRARY

The paper in this book is produced from pure wood
pulp, without the use of chlorine or any other substance
harmful to the environment. The energy used in its
production consists almost entirely of hydroelectricity
and heat generated from waste material, thereby
conserving fossil fuels and contributing little to the
greenhouse effect.

This edition published 1995 by
Wordsworth Editions Limited
Cumberland House, Crib Street
Ware, Hertfordshire SG12 9ET

ISBN 1 85326 558 6

Typeset in the UK by Antony Gray
Printed and bound in Denmark by Nørhaven

INTRODUCTION

Edward Everett Hale (1822–1909) was the son of Nathan Hale, owner and editor of the *Daily Advertiser*, at that time the only daily newspaper in New England. Edward grew up in an atmosphere of journalistic activity; moreover, throughout much of his life his home town, Boston, was the centre of literary activity in the country. He would have met in his father's house such eminent literary figures as James Russell Lowell, Henry W. Longfellow and Daniel Webster. But, because of his strong religious feelings, Edward chose to become a minister, rising in his profession to become the pastor of the South Congregational Church in Boston. He was a leading activist in the anti-slavery movement and later in the Chautuaqua school movement. Yet along with all these activities he was the author of over sixty books, one of his favourite modes of expression being the short story.

As one might expect from his background, Hale's fiction was designed to convey a message as well as to entertain. He once wrote out for a friend his basic rules for writing fiction: one, know what you want to say; two, say it; three, use your own language; four, leave out all fine passages; five, a short word is better than a long one; six, the fewer words, other things being equal, the better; seven, cut it to pieces.

Of his best known short story, 'A Man Without a Country', one can safely say that no other American short story ever achieved such widespread fame so swiftly. This extraordinary fame was due to certain historical factors as much as to the author's talent, for this story was written in the midst of the Civil War which threatened to sever the unity of the nation. As a consequence, the importance of patriotism had never been more in the public mind. In a sense 'A Man Without a Country' was a writer's response to that public mood. But since patriotism is a recurrent phenomenon, it is likely that the appeal of this unique work will remain timeless.

Specifically, the story was written in response to an actual situation. In 1863, an ex-Congressman from Ohio by the name of Vallandigham had made a vitriolic speech against the Federal government for which he had been arrested and sentenced to jail. However, Lincoln changed the sentence to deportation back into Confederate territory. When some of Vallandigham's sympathisers nominated him for governor of Ohio, Hale was so incensed that he wrote 'The Man Without a Country' to illustrate how a man exiled from his country for life would eventually come to realize how much his country meant to him. In the story the protagonist's name is Nolan, and his crime is that during some amateur army theatricals he, like Vallandigham, makes some scurrilous remarks about the Federal government that result in his being court-martialled and sentenced to eternal exile from his native land through confinement in one of the nation's navy vessels. Great care is taken that no one even utters the *name* of Nolan's country in his presence.

Throughout the long years of his exile Nolan is shifted from one ship to another, his only break from this limited existence being some guarded outings in various ports to which the vessels come for renewal of their supplies. It is a brilliant conception for a short story that is, to this day, capable of keeping a reader engrossed to the final sentence. What is particularly impressive is the variety of devices Hale uses to intensify the reader's illusion that he is reading an account of something that really happened and the inventiveness with which Hale thinks up interesting situations which tighten the screws on Nolan's remorse.

In his second most famous story, 'My Double and How He Undid Me', Hale writes about an unfortunate pastor who laments the way the lives of pastors are cluttered up by the endless, insufferably boring functions in which they have to participate. To use his own colourful style –

> . . . there were pitchforked in on us a great rowen-heap of humbugs, handed down from some unknown seed-time . . .

Driven to desperation, the pastor longs for a double to take his place in the boring half of his life. In a visit to the Monson Poorhouse to his astonishment he finds his exact replica, a poor, miserable, not-very-bright wretch with the same 'brickbat' scar over his right eyebrow. He takes the fellow home, cleans him up, provides him with outfits from his own wardrobe, gets him to memorise half a dozen one-sentence responses to use for almost any situation in which he will find himself, and sends him out to act as his double at all those boring functions that have been the pastor's nightmare. Needless to say, the double carries out his assignments with hilarious success and, in the course of describing these successes, Hale manages to ridicule a good deal of human pomposity, vanity and general tediousness. But inevitably, in an ingeniously conceived climax, the double manages in a tight situation before the governor of the state and many other bigwigs to do and say things so unseemly for a pastor as to undo him in the eyes of the world. But is he really undone? Well, that is the question Hale leaves us with at the end of this delightful little masterpiece.

The appeal of Hale's short story 'Christmas Waits in Boston' lies in its vivid recreation of a ritual which still awakens nostalgia – a Christmas sleigh-ride. What makes this sleigh-ride special is the route it follows through the streets of old Boston.

A romantic story of special interest concerns two young people, Julia and George, who are in love but whose chances of ever getting married seem hopeless due to the restrictions the girl's grandfather has placed on the kind of suitor he will let her marry. Hale provides a most unusual twist to this familiar Victorian theme. George is a newspaper editor very much on top of the news coming in of a revolution in South America that has resulted in the blockade of certain key ports. This blockade is a disaster for the grandfather who is in the shipping business and stands to lose a fortune as a result of it. With his inside knowledge about how the blockade will ultimately result in large profits instead of losses to exporters, George has an idea of how he can become in the old fellow's mind the perfect suitor for his granddaughter. How this plan works out provides both suspense and amusement.

Finally, anyone who read the tremendous bestseller a number of years ago about the epic escape of the explorer Ernest Shackleton and his crew in a rowing boat from their ship frozen in the Antarctic ice-cap will look forward to reading Hale's 'The Last Voyage of the Resolute' and will not be disappointed.

Dr Douglas R. Angus
Professor of English Emeritus
St Lawrence University

FURTHER READING

John R. Adams. *Edward Everett Hale*, Boston: Twayne Publishers, c. 1977

Edward Everett Hale, *The Life and Letters*, Boston: Little, Brown and Company, 1917

Edward Everett Hale, *A New England Boyhood*, Boston: Little Brown and Company, 1915

Jean Holloway, *Edward Everett Hale: A Biography*, Austin: University of Texas Press, 1956

Russell A. Sharp, Introduction to *The Man Without a Country*, The Riverside Literature Series, Boston: Houghton Mifflin Company, c. 1923

CONTENTS

THE MAN WITHOUT A COUNTRY
& other tales

The Man Without a Country

FROM THE INGHAM PAPERS

This story was written in the summer of 1863, as a contribution, however humble, towards the formation of a just and true national sentiment, or sentiment of love to the nation. It was at the time when Mr Vallandigham had been sent across the border. It was my wish, indeed, that the story might be printed before the autumn elections of that year – as my 'testimony' regarding the principles involved in them – but circumstances delayed its publication till the December number of the Atlantic appeared.

It is wholly a fiction, 'founded on fact'. The facts on which it is founded are these – that Aaron Burr sailed down the Mississippi River in 1805, again in 1806, and was tried for treason in 1807. The rest, with one exception to be noticed, is all fictitious.

It was my intention that the story should have been published with no author's name, other than that of Captain Frederic Ingham, USN. Whether writing under his name or my own, I have taken no liberties with history other than such as every writer of fiction is privileged to take – indeed, must take, if fiction is to be written at all.

The story having been once published, it passed out of my hands. From that moment it has gradually acquired different accessories, for which I am not responsible. Thus I have heard it said, that at one bureau of the Navy Department they say that Nolan was pardoned, in fact, and returned home to die. At another bureau, I am told, the answer to questions is, that, though it is true that an officer was kept abroad all his life, his name was not Nolan. A venerable friend of mine in Boston, who discredits all tradition, still recollects this 'Nolan court-martial'. One of the most accurate of my younger friends had noticed Nolan's death in the newspaper, but recollected 'that it was in September, and not in August'. A lady in Baltimore writes me, I believe in good faith, that Nolan has two widowed sisters residing in that neighbourhood. A correspondent of the Philadelphia Despatch *believed 'the article untrue, as the United States corvette* Levant *was lost at sea nearly three years since, between San Francisco and San*

Juan'. I may remark that this uncertainty as to the place of her loss rather adds to the probability of her turning up after three years in Lat. 2° 11' S., Long. 131° W. A writer in the New Orleans Picayune, *in a careful historical paper, explained at length that I had been mistaken all through; that Philip Nolan never went to sea, but to Texas; that there he was shot in battle, 21 March 1801, and by orders from Spain every fifth man of his party was to be shot, had they not died in prison. Fortunately, however, he left his papers and maps, which fell into the hands of a friend of the* Picayune's *correspondent. This friend proposes to publish them – and the public will then have, it is to be hoped, the true history of Philip Nolan, the man without a country.*

With all these continuations, however, I have nothing to do. I can only repeat that my Philip Nolan is pure fiction. I cannot send his scrapbook to my friend who asks for it, because I have it not to send.

I remembered, when I was collecting material for my story, that in General Wilkinson's galimatias, which he calls his 'Memoirs', is frequent reference to a business partner of his, of the name of Nolan, who, in the very beginning of this century, was killed in Texas. Whenever Wilkinson found himself in rather a deeper bog than usual, he used to justify himself by saying that he could not explain such or such a charge because 'the papers referring to it were lost when Mr Nolan was imprisoned in Texas'. Finding this mythical character in the mythical legends of a mythical time, I took the liberty to give him a cousin, rather more mythical, whose adventures should be on the seas. I had the impression that Wilkinson's friend was named Stephen – and as such I spoke of him in the early editions of this story. But long after this was printed, I found that the New Orleans paper was right in saying that the Texan hero was named Philip Nolan.

If I had forgotten him and his name, I can only say that Mr Jefferson, who did not forget him, abandoned him and his – when the Spanish government murdered him and imprisoned his associates for life. I have done my best to repair my fault, and to recall to memory a brave man, by telling the story of his fate, in a book called Philip Nolan's Friends. *To the historical statements in that book the reader is referred. That the Texan Philip Nolan played an important, though forgotten, part in our national history, the reader will understand – when I say that the terror of the Spanish government, excited by his adventures, governed all their policy regarding Texas and Louisiana also, till the last territory was no longer their own.*

If any reader considers the invention of a cousin too great a liberty to

*take in fiction, I venture to remind him that ' 'tis sixty years since';
and that I should have the highest authority in literature even for
much greater liberties taken with annals so far removed from our
time.*

*A Boston paper, in noticing the story of 'My Double', contained in
another part of this collection, said it was highly* improbable. *I have
always agreed with that critic. I confess I have the same opinion of this
story of Philip Nolan. It passes on ships which had no existence, is
vouched for by officers who never lived. Its hero is in two or three places
at the same time, under a process wholly impossible under any
conceivable administration of affairs. In reply, therefore, to a kind
adviser in Connecticut, who told me that the story must be apologised
for, because it was doing great injury to the national cause by asserting
such continued cruelty of the Federal government through a half-
century, I must be permitted to say that the public, being the Supreme
Court of the United States, 'may be supposed to know something'.*

E. E. H.
28 October 1876

I suppose that very few casual readers of the New York *Herald* of
13 August observed, in an obscure corner, among the 'Deaths', the
announcement –

NOLAN. Died, on board US corvette *Levant*, Lat. 2° 11' S.,
Long. 131° W., on the 11th of May, PHILIP NOLAN.

I happened to observe it, because I was stranded at the old Mission-
House in Mackinaw, waiting for a Lake Superior steamer which did not
choose to come, and I was devouring to the very stubble all the current
literature I could get hold of, even down to the deaths and marriages in
the *Herald*. My memory for names and people is good, and the reader
will see, as be goes on, that I had reason enough to remember Philip
Nolan. There are hundreds of readers who would have paused at that
announcement, if the officer of the *Levant* who reported it had chosen
to make it thus – 'Died, 11 May, THE MAN WITHOUT A COUNTRY.'
For it was as the 'man without a country' that poor Philip Nolan had
generally been known by the officers who had him in charge during
some fifty years, as, indeed, by all the men who sailed under them. I
dare say there is many a man who has taken wine with him once a
fortnight, in a three years' cruise, who never knew that his name was

'Nolan', or whether the poor wretch had any name at all.

There can now be no possible harm in telling this poor creature's story. Reason enough there has been till now, ever since Madison's administration went out in 1817, for very strict secrecy, the secrecy of honour itself, among the gentlemen of the navy who have had Nolan in successive charge. And certainly it speaks well for the *esprit de corps* of the profession, and the personal honour of its members, that to the press this man's story has been wholly unknown – and, I think, to the country at large also. I have reason to think, from some investigations I made in the Naval Archives when I was attached to the Bureau of Construction, that every official report relating to him was burned when Ross burned the public buildings at Washington. One of the Tuckers, or possibly one of the Watsons, had Nolan in charge at the end of the war; and when, on returning from his cruise, he reported at Washington to one of the Crowninshields – who was in the Navy Department when he came home – he found that the Department ignored the whole business. Whether they really knew nothing about it or whether it was a '*Non mi ricordo*', determined on as a piece of policy, I do not know. But this I do know, that since 1817, and possibly before, no naval officer has mentioned Nolan in his report of a cruise.

But, as I say, there is no need for secrecy any longer. And now the poor creature is dead, it seems to me worth while to tell a little of his story, by way of showing young Americans of today what it is to be a 'man without a country'.

Philip Nolan was as fine a young officer as there was in the 'Legion of the West', as the Western division of our army was then called. When Aaron Burr made his first dashing expedition down to New Orleans in 1805, at Fort Massac, or somewhere above on the river, he met, as the Devil would have it, this gay, dashing, bright young fellow, at some dinner-party, I think. Burr marked him, talked to him, walked with him, took him a day or two's voyage in his flat-boat, and, in short, fascinated him. For the next year, barrack-life was very tame to poor Nolan. He occasionally availed himself of the permission the great man had given him to write to him. Long, high-worded, stilted letters the poor boy wrote and rewrote and copied. But never a line did he have in reply from the gay deceiver. The other boys in the garrison sneered at him, because he sacrificed in this unrequited affection for a politician the time which they devoted to Monongahela, hazard, and high-low-jack. Bourbon, euchre, and poker were still unknown. But one day Nolan had his revenge. This time Burr came down the river, not as an attorney seeking a place for his office, but as a disguised conqueror. He had defeated I know not how many district-attorneys; he had dined at I know not how many public dinners; he had been heralded in I know not how many *Weekly Arguses*, and it was rumoured that he had an army behind him and an empire before him. It was a great day – his arrival – to poor Nolan. Burr had not been at the fort an hour before he sent for him. That evening he asked Nolan to take him out in his skiff, to show him a canebrake or a cotton-wood tree, as he said – really to seduce him; and by the time the sail was over, Nolan was enlisted body and soul. From that time, though he did not yet know it, he lived as a 'man without a country'.

What Burr meant to do I know no more than you, dear reader. It is none of our business just now. Only, when the grand catastrophe came, and Jefferson and the House of Virginia of that day undertook to break on the wheel all the possible Clarences of the then House of York, by the great treason-trial at Richmond, some of the lesser fry in that distant Mississippi Valley, which was farther from us than Puget's Sound is today, introduced the like novelty on their provincial stage, and, to while away the monotony of the summer at Fort Adams, got up, for *spectacles*, a string of court-martials on the officers there. One and another of the colonels and majors were tried, and, to fill out the list, little Nolan, against whom, Heaven knows, there was evidence enough – that he was sick of the service, had been willing to be false to it, and would have obeyed any order to march any-whither with anyone who would follow him had the order been signed, 'By command of His Exc. A. Burr.' The courts dragged on. The big flies escaped – rightly for all I know. Nolan was proved guilty enough, as I say; yet you and I would never have heard of him, reader, but that, when the president of the court asked him at the close, whether he wished to say anything to show that he had always been faithful to the United States, he cried out, in a fit of frenzy –

'Damn the United States! I wish I may never hear of the United States again!'

I suppose he did not know how the words shocked old Colonel Morgan, who was holding the court. Half the officers who sat in it had served through the Revolution, and their lives, not to say their necks, had been risked for the very idea which he so cavalierly cursed in his madness. He, on his part, had grown up in the West of those days, in the midst of 'Spanish plot', 'Orleans plot', and all the rest. He had been educated on a plantation where the finest company was a Spanish officer or a French merchant from Orleans. His education, such as it was, had been perfected in commercial expeditions to Vera Cruz, and I think he told me his father once hired an Englishman to be a private tutor for a winter on the plantation. He had spent half his youth with an older brother, hunting horses in Texas; and, in a word, to him 'United States' was scarcely a reality. Yet he had been fed by 'United States' for all the years since he had been in the army. He had sworn on his faith as a Christian to be true to 'United States'. It was 'United States' which gave him the uniform he wore, and the sword by his side. Nay, my poor Nolan, it was only because 'United States' had picked you out first as one of her own confidential men of honour that 'A. Burr' cared for you a straw more than for the flat-boat men who sailed his ark for him. I do not excuse Nolan; I only explain to the reader why he damned his country, and wished he might never hear her name again.

He never did hear her name but once again. From that moment, 23 September 1807, till the day he died, 11 May 1863, he never heard her name again. For that half-century and more he was a man without a country.

Old Morgan, as I said, was terribly shocked. If Nolan had compared George Washington to Benedict Arnold, or had cried, 'God save King George', Morgan would not have felt worse. He called the court into his private room, and returned in fifteen minutes, with a face like a sheet, to say –

'Prisoner, hear the sentence of the Court! The Court decides, subject to the approval of the President, that you never hear the name of the United States again.'

Nolan laughed. But nobody else laughed. Old Morgan was too solemn, and the whole room was hushed dead as night for a minute. Even Nolan lost his swagger in a moment. Then Morgan added –

'Mr Marshal, take the prisoner to Orleans in an armed boat, and deliver him to the naval commander there.'

The Marshal gave his orders and the prisoner was taken out of court.

'Mr Marshal,' continued old Morgan, 'see that no one mentions the United States to the prisoner. Mr Marshal, make my respects to Lieutenant Mitchell at Orleans, and request him to order that no one shall mention the United States to the prisoner while he is on board ship. You will receive your written orders from the officer on duty here this evening. The court is adjourned without day.'

I have always supposed that Colonel Morgan himself took the proceedings of the court to Washington City, and explained them to Mr Jefferson. Certain it is that the President approved them – certain, that is, if I may believe the men who say they have seen his signature.

Before the *Nautilus* got round from New Orleans to the Northern Atlantic coast with the prisoner on board the sentence had been approved, and he was a man without a country.

The plan then adopted was substantially the same which was necessarily followed ever after. Perhaps it was suggested by the necessity of sending him by water from Fort Adams and Orleans. The Secretary of the Navy – it must have been the first Crowninshield, though he is a man I do not remember – was requested to put Nolan on board a government vessel bound on a long cruise, and to direct that he should be only so far confined there as to make it certain that he never saw or heard of the country. We had few long cruises then, and the navy was very much out of favour; and as almost all of this story is traditional, as I have explained, I do not know certainly what his first cruise was. But the commander to whom he was entrusted – perhaps it was Tingey or Shaw, though I think it was one of the younger men – we are all old enough now – regulated the etiquette and the precautions of the affair, and according to his scheme they were carried out, I suppose, till Nolan died.

When I was second officer of the *Intrepid*, some thirty years after, I saw the original paper of instructions. I have been sorry ever since that I did not copy the whole of it. It ran, however, much in this way –

Washington
(with a date, which must have been late in 1807)

SIR – You will receive from Lieutenant Neale the person of Philip Nolan, late a Lieutenant in the United States Army.

This person on his trial by court-martial expressed with an oath the wish that he might 'never hear of the United States again'.

The Court sentenced him to have his wish fulfilled.

For the present, the execution of the order is entrusted by the President to this Department.

You will take the prisoner on board your ship, and keep him there with such precautions as shall prevent his escape.

You will provide him with such quarters, rations, and clothing as would be proper for an officer of his late rank, if he were a passenger on your vessel on the business of his government.

The gentlemen on board will make any arrangements agreeable to themselves regarding his society. He is to be exposed to no indignity of any kind, nor is he ever unnecessarily to be reminded that he is a prisoner.

But under no circumstances is he ever to hear of his country or to see any information regarding it; and you will specially caution all the officers under your command to take care, that, in the various indulgences which may be granted, this rule, in which his punishment is involved, shall not be broken.

It is the intention of the government that he shall never again see the country which he has disowned. Before the end of your cruise you will receive orders which will give effect to this intention.

Respectfully yours,

W. SOUTHARD
for the Secretary of the Navy.

If I had only preserved the whole of this paper, there would be no break in the beginning of my sketch of this story. For Captain Shaw, if it were he, handed it to his successor in the charge, and he to his, and I suppose the commander of the *Levant* has it today as his authority for keeping this man in this mild custody.

The rule adopted on board the ships on which I have met 'the man without a country' was, I think, transmitted from the beginning. No mess liked to have him permanently, because his presence cut off all talk of home or of the prospect of return, of politics or letters, of peace or of war – cut off more than half the talk men liked to have at sea. But it was always thought too hard that he should never meet the rest of us, except to touch hats, and we finally sank into one system. He was not permitted to talk with the men, unless an officer was by. With officers he had unrestrained intercourse, as far as they and he chose. But he grew shy, though he had favourites: I was one. Then the captain always asked him to dinner on Monday. Every mess in succession took up the invitation in its turn. According to the size of the ship, you had him at your mess more or less often at dinner. His breakfast he ate in his own state-room – he always had a state-room – which was where a sentinel or somebody on the watch could see the door. And whatever else he ate or drank, he ate or drank alone. Sometimes, when the marines or sailors had any special jollification, they were permitted to invite 'Plain-Buttons', as they called him. Then Nolan was sent with some officer, and the men were forbidden to speak of home while he was there. I believe the theory was that the sight of his punishment did them good. They called him 'Plain-Buttons', because, while he always chose to wear a regulation army-uniform, he was not permitted to wear the army-button, for the reason that it bore either the initials or the insignia of the country he had disowned.

I remember, soon after I joined the navy, I was on shore with some of the older officers from our ship and from the *Brandywine*, which we had met at Alexandria. We had leave to make a party and go up to Cairo and the Pyramids. As we jogged along (you went on donkeys then), some of the gentlemen (we boys called them 'Dons', but the phrase was long since changed) fell to talking about Nolan, and someone told the system which was adopted from the first about his books and other reading. As he was almost never permitted to go on shore, even though the vessel lay in port for months, his time at the best hung heavy; and everybody was permitted to lend him books, if they were not published in America and made no allusion to it. These were common enough in the old days, when people in the other hemisphere talked of the United States as little as we do of Paraguay. He had almost all the foreign papers that came into the ship, sooner or later; only somebody must go over them first, and cut out any advertisement or stray paragraph that alluded to America. This was a little cruel sometimes, when the back of what was cut out might be as innocent as Hesiod. Right in the midst of one of Napoleon's battles, or one of Canning's speeches, poor Nolan would find a great hole, because on the back of the page of that paper there had been an advertisement of a packet for New York, or a scrap from the President's message. I say this was the first time I ever heard of this plan, which afterwards I had enough and more than enough to do with. I remember it, because poor Phillips, who was of the party, as soon as the allusion to reading was made, told a story of something which happened at the Cape of Good Hope on Nolan's first voyage; and it is the only thing I ever knew of that voyage. They had touched at the Cape, and had done the civil thing with the English Admiral and the fleet, and then, leaving for a long cruise up the Indian Ocean, Phillips had borrowed a lot of English books from an officer, which, in those days, as indeed in these, was quite a windfall. Among them, as the Devil would order, was the *Lay of the Last Minstrel*, which they had all of them heard of, but which most of them had never seen. I think it could not have been published long. Well, nobody thought there could be any risk of anything national in that, though Phillips swore old Shaw had cut out the *Tempest* from Shakespeare before he let Nolan have it, because he said 'the Bermudas ought to be ours, and, by Jove, should be one day'. So Nolan was permitted to join the circle one afternoon when a lot of them sat on deck smoking and reading aloud. People do not do such things so often now; but when I was young we got rid of a great deal of time so. Well, so it happened that in his turn Nolan took the book and read to the others; and he read very well, as I know.

Nobody in the circle knew a line of the poem, only it was all magic and Border chivalry, and was ten thousand years ago. Poor Nolan read steadily through the fifth canto, stopped a minute and drank something, and then began, without a thought of what was coming –

> 'Breathes there the man, with soul so dead,
> Who never to himself hath said' –

It seems impossible to us that anybody ever heard this for the first time; but all these fellows did then, and poor Nolan himself went on, still unconsciously or mechanically –

> 'This is my own, my native land!'

Then they all saw something was to pay; but he expected to get through, I suppose, turned a little pale, but plunged on –

> 'Whose heart hath ne'er within him burned,
> As home his footsteps he hath turned
> From wandering on a foreign strand? –
> If such there breathe, go, mark him well' –

By this time the men were all beside themselves, wishing there was any way to make him turn over two pages; but he had not quite presence of mind for that; he gagged a little, coloured crimson, and staggered on –

> 'For him no minstrel raptures swell;
> High though his titles, proud his name,
> Boundless his wealth as wish can claim
> Despite these titles, power, and pelf,
> The wretch, concentred all in self' –

and here the poor fellow choked, could not go on, but started up, swung the book into the sea, vanished into his state-room, 'And by Jove,' said Phillips, 'we did not see him for two months again. And I had to make up some beggarly story to that English surgeon why I did not return his Walter Scott to him.'

That story shows about the time when Nolan's braggadocio must have broken down. At first, they said, he took a very high tone, considered his imprisonment a mere farce, affected to enjoy the voyage, and all that; but Phillips said that after he came out of his state-room he never was the same man again. He never read aloud again, unless it was the Bible or Shakespeare, or something else he was sure of. But it was not that merely. He never entered in with the other young men exactly as a companion again. He was always shy after-wards, when I knew him – very seldom spoke, unless he was spoken to, except to a very few friends. He lighted up occasionally – I remember late in his life hearing him fairly eloquent on something which had been suggested to him by one of Fléchier's sermons – but generally he had the nervous, tired look of a heart-wounded man.

When Captain Shaw was coming home – if, as I say, it was Shaw – rather to the surprise of everybody they made one of the Windward Islands, and lay off and on for nearly a week. The boys said the officers were sick of salt-junk, and meant to have turtle soup before they came home. But after several days the *Warren* came to the same rendezvous; they exchanged signals; she sent to Phillips and these homeward-bound men letters and papers, and told them she was outward-bound, perhaps to the Mediterranean, and took poor Nolan and his traps on the boat back to try his second cruise. He looked very blank when he was told to get ready to join her. He had known enough of the signs of the sky to know that till that moment he was going 'home'. But this was a distinct evidence of something he had not thought of, perhaps – that there was no going home for him, even to a prison. And this was the first of some twenty such transfers, which brought him sooner or later into half our best vessels, but which kept him all his life at least some hundred miles from the country he had hoped he might never hear of again.

It may have been on that second cruise – it was once when he was up the Mediterranean – that Mrs Graff, the celebrated Southern beauty of those days, danced with him. They had been lying a long time in the Bay of Naples, and the officers were very intimate in the English fleet, and there had been great festivities, and our men thought they must give a great ball on board the ship. How they ever did it on board the *Warren* I am sure I do not know. Perhaps it was not the *Warren*, or perhaps ladies did not take up so much room as they do now. They wanted to use Nolan's state-room for something, and they hated to do it without asking him to the ball; so the captain said they might ask him, if they would be responsible that he did not talk with the wrong people, 'who would give him intelligence'. So the dance went on, the finest party that had ever been known, I dare say; for I never heard of a man-of-war ball that was not. For ladies they had the family of the American consul, one or two travellers who had adventured so far, and a nice bevy of English girls and matrons, perhaps Lady Hamilton herself.

Well, different officers relieved each other in standing and talking with Nolan in a friendly way, so as to be sure that nobody else spoke to him. The dancing went on with spirit, and after a while even the fellows who took this honorary guard of Nolan ceased to fear any *contretemps*. Only when some English lady – Lady Hamilton, as I said, perhaps – called for a set of 'American dances', an odd thing happened. Everybody then danced contra-dances. The black band, nothing loath, conferred as to what American dances were, and started off with 'Virginia Reel', which they followed with 'Money-Musk', which, in its turn in those days, should have been followed by 'The Old Thirteen'. But just as Dick, the leader, tapped for his fiddles to begin, and bent forward, about to say, in true negro state, ' "The Old Thirteen", gentlemen and ladies!' as he had said ' "Virginny Reel", if you please!' and ' "Money-Musk", if you please!' the captain's boy tapped him on the shoulder, whispered to him, and he did not announce the name of the dance; he merely bowed, began on the air, and they all fell to – the officers teaching the English girls the figure, but not telling them why it had no name.

But that is not the story I started to tell. – As the dancing went on, Nolan and our fellows all got at ease, as I said – so much so, that it seemed quite natural for him to bow to that splendid Mrs Graff, and say –

'I hope you have not forgotten me, Miss Rutledge. Shall I have the honour of dancing?'

He did it so quickly, that Fellows, who was by him, could not hinder him. She laughed and said –

'I am not Miss Rutledge any longer, Mr Nolan; but I will dance all the same,' just nodded to Fellows, as if to say he must leave Mr Nolan to her, and led him off to the place where the dance was forming.

Nolan thought he had got his chance. He had known her at Philadelphia, and at other places had met her, and this was a Godsend. You could not talk in contra-dances, as you do in cotillons, or even in the pauses of waltzing; but there were chances for tongues and sounds, as well as for eyes and blushes. He began with her travels, and Europe, and Vesuvius, and the French; and then, when they had worked down, and had that long talking-time at the bottom of the set, he said, boldly – a little pale, she said, as she told me the story, years after –

'And what do you hear from home, Mrs Graff?'

And that splendid creature looked through him. Jove! how she must have looked through him!

'Home!! Mr Nolan!!! I thought you were the man who never wanted to hear of home again!' – and she walked directly up the deck to her husband, and left poor Nolan alone, as he always was. – He did not dance again.

I cannot give any history of him in order; nobody can now; and, indeed, I am not trying to. These are the traditions, which I sort out, as I believe them, from the myths which have been told about this man for forty years. The lies that have been told about him are legion. The fellows used to say he was the 'Iron Mask'; and poor George Pons went to his grave in the belief that this was the author of *Junius*, who was being punished for his celebrated libel on Thomas Jefferson. Pons was not very strong in the historical line. A happier story than either of these I have told is of the War. That came along soon after. I have heard this affair told in three or four ways – and, indeed, it may have happened more than once. But which ship it was on I cannot tell. However, in one, at least, of the great frigate-duels with the English, in which the navy was really baptised, it happened that a round-shot from the enemy entered one of our ports square, and took right down the officer of the gun himself, and almost every man of the gun's crew. Now you may say what you choose about courage, but that is not a nice thing to see. But, as the men who were not killed picked themselves up, and as they and the surgeon's people were carrying off the bodies, there appeared Nolan, in his shirt-sleeves, with the rammer in his hand, and, just as if he had been the officer, told them off with authority – who should go to the cockpit with the wounded men, who should stay with him – perfectly cheery, and with that way which makes men feel sure all is right and is going to be right. And he finished loading the gun with his own hands, aimed it, and bade the men fire. And there he stayed, captain of that gun, keeping those fellows in spirits, till the enemy struck – sitting on the carriage while the gun was cooling, though he was exposed all the time – showing them easier ways to handle heavy shot – making the raw hands laugh at their own blunders – and when the gun cooled again, getting it loaded and fired twice as often as any other gun on the ship. The captain walked forward by way of encouraging the men, and Nolan touched his hat and said –

'I am showing them how we do this in the artillery, sir.'

And this is the part of the story where all the legends agree; and the Commodore said –

'I see you do, and I thank you, sir; and I shall never forget this day, sir, and you never shall, sir.'

And after the whole thing was over, and he had the Englishman's sword, in the midst of the state and ceremony of the quarter-deck, he said –

'Where is Mr Nolan? Ask Mr Nolan to come here.'

And when Nolan came, the captain said –

'Mr Nolan, we are all very grateful to you today; you are one of us today; you will be named in the despatches.'

And then the old man took off his own sword of ceremony, and gave it to Nolan, and made him put it on. The man told me this who saw it. Nolan cried like a baby, and well he might. He had not worn a sword since that infernal day at Fort Adams. But always afterwards on occasions of ceremony, he wore that quaint old French sword of the Commodore's.

The captain did mention him in the despatches. It was always said he asked that he might be pardoned. He wrote a special letter to the Secretary of War. But nothing ever came of it. As I said, that was about the time when they began to ignore the whole transaction at Washington, and when Nolan's imprisonment began to carry itself on because there was nobody to stop it without any new orders from home.

I have heard it said that he was with Porter when he took possession of the Nukahiwa Islands. Not this Porter, you know, but old Porter, his father, Essex Porter – that is, the old Essex Porter, not this Essex. As an artillery officer, who had seen service in the West, Nolan knew more about fortifications, embrasures, ravelins, stockades, and all that, than any of them did; and he worked with a right good will in firing that battery all right. I have always thought it was a pity Porter did not leave him in command there with Gamble. That would have settled all the question about his punishment. We should have kept the islands, and at this moment we should have one station in the Pacific Ocean. Our French friends, too, when they wanted this little watering-place, would have found it was preoccupied. But Madison and the Virginians, of course, flung all that away.

All that was near fifty years ago. If Nolan was thirty then, he must have been near eighty when he died. He looked sixty when he was forty. But he never seemed to me to change a hair afterwards. As I imagine his life, from what I have seen and heard of it, he must have been in every sea, and yet almost never on land. He must have known, in a formal way, more officers in our service than any man living knows. He told me once, with a grave smile, that no man in the world lived so methodical a life as he. 'You know the boys say I am the Iron Mask, and you know how busy he was.' He said it did not do for anyone to try to read all the time, more than to do anything else all the time; but that he read just five hours a day. 'Then,' he said, 'I keep up my note-books, writing in them at such and such hours from what I have been reading; and I include in these my scrapbooks.' These were very curious indeed. He had six or eight, of different subjects. There was one of History, one of Natural Science, one which he called 'Odds and Ends'. But they were not merely books of extracts from newspapers. They had bits of plants and ribbons, shells tied on, and carved scraps of bone and wood, which he had taught the men to cut for him, and they were beautifully illustrated. He drew admirably. He had some of the funniest drawings there, and some of the most pathetic, that I have ever seen in my life. I wonder who will have Nolan's scrapbooks.

Well, he said his reading and his notes were his profession, and that they took five hours and two hours respectively of each day. 'Then,' said he, 'every man should have a diversion as well as a profession. My Natural History is my diversion.' That took two hours a day more. The men used to bring him birds and fish, but on a long cruise he had to satisfy himself with centipedes and cockroaches and such small game. He was the only naturalist I ever met who knew anything about the habits of the house-fly and the mosquito. All those people can tell you whether they are *Lepidoptera* or *Steptopotera;* but as for telling how you can get rid of them, or how they get away from you when you strike them – why Linnæus knew as little of that as John Foy the idiot did. These nine hours made Nolan's regular daily 'occupation'. The rest of the time he talked or walked. Till he grew very old, he went aloft a great deal. He always kept up his exercise; and I never heard that he was ill. If any other man was ill, he was the kindest nurse in the world; and he knew more than half the surgeons do. Then if anybody was sick or died, or if the captain wanted him to, on any other occasion, he was always ready to read prayers. I have said that he read beautifully.

My own acquaintance with Philip Nolan began six or eight years after the War, on my first voyage after I was appointed a midshipman. It was in the first days after our Slave-Trade treaty, while the Reigning House, which was still the House of Virginia, had still a sort of sentimentalism about the suppression of the horrors of the Middle Passage, and something was sometimes done that way. We were in the South Atlantic on that business. From the time I joined, I believe I thought Nolan was a sort of lay chaplain – a chaplain with a blue coat. I never asked about him. Everything in the ship was strange to me. I knew it was green to ask questions, and I suppose I thought there was a 'Plain-Buttons' on every ship. We had him to dine in our mess once a week, and the caution was given that on that day nothing was to be said about home. But if they had told us not to say anything about the planet Mars or the Book of Deuteronomy, I should not have asked why; there were a great many things which seemed to me to have as little reason. I first came to understand anything about 'the man without a country' one day when we overhauled a dirty little schooner which had slaves on board. An officer was sent to take charge of her, and, after a few minutes, he sent back his boat to ask that someone might be sent him who could speak Portuguese. We were all looking over the rail when the message came, and we all wished we could interpret, when the captain asked who spoke Portuguese. But none of the officers did; and just as the captain was sending forward to ask if any of the people could, Nolan stepped out and said he should be glad to interpret, if the captain wished, as he understood the language. The captain thanked him, fitted out another boat with him, and in this boat it was my luck to go.

When we got there, it was such a scene as you seldom see, and never want to. Nastiness beyond account, and chaos run loose in the midst of the nastiness. There were not a great many of the negroes; but by way of making what there were understand that they were free, Vaughan had had their hand-cuffs and ankle-cuffs knocked off, and, for conven- ience' sake, was putting them upon the rascals of the schooner's crew. The negroes were, most of them, out of the hold, and swarming all round the dirty deck, with a central throng surrounding Vaughan and addressing him in every dialect, and *patois* of a dialect, from the Zulu click up to the Parisian of Beledeljereed.

As we came on deck, Vaughan looked down from a hogshead, on which he had mounted in desperation, and said –

'For God's love, is there anybody who can make these wretches understand something? The men gave them rum, and that did not quiet them. I knocked that big fellow down twice, and that did not soothe him. And then I talked Choctaw to all of them together; and I'll be hanged if they understood that as well as they understood the English.'

Nolan said he could speak Portuguese, and one or two fine-looking Kroomen were dragged out, who, as it had been found already, had worked for the Portuguese on the coast at Fernando Po.

'Tell them they are free,' said Vaughan; 'and tell them that these rascals are to be hanged as soon as we can get rope enough.'

Nolan 'put that into Spanish' – that is, he explained it in such Portuguese as the Kroomen could understand, and they in turn to such of the negroes as could understand them. Then there was such a yell of delight, clinching of fists, leaping and dancing, kissing of Nolan's feet, and a general rush made to the hogshead by way of spontaneous worship of Vaughan, as the *deus ex machina* of the occasion.

'Tell them,' said Vaughan, well pleased, 'that I will take them all to Cape Palmas.'

This did not answer so well. Cape Palmas was practically as far from the homes of most of them as New Orleans or Rio Janeiro was; that is, they would he eternally separated from home there. And their interpreters, as we could understand, instantly said, '*Ah, non Palmas,*' and began to propose infinite other expedients in most voluble language. Vaughan was rather disappointed at this result of his liberality, and asked Nolan eagerly what they said. The drops stood on poor Nolan's white forehead, as he hushed the men down, and said –

'He says, "Not Palmas." He says, "Take us home, take us to our own country, take us to our own house, take us to our own piccaninnies and our own women." He says he has an old father and mother who will die if they do not see him. And this one says he left his people all sick, and paddled down to Fernando to beg the white doctor to come and help them, and that these devils caught him in the bay just in sight of home, and that he has never seen anybody from home since then. And this one says,' choked out Nolan, 'that he has not heard a word from his home in six months, while he has been locked up in an infernal barracoon.'

Vaughan always said he grew grey himself while Nolan struggled through this interpretation. I, who did not understand anything of the passion involved in it, saw that the very elements were melting with fervent heat, and that something was to pay somewhere. Even the negroes themselves stopped howling, as they saw Nolan's agony, and Vaughan's almost equal agony of sympathy. As quick as he could get words, he said –

'Tell them yes, yes, yes; tell them they shall go to the Mountains of the Moon, if they will. If I sail the schooner through the Great White Desert, they shall go home!'

And after some fashion Nolan said so. And then they all fell to kissing him again, and wanted to rub his nose with theirs.

But he could not stand it long; and getting Vaughan to say he might go back, he beckoned me down into our boat. As we lay back in the stern-sheets and the men gave way, he said to me – 'Youngster, let that show you what it is to be without a family, without a home, and without a country. And if you are ever tempted to say a word or to do a thing that shall put a bar between you and your family, your home, and your country, pray God in his mercy take you that instant home to his own heaven. Stick by your family, boy; forget you have a self, while you do everything for them. Think of your home boy; write and send, and talk about it. Let it be nearer and nearer to your thought, the farther you have to travel from it; and rush back to it, when you are free, as that poor black slave is doing now. And for your country, boy,' and the words rattled in his throat, 'and for that flag,' and he pointed to the ship, 'never dream a dream but of serving her as she bids you, though the service carry you through a thousand hells. No matter what happens to you, no matter who flatters you or who abuses you, never look at another flag, never let a night pass but you pray God to bless that flag. Remember, boy, that behind all these men you have to do with, behind officers, and government, and people even, there is the Country Herself, your Country, and that you belong to Her as you belong to your own mother. Stand by Her, boy, as you would stand by your mother, if those devils there had got hold of her today!'

I was frightened to death by his calm, hard passion; but I blundered out, that I would, by all that was holy, and that I had never thought of doing anything else. He hardly seemed to hear me; but he did, almost in a whisper, say – 'O, if anybody had said so to me when I was of your age!'

I think it was this half-confidence of his, which I never abused, for I never told this story till now, which afterward made us great friends. He was very kind to me. Often he sat up, or even got up, at night, to walk the deck with me, when it was my watch. He explained to me a great deal of my mathematics, and I owe to him my taste for mathematics. He lent me books, and helped me about my reading. He never alluded so directly to his story again; but from one and another officer I have learned, in thirty years, what I am telling. When we parted from him in St Thomas harbour, at the end of our cruise, I was more sorry than I can tell. I was very glad to meet him again in 1830; and later in life, when I thought I had some influence in Washington, I moved heaven and earth to have him discharged. But it was like getting a ghost out of prison. They pretended there was no such man, and never was such a man. They will say so at the Department now! Perhaps they do not know. It will not be the first thing in the service of which the Department appears to know nothing!

There is a story that Nolan met Burr once on one of our vessels, when a party of Americans came on board in the Mediterranean. But this I believe to be a lie; or, rather, it is a myth, *ben trovato*, involving a tremendous blowing-up with which he sank Burr – asking him how he liked to be 'without a country'. But it is clear from Burr's life, that nothing of the sort could have happened; and I mention this only as an illustration of the stories which get a-going where there is the least mystery at bottom.

So poor Philip Nolan had his wish fulfilled. I know but one fate more dreadful; it is the fate reserved for those men who shall have one day to exile themselves from their country because they have attempted her ruin, and shall have at the same time to see the prosperity and honour to which she rises when she has rid herself of them and their iniquities. The wish of poor Nolan, as we all learned to call him, not because his punishment was too great, but because his repentance was so clear, was precisely the wish of every Bragg and Beauregard who broke a soldier's oath two years ago, and of every Maury and Barron who broke a sailor's. I do not know how often they have repented. I do know that they have done all that in them lay that they might have no country – that all the honours, associations, memories, and hopes which belong to 'country' might be broken up into little shreds and distributed to the winds. I know, too, that their punishment, as they vegetate through what is left of life to them in wretched Boulognes and Leicester Squares, where they are destined to upbraid each other till they die, will have all the agony of Nolan's, with the added pang that everyone who sees them will see them to despise and to execrate them. They will have their wish, like him.

For him, poor fellow, he repented of his folly, and then, like a man, submitted to the fate he had asked for. He never intentionally added to the difficulty or delicacy of the charge of those who had him in hold. Accidents would happen; but they never happened from his fault. Lieutenant Truxton told me, that, when Texas was annexed, there was a careful discussion among the officers, whether they should get hold of Nolan's handsome set of maps, and cut Texas out of it – from the map of the world and the map of Mexico. The United States had been cut out when the atlas was bought for him. But it was voted, rightly enough, that to do this would be virtually to reveal to him what had happened, or, as Harry Cole said, to make him think Old Burr had succeeded. So it was from no fault of Nolan's that a great botch happened at my own table, when, for a short time, I was in command of the *George Washington* corvette, on the South American station. We were lying in the La Plata, and some of the officers, who had been on shore, and had just joined again, were entertaining us with accounts of their misadventures in riding the half-wild horses of Buenos Aires. Nolan was at table, and was in an unusually bright and talkative mood.

Some story of a tumble reminded him of an adventure of his own, when he was catching wild horses in Texas with his adventurous cousin, at a time when he must have been quite a boy. He told the story with a good deal of spirit – so much so, that the silence which often follows a good story hung over the table for an instant, to be broken by Nolan himself. For he asked perfectly unconsciously –

'Pray, what has become of Texas? After the Mexicans got their independence, I thought that province of Texas would come forward very fast. It is really one of the finest regions on earth; it is the Italy of this continent. But I have not seen or heard a word of Texas for near twenty years.'

There were two Texan officers at the table. The reason he had never heard of Texas was that Texas and her affairs had been painfully cut out of his newspapers since Austin began his settlements; so that, while he read of Honduras and Tamaulipas, and, till quite lately, of California – this virgin province, in which his brother had travelled so far, and, I believe, had died, had ceased to be to him. Waters and Williams, the two Texas men, looked grimly at each other, and tried not to laugh. Edward Morris had his attention attracted by the third link in the chain of the captain's chandelier. Watrous was seized with a convulsion of sneezing. Nolan himself saw that something was to pay, he did not know what. And I, as master of the feast, had to say –

'Texas is out of the map, Mr Nolan. Have you seen Captain Back's curious account of Sir Thomas Roe's Welcome?'

After that cruise I never saw Nolan again. I wrote to him at least twice a year, for in that voyage we became even confidentially intimate; but he never wrote to me. The other men tell me that in those fifteen years he *aged* very fast, as well he might indeed, but that he was still the same gentle, uncomplaining, silent sufferer that he ever was, bearing as best he could his self-appointed punishment – rather less social, perhaps, with new men whom he did not know, but more anxious, apparently, than ever to serve and befriend and teach the boys, some of whom fairly seemed to worship him. And now it seems the dear old fellow is dead. He has found a home at last, and a country.

Since writing this, and while considering whether or no I would print it, as a warning to the young Nolans and Vallandighams and Tatnalls of today of what it is to throw away a country, I have received from Danforth, who is on board the *Levant*, a letter which gives an account of Nolan's last hours. It removes all my doubts about telling this story.

To understand the first words of the letter, the non-professional reader should remember that after 1817, the position of every officer who had Nolan in charge was one of the greatest delicacy. The government had failed to renew the order of 1807 regarding him. What was a man to do? Should he let him go? What, then, if he were called to account by the Department for violating the order of 1807? Should he keep him? What, then, if Nolan should be liberated someday, and should bring an action for false imprisonment or kidnapping against every man who had had him in charge? I urged and pressed this upon Southard, and I have reason to think that other officers did the same thing. But the Secretary always said, as they so often do at Washington, that there were no special orders to give, and that we must act on our own judgment. That means, 'If you succeed, you will be sustained if you fail, you will be disavowed.' Well, as Danforth says, all that is over now, though I do not know but I expose myself to a criminal prosecution on the evidence of the very revelation I am making.

Here is the letter –

Levant, 2° 11' S., 131° W.

DEAR FRED – I try to find heart and life to tell you that it is all over with dear old Nolan. I have been with him on this voyage more than I ever was, and I can understand wholly now the way in which you used to speak of the dear old fellow. I could see that he was not strong, but I had no idea the end was so near. The doctor has been watching him very carefully, and yesterday morning came to me and told me that Nolan was not so well, and had not left his state-room – a thing I never remember before. He had let the doctor come and see him as he lay there,– the first time the doctor had been in the state-room – and he said he should like to see me. O dear! do you remember the mysteries we boys used to invent about his room, in the old *Intrepid* days? Well, I went in, and there, to be sure, the poor fellow lay in his berth, smiling pleasantly as he gave me his hand, but looking very frail. I could not help a glance round, which showed me what a little shrine he had made of the box he was lying in. The stars and stripes were triced up above and around a picture of Washington, and he had painted a majestic eagle, with lightnings blazing from his beak and his foot just clasping the whole globe, which his wings overshadowed. The dear old boy saw my glance, and said, with a sad smile, 'Here, you see, I have a country!' And then he pointed to the foot of his bed, where I had not seen before a great map of the United States, as he had drawn it from memory, and which he had there to look upon as he lay. Quaint, queer old names were on it, in large letters – 'Indiana Territory', 'Mississippi Territory' and 'Louisiana Territory', as I suppose our fathers learned such things – but the old fellow had patched in Texas, too; he had carried his western boundary all the way to the Pacific, but on that shore he had defined nothing.

'O Danforth,' he said, 'I know I am dying. I cannot get home. Surely you will tell me something now? – Stop! stop! Do not speak till I say what I am sure you know, that there is not in this ship, that there is not in America – God bless her! – a more loyal man than I. There cannot be a man who loves the old flag as I do, or prays for it as I do, or hopes for it as I do. There are thirty-four stars in it now, Danforth. I thank God for that, though I do no know what their names are. There has never been one taken away – I thank God for that. I know by that that there has never been any successful Burr. O Danforth, Danforth,' he sighed out, 'how like a wretched night's dream a boy's idea of personal fame or of separate sovereignty seems, when one look back on it after such a life as mine! But tell me – tell me something – tell me everything, Danforth before I die!'

Ingham, I swear to you that I felt like a monster that I had not told him everything before. Danger or no danger, delicacy or no delicacy, who was I, that I should have been acting the tyrant all this time over this dear, sainted old man, who had years ago expiated in his whole manhood's life, the madness of a boy's treason? 'Mr Nolan,' said I, 'I will tell you everything you ask about. Only, where shall I begin?'

O the blessed smile that crept over his white face! and he pressed my hand and said, 'God bless you!' 'Tell me their names,' he said, and he pointed to the stars on the flag. 'The last I know is Ohio. My father lived in Kentucky. But I have guessed Michigan and Indiana and Mississippi – that was where Fort Adams is – they make twenty. But where are your other fourteen? You have not cut up any of the old ones, I hope?'

Well, that was not a bad text, and I told him the names in as good order as I could, and he bade me take down his beautiful map and draw them in as I best could with my pencil. He was wild with delight about Texas, told me how his cousin died there; he had marked a gold cross near where he supposed his grave was; and he had guessed at Texas. Then he was delighted as he saw California and Oregon; that, he said, he had suspected partly, because he had never been permitted to land on that shore, though the ships were there so much. 'And the men,' said he, laughing, 'brought off a good deal besides furs.' Then he went back – heavens, how far! – to ask about the *Chesapeake*, and what was done to Barron for surrendering her to the *Leopard*, and whether Burr ever tried again – and he ground his teeth with the only passion he showed. But in a moment that was over, and he said, 'God forgive me, for I am sure I forgive him.' Then he asked about the old war – told me the true story of his serving the gun the day we took the *Java* – asked about dear old David Porter, as he called him. Then he settled down more quietly, and very happily, to hear me tell in an hour the history of fifty years.

How I wished it had been somebody who knew something! But I did as well as I could. I told him of the English war. I told him about Fulton and the steamboat beginning. I told him about old Scott, and Jackson; told him all I could think of about the Mississippi, and New Orleans, and Texas, and his own old Kentucky. And do you think, he asked who was in command of the 'Legion of the West'. I told him it was a very gallant officer named Grant, and that, by our last news, he was about to establish his headquarters at Vicksburg. Then, 'Where was Vicksburg?' I worked that out on the map; it was about a hundred miles, more or less, above his old Fort Adams; and I thought Fort Adams must be a ruin now. 'It must be at old Vick's plantation at Walnut Hills,' said he – 'well, that is a change!'

I tell you, Ingham, it was a hard thing to condense the history of half a century into that talk with a sick man. And I do not now know what I told him – of emigration, and the means of it – of steamboats, and railroads, and telegraphs – of inventions, and books, and literature – of the colleges, and West Point, and the Naval School – but with the queerest interruptions that ever you heard. You see it was Robinson Crusoe asking all the accumulated questions of fifty-six years!

I remember he asked, all of a sudden, who was President now; and when I told him; he asked if Old Abe was General Benjamin Lincoln's son. He said he met old General Lincoln, when he was quite a boy himself, at some Indian treaty. I said no, that Old Abe was a Kentuckian like himself, but I could not tell him of what family he had worked up from the ranks. 'Good for him!' cried Nolan; 'I am glad of that as I have brooded and wondered, I have thought our danger was in keeping up those regular successions in the first families.' Then I got talking about my visit to Washington. I told him of meeting the Oregon Congressman, Harding; I told him about the Smithsonian, and the Exploring Expedition; I told him about the Capitol, and the statues for the pediment, and Crawford's Liberty, and Greenough's Washington: Ingham, I told him everything I could think of that would show the grandeur of his country and its prosperity; but I could not make up my mouth to tell him a word about this infernal Rebellion!

And he drank it in, and enjoyed it as I cannot tell you. He grew more and more silent, yet I never thought he was tired or faint. I gave him a glass of water, but he just wet his lips, and told me not to go away. Then he asked me to bring the Presbyterian *Book of Public Prayer*, which lay there, and said, with a smile, that it would open at the right place – and so it did. There was his double red mark down the page; and I knelt down and read, and he repeated with me, 'For ourselves and our country, O gracious God, we thank Thee, that, notwithstanding our manifold transgressions of Thy holy laws, Thou hast continued to us Thy marvellous kindness,' – and so to the end of that thanksgiving. Then he turned to the end of the same book, and I read the words more familiar to me – 'Most heartily we beseech Thee with Thy favour to behold and bless Thy servant, the President of the United States, and all others in authority,' – and the rest of the Episcopal collect. 'Danforth,' said he, 'I have repeated those prayers night and morning, it is now fifty-five years.' And then he said he would go to sleep. He bent me down over him and kissed me; and he said, 'Look in my Bible Danforth, when I am gone.' And I went away.

But I had no thought it was the end. I thought he was tired and would sleep. I knew he was happy and I wanted him to be alone.

But in an hour, when the doctor went in gently; he found Nolan had breathed his life away with smile. He had something pressed close to his lips. It was his father's badge of the Order of the Cincinnati.

We looked in his Bible, and there was a slip of paper at the place where he had marked the text –

'They desire a country, even a heavenly: wherefore God is not ashamed to be called their God: for he hath prepared for them a city.'

On this slip of paper he had written –

'Bury me in the sea; it has been my home, and I love it. But will not someone set up a stone for my memory at Fort Adams or at Orleans, that my disgrace may not be more than I ought to bear?

Say on it –

> In memory of
> **PHILIP NOLAN**
> Lieutenant in the Army of the United States.
> He loved his country as no other man has
> loved her, but no man deserved
> less at her hands.'

The Last of the Florida

FROM THE INGHAM PAPERS

The Florida, *Anglo-Rebel pirate, after inflicting horrible injuries on the commerce of America and the good name of England, was cut out by Captain Collins, from the Bay of Bahia, by one of those fortunate mistakes in international law which endear brave men to the nations in whose interest they are committed. When she arrived here the government was obliged to disavow the act. The question then was, as we had her by mistake, what we should do with her. At that moment the National Sailors' Fair was in full blast at Boston, and I offered my suggestion in answer in the following article, which was published 19 November 1864, in the* Boatswain's Whistle, *a little paper issued at the fair.*

The government did not take the suggestion. Very unfortunately, before the Florida *was got ready for sea, she was accidentally sunk in a collision with a tug off Fort Monroe, and the heirs of the Confederate government or the English bond-holders must look there for her, if the Brazilian government will give them permission.*

For the benefit of the New York Observer *I will state that a despatch sent round the world in a spiral direction westward 1,200 times, would not really arrive at its destination four years before it started. It is only a joke which suggests it.*

SPECIAL DISPATCH

LETTER FROM CAPTAIN INGHAM, IN COMMAND OF THE *FLORIDA*
Received four years in advance of the mail by a lightning express, which has gained that time by running round the world 1,200 times in a spiral direction westward on its way from Brazil to our publication-office. Mrs Ingham's address not being known, the letter is printed for her information.   No. 29.

Bahia, Brazil, 1 April 1868

MY DEAR WIFE – We are here at last, thank fortune; and I shall surrender the old pirate today to the officers of government. We have been saluted, are to be fêted, and perhaps I shall be made a Knight Commander of the Golden Goose. I never was so glad as when I saw the lights on the San Esperitu headland, which makes the south point of this Bahia or bay.

You will not have received my No. 28 from Loando, and may have missed 26 and 24, which I gave to *outward* bound whalemen. I always doubted whether you got 1, 7, 9, and 11. And for me I have no word of you since you waved your handkerchief from the window in Springfield Street on the morning of the 1 June 1865, nearly four years. My dear child, you will not know me.

Let me then repeat, very briefly, the outline of this strange cruise; and when the letters come, you can fill in the blanks.

The government had determined that the *Florida* must be returned to the neutral harbour whence she came. They had put her in complete repair, and six months of diplomacy had made the proper apologies to the Brazilian government. Meanwhile Collins, who had captured her by mistake, had, by another mistake, been made an admiral, and was commanding a squadron; and to ensure her safe and respectful delivery, I, who had been waiting service, was unshelved, and, as you know, bidden to take command.

She was in apple-pie order. The engines had been cleaned up; and I thought we could make a quick thing of it. I was a little dashed when I found the crew was small; but I have been glad enough since that we had no more mouths. No one but myself knew our destination. The men thought we were to take despatches to the Gulf squadron.

You remember I had had only verbal orders to take command, and after we got outside the bay I opened my sealed despatches. The gist of them was in these words –

'You will understand that the honour of this government is pledged for the *safe* delivery of the *Florida* to the government of Brazil. You will therefore hazard nothing to gain speed. The quantity of your coal has been adjusted with the view to give your vessel her best trim, and the supply is not large. You will husband it with care – taking every precaution to arrive in Bahia *safely* with your charge, in such time as *your best discretion* may suggest to you.'

'*Your best discretion*' was underscored.

I called Prendergast, and showed him the letter. Then we called the engineer and asked about the coal. He had not been into the bunkers, but went and returned with his face white, through the black grime, to report 'not four days' consumption'. By some cursed accident, he said, the bunkers had been filled with barrels of salt-pork and flour!

On this, I ordered a light and went below. There had been some fatal misunderstanding somewhere. The vessel was fitted out as for an arctic voyage. Everywhere hard-bread, flour, pork, beef, vinegar, sauerkraut; but, clearly enough, not, at the very best, five days of coal!

And I was to get to Brazil with this old pirate transformed into a provision ship, 'at my best discretion'.

'Prendergast,' said I, 'we will take it easy. Were you ever in Bahia?'

'Took flour there in '55, and lay waiting for india-rubber from July to October. Lost six men by yellow-jack.'

Prendergast was from the merchant marine. I had known him since we were children. 'Ethan,' said I, 'in my best discretion it would be bad to arrive there before the end of October. Where would you go?'

I cannot say he took the responsibility. He would not take it. You know, my dear, of course, that it was I who suggested Upernavik. From the days of the old marbled paper Northern Regions – through the quarto Ross and Parry and Back and the nephew Ross and Kane and McClure and McClintock, you know, my dear, what my one passion has been – to see those floes and icebergs for myself. Surely you forgive me, or at least excuse me. Do not you? Here was this fast steamer under me. I ought not to be in Bahia before October 25. It was June 1. Of course we went to Upernavik.

I will not say I regret it now. Yet I will say that on that decision, cautiously made, though it was 'on my discretion', all our subsequent misfortunes hang. The Danes were kind to us – the Governor especially, though I had to carry the poor fellow bad news about the Duchies and the Danish war, which was all fresh then. He got up a dance for us, I remember, and there I wrote No. 1 to you. I could not of course help – when we left him – running her up a few degrees to the north, just to see whether there is or is not that passage between Igloolik and Prince Rupert's Headland (and by the way there *is*). After we passed Igloolik, there was such splendid weather, that I just used up a little coal to drive her along the coast of King William's Land; and there, as we waited for a little duck-shooting on the edge of a floe one day, as our luck ordered, a party of natives came on board, and we treated them with hard-tack crumbs and whale oil. They fell to dancing, and we to laughing – they danced more and we laughed more, till the oldest woman tumbled in her bear-skin bloomers, and came with a smash right on the little cast-iron frame by the wheel, which screened binnacle and compass. My dear child, there was such a hullalu and such a mess together as I remember now. We had to apologise; the doctor set her head as well as he could. We gave them gingerbread from the cabin, to console them, and got them off without a fight. But the next morning when I cast off from the floe, it proved the beggars had stolen the compass card, needle and all.

My dear Mary, there was not another bit of magnetised iron in the ship. The government had been very shy of providing instruments of any kind for Confederate cruisers. Poor Ethan had traded off two compasses only the day before for whalebone spears and skin breeches, neither of which knew the north star from the ace of spades. And this thing proved of more importance than you will think; it really made me feel that the stuff in the books and the sermons about the mariners' needle was not quite poetry.

As you shall see, if I ever get through. (Since I began, I have seen the Consul – and heard the glorious news from home – and am to be presented to the port authorities tomorrow.) It was the most open summer, Mary, ever known there. If I had not had to be here in October, I would have driven right through Lancaster Sound, by Baring's Island, and come out into the Pacific. But here was the honour of the country, and we merely stole back through the Straits. It was well enough there – all daylight, you know. But after we passed Cape Farewell, we worked her into such fogs, child, as you never saw out of Hyde Park. Did not I long for that compass-card! We sailed, and we sailed, and we sailed. For thirty-seven days I did not get an observation, nor speak a ship! October! It was October before we were warm. At noon we used to sail where we thought it was lightest. At night I used to keep two men up for a lookout, lash the wheel, and let her drift like a Dutchman. One way as good as another. Mary, when I saw the sun at last, enough to get any kind of observation, we were wellnigh three hundred miles northeast of Iceland! Talk of fogs to me!

Well, I set her south again, but how long can you know if you are sailing south, in those places where the northeast winds and Scotch mists come from. Thank Heaven, we got south, or we should have frozen to death. We got into November, and we got into December. We were as far south as 37° 29'; and were in 31° 17' west on New Year's Day 1866, when the second officer wished me a happy new year, congratulated me on the fine weather, said we should get a good observation, and asked me for the new nautical almanac! You know they are only calculated for five years. We had two Greenwich ones on board, and they ran out 31 December 1865. But the government had been as stingy in almanacs as in coal and compasses. They did not mean to keep the Confederacy in almanacs.

That was the beginning of our troubles. I had to take the old almanac, with Prendergast, and we figured like Cocker, and always kept ahead with a month's tables. But somehow – I feel sure we were right – but something was wrong; and after a few weeks the lunars used to come out in the most beastly way, and we always proved to be on the top of the Andes or in the Marquesas Islands, or anywhere but in the Atlantic Ocean. Well then, by good luck, we spoke to the *Winged Batavian*; could not speak a word of Dutch, nor he a word of English; but he let Ethan copy his tables, and so we ran for St Sacrament. I posted 8, 9, and 10 there; I gave the Dutchman 7, which I hope you got, but fear.

Well, this story is running long; but at St Sacrament we started again, but, as ill-luck would have it, without a clean bill of health. At that time I could have run into Bahia with coal – of which I had bought some – in a week. But there was fever on shore – and bad – and I knew we must make pratique when we came into the outer harbour here; so, rather than do that, we stretched down the coast, and met that cyclone I wrote you about, and had to put into Loando. Understand, this was the first time we went into Loando. I have learned that wretched hole well enough since. And it was as we were running out of Loando, that, in reversing the engine too suddenly, lest we should smash up an old Portuguese woman's bum-boat, that the slides or supports of the piston-rod just shot out of the grooves they run in on the top, came cleverly down on the outside of the carriage, gave that odious *g-r-r-r*, which I can hear now, and then, *dump* – down came the whole weight of the walking-beam, bent rod and carriages all into three figure 8s, and there we were! I had as lief run the boat with a clothes-wringer as with that engine, any day, from then to now.

Well, we tinkered, and the Portuguese dockyard people tinkered. We took out this, and they took out that. It was growing sickly, and I got frightened, and finally I shipped the propeller and took it on board, and started under such canvas as we had left – not much after the cyclone – for the North and the South together had rather rotted the original duck.

Then – as I wrote you in No. 11 – it was too late to get to Bahia before that summer's sickly season, and I stretched off to cooler regions again, 'in my best discretion'. That was the time when we had the fever so horribly on board; and but for Wilder the surgeon, and the Falkland

Islands, we should be dead, every man of us, now. But we touched in Queen's Bay just in time. The Governor (who is his own only subject) was very cordial and jolly and kind. We all went ashore, and pitched tents, and ate ducks and penguins till the men grew strong. I scraped her, nearly down to the bends, for the grass floated by our side like a mermaid's hair as we sailed, and the once swift *Florida* would not make four knots an hour on the wind; and this was the ship I was to get into Bahia in good order, at my best discretion!

Meanwhile none of these people had any news from America. The last paper at the Falkland Islands was the *London Times* of 1864, abusing the Yankees. As for the Portuguese, they were like the people Logan saw at Vicksburg. 'They don't know anything good!' said he; 'they don't know anything at all!' It was really more for news than for water I put into Santa Lucia – and a pretty mess I made of it there. We looked so like pirates (as at bottom the old tub is), that they took all of us who landed to the guard-house. None of us could speak Santa Lucia, whatever that tongue may be, nor understand it. And it was not till Ethan fired a shell from the 100-pound Parrott over the town that they let us go. I hope the dogs sent you my letters. I suppose there was another infringement of neutrality. But if the Brazilian government sends this ship to Santa Lucia, I shall not command her, that's all!

Well! what happened at Loando the second time, Valencia, and Puntos Pimos, and Nueva Salamanca, and Loando this last time, you know and will know, and why we loitered so. At last, thank fortune, here we are. Actually, Mary, this ship logged on the average only thirty-two knots a day for the last week before we got her into port.

Now think of the ingratitude of men! I have brought her in here, 'according to my best discretion', and do you believe, these hidalgos, or dons, or senores, or whatever they are, had forgotten she existed. And when I showed them to her, they said in good Portugal that I was a liar. Fortunately the Consul is our old friend Kingsley. He was delighted to see me; thought I was at the bottom of the sea. From him we learned that the Confederacy was blown sky-high long ago. And from all I can learn, I may have the *Florida* back again for my own private yacht or peculium, unless she goes to Santa Lucia.

Not I, my friends! Scrape her, and mend her, and give her to the marines – and tell them her story; but do not entrust her again to my own Polly's own

FREDERIC INGHAM

A Piece of Possible History

This essay was first published in the Monthly Religious Magazine, Boston, *for October 1851. One or another professor of chronology has since taken pains to tell me that it is impossible. But until they satisfy themselves whether Homer ever lived at all, I shall hold to the note which I wrote to Miss Dryasdust's cousin, which I printed originally at the end of the article, and which will be found there in this collection. The difficulties in the geography are perhaps worse than those of chronology.*

A summer bivouac had collected together a little troop of soldiers from Joppa, under the shelter of a grove, where they had spread their sheepskins, tethered their horses, and pitched a single tent. With the carelessness of soldiers, they were chatting away the time till sleep might come, and help them to tomorrow with its chances; perhaps of fight, perhaps of another day of this camp indolence. Below the garden slope where they were lounging, the rapid torrent of Kishon ran brawling along. A full moon was rising above the rough edge of the Eastern hills, and the whole scene was alive with the loveliness of an Eastern landscape.

As they talked together, the strains of a harp came borne down the stream by the wind, mingling with the rippling of the brook.

'The boys were right,' said the captain of the little company. 'They asked leave to go up the stream to spend their evening with the Carmel-men; and said that they had there a harper, who would sing and play for them.'

'Singing at night, and fighting in the morning! It is the true soldier's life,' said another.

'Who have they there?' asked a third.

'One of those Ziklag-men,' replied the chief. 'He came into camp a few days ago, seems to be an old favourite of the king's, and is posted with his men, by the old tomb on the edge of the hill. If you cross the brook, he is not far from the Carmel post; and some of his young men have made acquaintance there.'

'One is not a soldier for nothing. If we make enemies at sight, we make friends at sight too.'

'Echish here says that the harper is a Jew.'

'What! – a deserter?'

'I do not know that; that is the king's lookout. Their company came up a week ago, were reviewed the day I was on guard at the outposts, and they had this post I tell you of assigned to them. So the king is satisfied; and, if he is, I am.'

'Jew or Gentile, Jehovah's man or Dagon's man,' said one of the younger soldiers, with a half-irreverent tone, 'I wish we had him here to sing to us.'

'And to keep us awake,' yawned another.

'Or to keep us from thinking of tomorrow,' said a third.

'Can nobody sing here, or play, or tell an old-time story?'

There was nobody. The only two soldiers of the post, who affected musical skill, were the two who had gone up to the Carmelites' bivouac; and the little company of Joppa – catching louder notes and louder, as the bard's inspiration carried him farther and farther away – crept as far up the stream as the limits of their station would permit; and lay, without noise, to catch, as they best could, the rich tones of the music as it swept down the valley.

Soothed by the sound, and by the moonlight, and by the summer breeze, they were just in mood to welcome the first interruption which broke the quiet of the night. It was the approach of one of their company, who had been detached to Accho a day or two before; and who came hurrying in to announce the speedy arrival of companions, for whom he bespoke a welcome. Just as they were to leave Accho, he said, that day, on their return to camp, an Ionian trading-vessel had entered port. He and his fellow-soldiers had waited to help her moor, and had been chatting with her seamen. They had told them of the chance of battle to which they were returning; and two or three of the younger Ionians, enchanted at the relief from the sea's imprisonment, had begged them to let them volunteer in company with them. These men had come up into the country with the soldiers, therefore; and he who had broken the silence of the listeners to the distant serenade had hurried on to tell his comrades that such visitors were on their way.

They soon appeared on foot, but hardly burdened by the light packs they bore.

A soldier's welcome soon made the Ionian sailors as much at home with the men of the bivouac, as they had been through the day with the detachment from the sea-board. A few minutes were enough to draw, out sheepskins for them to lie upon, a skin of wine for their thirst, a bunch of raisins and some oat-cakes for their hunger; a few minutes more had told the news which each party asked from the other; and then these sons of the sea and these war-bronzed Philistine's were as much at ease with each other as if they had served under the same sky for years.

'We were listening to music,' said the old chief, 'when you came up. Some of our young men have gone up, indeed, to the picket yonder, to hear the harper sing, whose voice you catch sometimes, when we are not speaking.'

'You find the Muses in the midst of arms, then,' said one of the young Ionians.

'Muses?' said the old Philistine, laughing. 'That sounds like you Greeks. Ah! sir, in our rocks here we have few enough Muses, but those who carry these lances, or teach us how to trade with the islands for tin.'

'That's not quite fair,' cried another. 'The youngsters who are gone sing well; and one of them has a harp I should be glad you should see. He made it himself from a gnarled olive-root.' And he turned to look for it.

'You'll not find it in the tent: the boy took it with him. They hoped the Ziklag minstrel might ask them to sing, I suppose.'

'A harp of olive-wood,' said the Ionian, 'seems Muse-born and Pallas-blessed.'

And, as he spoke, one of the new-comers of the Philistines leaned over, and whispered to the chief – 'He is a bard himself, and we made him promise to sing to us. I brought his harp with me that he might cheer up our bivouac. Pray, do you ask him.'

The old chief needed no persuasion; and the eyes of the whole force brightened as they found they had a minstrel 'of their own' now, when the old man pressed the young Ionian courteously to let them hear him – 'I told you, sir, that we had no Muses of our own; but we welcome all the more those who come to us from overseas.'

Homer smiled; for it was Homer whom he spoke to – Homer still in the freshness of his unblinded youth. He took the harp which the young Philistine handed to him, thrummed upon its chords, and as he tuned them said – 'I have no harp of olive-wood; we cut this out, it was years ago, from an old oleander in the marshes behind Colophon. What will you hear, gentlemen?'

'The poet chooses for himself,' said the courtly old captain.

'Let me sing you, then, of the *Olive Harp*'; and he struck the chords in a gentle, quieting harmony, which attuned itself to his own spirit, pleased as he was to find music and harmony and the olive of peace in the midst of the rough bivouac, where he had come up to look for war. But he was destined to be disappointed. Just as his prelude closed, one of the young soldiers turned upon his elbow, and whispered contemptuously to his neighbour – 'Always *olives*, always *peace:* that's all your music's good for!'

The boy spoke too loud, and Homer caught the discontented tone and words with an ear quicker than the speaker had given him credit for. He ended the prelude with a sudden crash on the strings, and said shortly, 'And what is better to sing of than the olive?'

The more courteous Philistines looked sternly on the young soldier; but he had gone too far to be frightened, and he flashed back – 'War is better. My broadsword is better. If I could sing, I would sing to your Ares; we call him Mars!'

Homer smiled gravely. 'Let it be so,' said he; and, in a lower tone, to the captain, who was troubled at the breach of courtesy, he added, 'Let the boy see what war and Mars are for.'

He struck another prelude and began. Then was it that Homer composed his 'Hymn to Mars'. In wild measure, and impetuous, he swept along through the list of Mars's titles and attributes; then his key changed, and his hearers listened more intently, more solemnly, as in a graver strain, with slower music, and an almost awed dignity of voice, the bard went on –

> 'Helper of mortals, hear!
> As thy fires give
> The present boldnesses that strive
> In youth for honour;
> So would I likewise wish to have the power
> To keep off from my head thy bitter hour,
> And quench the false fire of my soul's low kind,
> By the fit ruling of my highest mind!
> Control that sting of wealth
> That stirs me on still to the horrid scath
> Of hideous battle!
>
> Do thou, O ever blessed! give me still
> Presence of mind to put in act my will,
> Whate'er the occasion be;
> And so to live, unforced by any fear,
> Beneath those laws of peace, that never are

> Affected with pollutions popular
> 　　Of unjust injury,
> As to bear safe the burden of hard fates,
> Of foes inflexive, and inhuman hates!'

The tones died away; the company was hushed for a moment; and the old chief then said gravely to his petulant follower, 'That is what *men* fight for, boy.' But the boy did not need the counsel. Homer's manner, his voice, the music itself, the spirit of the song, as much as the words, had overcome him; and the boasting soldier was covering his tears with his hands.

Homer felt at once (the prince of gentlemen he) that the little outbreak, and the rebuke of it, had jarred the ease of their unexpected meeting. How blessed is the presence of mind with which the musician of real genius passes from song to song, 'what e'er the occasion be!' With the ease of genius he changed the tone of his melody again, and sang his own hymn, 'To Earth, the Mother of all'.

The triumphant strain is one which harmonises with every senti-ment; and he commanded instantly the rapt attention of the circle. So engrossed was he, that he did not seem to observe, as he sang, an addition to their company of some soldiers from above in the valley, just as he entered on the passage –

> 'Happy, then, are they
> Whom thou, O great in reverence!
> Are bent to honour. They shall all things find
> In all abundance! All their pastures yield
> Herds in all plenty. All their roofs are filled
> 　　With rich possessions.
> 　High happiness and wealth attend them,
> 　While, with laws well-ordered, they
> 　Cities of happy households sway;
> And their sons exult in the pleasure of youth,
> And their daughters dance with the flower-decked girls,
> Who play among the flowers of summer!
> Such are the honours thy full hands divide;
> Mother of Gods and starry Heaven's bride!'

A buzz of pleasure and a smile ran round the circle, in which the new-comers joined. They were the soldiers who had been to hear and join the music at the Carmel-men's post. The tones of Homer's harp had tempted them to return; and they had brought with them the Hebrew minstrel, to whom they had been listening. It was the outlaw David, of Bethlehem Ephrata.

David had listened to Homer more intently than anyone; and, as the pleased applause subsided, the eyes of the circle gathered upon him, and the manner of all showed that they expected him, in minstrel-fashion, to take up the same strain.

He accepted the implied invitation, played a short prelude, and taking Homer's suggestion of topic, sang in parallel with it –

> 'I will sing a new song unto thee, O God!
> Upon psaltery and harp will I sing praise to thee.
> Thou art He that giveth salvation to kings,
> That delivereth David, thy servant, from the sword.
> Rid me and save me from those who speak vanity,
> Whose right hand is a right hand of falsehood –
> That our sons may be as plants in fresh youth;
> That our daughters may be as corner-stones –
> The polished stones of our palaces;
> That our garners may be full with all manner of store;
> That our sheep may bring forth thousands and ten
>   thousands in the way;
> That there may be no cry nor complaint in our streets
> Happy is the people that is in such a case;
> Yea, happy is the people whose God is the Lord!'

The melody was triumphant; and the enthusiastic manner yet more so. The Philistines listened delighted – too careless of religion, they, indeed not to be catholic in presence of religious enthusiasm; and Homer wore the exalted expression which his face seldom wore. For the first time since his childhood, Homer felt that he was not alone in the world!

Who shall venture to tell what passed between the two minstrels, when Homer, leaving his couch, crossed the circle at once, flung himself on the ground by David's side, gave him his hand; when they looked each other in the face, and sank down into the rapid murmuring of talk, which constant gesture illustrated, but did not fully explain to the rough men around them? They respected the poets' colloquy for a while; but then, eager again to hear one harp or the other, they persuaded one of the Ionian sailors to ask Homer again to sing to them.

It was hard to persuade Homer. He shook his head, and turned back to the soldier-poet.

'What should *I* sing?' he said.

They did not enter into his notion: hearers will not always. And so, taking his question literally, they replied, 'Sing? Sing us of the snow-storm, the storm of stones, of which you sang at noon.'

Poor Homer! It was easier to do it than to be pressed to do it; and he struck his harp again –

> 'It was as when, some wintry day, to men
>   Jove would, in might, his sharp artillery show,
> He wills his winds to sleep, and over plain
>   And mountains pours, in countless flakes, his snow.
> Deep it conceals the rocky cliffs and hills,
>   Then covers all the blooming meadows o'er,
> All the rich monuments of mortals' skill,
>   All ports and rocks that break the ocean-shore.
> Rock, haven, plain, are buried by its fall;
> But the near wave, unchanging, drinks it all.
> So while these stony tempests veil the skies,
> While this on Greeks, and that on Trojans flies,
> The walls unchanged above the clamour rise.'

The men looked round upon David, whose expression, as he returned the glance, showed that he had enjoyed the fragment as well as they. But when they still looked expectant, he did not decline the unspoken invitation; but, taking Homer's harp, sang, as if the words were familiar to him –

> 'He giveth snow like wool;
> He scattereth the hoar-frost like ashes;
> He casteth forth his ice like morsels;
> Who can stand before his cold?
> He sendeth forth his word, and melteth them;
> He causeth his wind to blow, and the waters flow.'

'Always this "*He*," ' said one of the young soldiers to another.

'Yes,' he replied; 'and it was so in the beginning of the evening, when we were above there.'

'There is a strange difference between the two men, though the one plays as well as the other, and the Greek speaks with quite as little foreign accent as the Jew, and their subjects are the same.'

'Yes,' said the young Philistine harper; 'if the Greek should sing one of the Hebrew's songs, you would know he had borrowed it, in a moment.'

'And so, if it were the other way.'

'Of course,' said their old captain, joining in this conversation. 'Homer, if you call him so, sings the thing made: David sings the maker. Or, rather, Homer thinks of the thing made: David thinks of the maker, whatever they sing.'

'I was going to say that Homer would sing of cities; and David, of the life in them.'

'It is not what they say so much, as the way they look at it. The Greek sees the outside – the beauty of the thing; the Hebrew – '

'Hush!'

For David and his new friend had been talking too. Homer had told him of the storm at sea they met a few days before; and David, I think, had spoken of a mountain-tornado, as he met it years before. In the excitement of his narrative he struck the harp, which was still in his hand, and sang –

> 'Then the earth shook and trembled,
> The foundations of the hills moved and were shaken,
>   Because He was wroth;
> There went up a smoke out of his nostrils,
> And fire out of his mouth devoured;
>   It burned with living coal.
>   He bowed the heavens also, and came down,
> And darkness was under his feet;
> He rode upon a cherub and did fly,
> Yea, he did fly upon the wings of the wind.
> He made darkness his resting-place,
> His pavilions were dark waters and clouds of the skies;
> At the brightness before him his clouds passed by,
>   Hail-stones and coals of fire.
> The Lord also thundered in the heavens,
> And the highest gave his voice;
>   Hail-stones and coals of fire.
>   Yea, he sent out his arrows, and scattered them,
> And he shot out his lightnings, and discomfited them.
>   Then the channels of waters were seen,
> And the foundations of the world were made known,
>   At thy rebuke, O Lord!

At the blast of the breath of thy nostrils.
He sent from above, he took me,
He drew me out of many waters.'

'Mine were but a few verses,' said Homer. 'I am more than repaid by yours. Imagine Neptune, our sea-god, looking on a battle –

There he sat high, retired from the seas;
There looked with pity on his Grecians beaten;
There burned with rage at the god-king who slew them.
Then he rushed forward from the rugged mountains,
        Quickly descending;
He bent the forests also as he came down,
And the high cliffs shook under his feet.
        Three times he trod upon them,
And with his fourth step reached the home he sought for.

There was his palace, in the deep waters of the seas,
Shining with gold, and builded forever.
There he yoked him his swift-footed horses;
Their hoofs are brazen, and their manes are golden.
        He binds them with golden thongs,
        He seizes his golden goad,
He mounts upon his chariot, and doth fly:
Yes! he drives them forth into the waves!
And the whales rise under him from the depths,
        For they know he is their king;
And the glad sea is divided into parts,
That his steeds may fly along quickly;
And his brazen axle passes dry between the waves,
        So, bounding fast, they bring him to his Grecians.'

And the poets sank again into talk.
'You see it,' said the old Philistine. 'He paints the picture. David sings the life of the picture.'
'Yes: Homer sees what he sings; David feels his song.'
'Homer's is perfect in its description.'
'Yes; but for life, for the soul of the description, you need the Hebrew.'
'Homer might be blind; and, with that fancy and word-painting power of his, and his study of everything new, he would paint pictures as he sang, though unseen.'

'Yes,' said another; 'but David – ' And he paused.

'But David?' asked the chief.

'I was going to say that he might be blind, deaf, imprisoned, exiled, sick, or all alone, and that yet he would never know he was alone; feeling as he does as he must to sing so, of the presence of this Lord of his!'

'He does not think of a snowflake, but as sent from him."

'While the snowflake is reminding Homer of that hard, worrying, slinging work of battle. He must have seen fight himself.'

They were hushed again. For, though they no longer dared ask the poets to sing to them – so engrossed were they in each other's society – the soldiers were hardly losers from this modest courtesy. For the poets were constantly arousing each other to strike a chord, or to sing some snatch of remembered song. And so it was that Homer, apropos of I do not know what, sang in a sad tone –

> 'Like leaves on trees the race of man is found,
> Now green in youth, now withering on the ground:
> Another race the following spring supplies;
> They fall successive, and successive rise.
> So generations in their course decay,
> So flourish these, when those have passed away.'

David waited for a change in the strain; but Homer stopped. The young Hebrew asked him to go on; but Homer said that the passage which followed was mere narrative, from a long narrative poem. David looked surprised that his new friend had not pointed a moral as he sang; and said simply, 'We sing that thus –

> As for man, his days are as grass;
> As a flower of the field, so he flourisheth;
> For the wind passeth over it, and it is gone,
> And the place thereof shall know it no more.
> > But the mercy of the Lord
> > Is from everlasting to everlasting
> > > Of them that fear him;
> > > And his righteousness
> > > Unto children's children,
> > > > To such as keep his covenant,
> > As remember his commandments to do them!'

Homer's face flashed delighted. 'I, like you, "keep his covenant",' he cried; and then without a lyre, for his was still in David's hands, he sang, in clear tone –

> 'Thou bid'st me birds obey – I scorn their flight,
> If on the left they rise, or on the right!
> Heed them who may, the will of Jove I own,
> Who mortals and immortals rules alone!'

'That is more in David's key,' said the young Philistine harper, seeing that the poets had fallen to talk together again. 'But how would it sound in one of the hymns on one of our feast-days? "Who mortals and immortals rules alone." '

'How, indeed?' cried one of his young companions. 'There would be more sense in what the priests say and sing, if each were not quarrelling for his own – Dagon against Astarte, and Astarte against Dagon.'

The old captain bent over, that the poets might not hear him, and whispered – 'There it is that the Hebrews have so much more heart than we in such things. Miserable fellows though they are, so many of them, yet, when I have gone through their whole land with the caravans, the chances have been that any serious-minded man spoke of no God but this "*He*" of David's.'

'What is his name?'

'They do not know themselves, I believe.'

'Well, as I said an hour ago, God's man or Dagon's man – for those are good names enough for me – I care little; but I should like to sing as that young fellow does.'

'My boy,' said the old man, 'have not you heard him enough to see that it is not *he* that sings, near as much as this love of his for a Spirit he does not name? It is that spirited heart of his that sings.'

'*You* sing like him? Find his life, boy; and perhaps it may sing for you.'

'We should be more manly men, if he sang to us every night.'

'Or if the other did,' said an Ionian sailor.

'Yes,' said the chief. 'And yet, I think, if your countryman sang every night to me, he would make me want the other. Whether David's singing would send me to his, I do not feel sure. But how silly to compare them! As well compare the temple in Accho with the roar of a whirlwind – '

'Or the point of my lance with the flight of an eagle. The men are in two worlds.'

'O, no! that is saying too much. You said that one could paint pictures – '

' – Into which the other puts life. Yes, I did say so. We are fortunate that we have them together.'

'For this man sings of men quite as well as the other does; and to have the other sing of God – '

' – Why, it completes the song. Between them they bring the two worlds together.'

'He bows the heavens, and comes down,' said the boy of the olive-harp, trying to hum David's air.

'Let us ask them – '

And just then there rang along the valley the sound of a distant conch-shell. The soldiers groaned, roused up, and each looked for his own side-arms and his own skin.

But the poets talked on unheeding.

The old chief knocked down a stack of lances; but the crash did not rouse them. He was obliged himself to interrupt their eager converse.

'I am sorry to break in; but the night-horn has sounded to rest, and the guard will be round to inspect the posts. I am sorry to hurry you away, sir,' he said to David.

David thanked him courteously.

'Welcome the coming, speed the parting guest,' said Homer, with a smile.

'We will all meet tomorrow. And may tonight's dreams be good omens!'

'If we dream at all,' said Homer again –

> 'Without a sign his sword the brave man draws,
> And asks no omen but his country's cause.'

They were all standing together, as he made this careless reply to the captain; and one of the young men drew him aside, and whispered that David was in arms against his country.

Homer was troubled that he had spoken as he did. But the young Jew looked little as if he needed sympathy. He saw the doubt and regret which hung over their kindly faces; told them not to fear for him; singing, as he bade them good-night, and with one of the Carmel-men walked home to his own outpost –

> 'The Lord who delivered me from the paw of the lion,
> The Lord who delivered me from the paw of the bear,
> He will deliver me.'

And he smiled to think how his Carmelite companion would start, if he knew when first he used those words.

So they parted, as men who should meet on the morrow.

But God disposes.

David had left tomorrow's dangers for tomorrow to care for. It seemed to promise him that he must be in arms against Saul. But, unlike us in our eagerness to anticipate our conflicts of duty, David waited.

And the Lord delivered him. While they were singing by the brookside, the proud noblemen of the Philistine army had forced an interview with their king; and, in true native Philistine arrogance, insisted that 'this Hebrew' and his men should be sent away.

With the light of morning the king sent for the minstrel, and courteously dismissed him, because 'the princes of the Philistines have said, "He shall not go up with us to the battle." '

So David marched his men to Ziklag.

And David and Homer never met on earth again.

Note – This will be a proper place to print the following note, which I was obliged to write to a second cousin of Miss Dryasdust after she had read the MS of the article above –

Dear Madam – I thank you for your kind suggestion, in returning my paper, that it involves a piece of impossible history. You inform me, that, 'according to the nomenclatured formulas and homophonic analogies of Professor Gouraud, of never-to-be-forgotten memory, "A needle is less useful for curing a deaf head, than for putting ear-rings into a Miss's lily-ears"; and that this shows that the second king of Judah, named David (or Deaf-head) began to reign in 1055 BC, and died 1040 BC'; and further, that, according to the same authority, 'Homer flourished when the Greeks were fond of his poetry'; which, being interpreted, signifies that he flourished in 914 BC, and, consequently, could have had no more to do with David than to plant ivy over his grave, in some of his voyages to Phœnicia.

I thank you for the suggestion. I knew the unforgetting professor; and I do not doubt that he remembered David and Homer as his near friends. But, of course, to such a memory, a century or two might easily slip aside.

Now, did you look up Clement? And did you not forget the Arundelian Marbles? For, if you will take the long estimates, you will find that some folks think Homer lived as long ago as the year 1150, and some that it was as short ago as 850. And some set David as long ago as 1170, and some bring him down to a hundred and fifty years later. These are the long measures and the short measures. So the long and short of it is, that you can keep the two poets 320 years apart, while I have rather more than a century which I can select any night of, for a bivouac scene, in which to bring them together. Believe me, my dear Miss D., always yours, &c.

Confess that you forgot the Arundelian Marbles!

The South American Editor

I am tempted to include this little burlesque in this collection simply in memory of the Boston Miscellany, *the magazine in which it was published, which won for itself a brilliant reputation in its short career. There was not a large staff of writers for the* Miscellany, *but many of the names then unknown have since won distinction. To quote them in the accidental order in which I find them in the table of contents, where they are arranged by the alphabetical order of the several papers, the* Miscellany *contributors were Edward Everett, George Lunt, Nathan Hale, Jr., Nathaniel Hawthorne, N. P. Willis, W. W. Story, J. R. Lowell, C. N. Emerson, Alexander H. Everett, Sarah P. Hale, W. A. Jones, Cornelius Matthews, Mrs Kirkland, J. W. Ingraham, H. T. Tuckerman, Evart A. Duyckinck, Francis A. Durivage, Mrs J. Webb, Charles F. Powell, Charles W. Storey, Lucretia P. Hale, Charles F. Briggs, William E. Channing, Charles Lanman, G. H. Hastings, and Elizabeth B. Barrett, now Mrs Browning, some of whose earliest poems were published in this magazine. These are all the contributors whose names appear, excepting the writers of a few verses. They furnished nine tenths of the contents of the magazine. The two Everetts, Lowell, William Story, and my brother, who was the editor, were the principal contributors. And I am tempted to say that I think they all put some of their best work upon this magazine.*

The misfortune of the Miscellany, *I suppose, was that its publishers had no capital. They had to resort to the claptraps of fashion-plates and other engravings in the hope of forcing an immediate sale upon persons who, caring for fashion-plates, did not care for the literary character of the enterprise. It gave a very happy escape-pipe. however, for the high spirits of some of us who had just left college, and, through my brother's kindness, I was sometimes permitted to contribute to the journal. In memory of those early days of authorship, I select 'The South American Editor' to publish here. For the benefit of the* New York Observer, *I will state that the story is not true. And lest any should complain that it advocates elopements, I beg to observe, in the seriousness of mature life, that the proposed elopement did not succeed, and that the parties who proposed it are represented as having no guardians or keepers but themselves. The article was first published in 1842.*

It is now more than six years since I received the following letter from an old classmate of mine, Harry Barry, who had been studying divinity, and was then a settled minister. It was an answer to a communication I had sent him the week before.

Topsham, R. I., 22 January 1836

To say the truth, my dear George, your letter startled me a little. To think that I, scarcely six months settled in the profession, should be admitted so far into the romance of it as to unite forever two young runaways like yourself and Miss Julia What's-her-name is at least curious. But, to give you your due, you have made a strong case of it, and as Miss – (what is her name, I have not yours at hand) is not under any real guardianship, I do not see but I am perfectly justified in complying with your rather odd request. You see I make a conscientious matter of it.

Write me word when it shall be, and I will be sure to be ready. Jane is of course in my counsels, and she will make your little wife feel as much at home as in her father's parlour. Trust us for secrecy.

I met her last week . . .

But the rest of the letter has nothing to do with the story.

The elopement alluded to in it (if the little transaction deserves so high-sounding a name) was, in every sense of the words, strictly necessary. Julia Wentworth had resided for years with her grandfather, a pragmatic old gentleman, to whom from pure affection she had long yielded an obedience which he would have had no right to extort, and which he was sometimes disposed to abuse. He had declared in the most ingenuous manner that she should never marry with his consent any man of less fortune that her own would be; and on his consent rested the prospect of her inheriting his property.

Julia and I, however, care little for money now, we cared still less then; and her own little property and my own salary made us esteem ourselves entirely independent of the old gentleman and his will.

His intention respecting the poor girl's marriage was thundered in his ears at least once a week;, so that we both knew that I had no need to make court to him; indeed, I had never seen him, always having met her in walking, or in the evening at party, spectacle, concert, or lecture.

He had lately been more domineering than usual, and I had but little difficulty in persuading the dear girl to let me write to Harry Barry, to make the arrangement to which he assented in the letter which I have copied above. The reasoning which I pressed upon her is obvious. We loved each other – the old gentleman could not help that; and as he managed to make us very uncomfortable in Boston, in the existing state of affairs, we naturally came to the conclusion that the sooner we changed that state the better. Our excursion to Topsham would, we supposed, prove a very disagreeable business to him; but we knew it would result very agreeably for us, and so, though with a good deal of maidenly compunction and granddaughterly compassion on Julia's part, we outvoted him.

I have said that I had no fortune to enable me to come near the old gentleman's *beau ideal* of a grandson-in-law. I was then living on my salary as a South American editor. Does the reader know what that is? The South American editor of a newspaper has the uncontrolled charge of its South American news. Read any important commercial paper for a month, and at the end of it tell me if you have any clear conception of the condition of the various republics (!) of South America. If you have, it is because that journal employs an individual for the sole purpose of setting them in the clearest order before you, and that individual is its South American editor. The general-news editor of the paper will keep the run of all the details of all the histories of all the rest of the world, but he hardly attempts this in addition. If he does, he fails. It is therefore necessary, from the most cogent reasons, that any American news office which has a strong regard for the consistency or truth of its South American intelligence shall employ some person competent to take the charge which I held in the establishment of the Boston *Daily Argus* at the time of which I am speaking. Before that enterprising paper was sold, I was its 'South American man'; this being my only employment, except-ing that by a special agreement, in consideration of an addition to my salary, I was engaged to attend to the news from St Domingo, Guatemala, and Mexico.*

---

* I do not know that this explanation is at all clear. Let me, as the mathematicians say, give an instance which will illustrate the importance of this profession. It is now a few months since I received the following note from a distinguished member of the Cabinet –

Washington, January 1842
Dear Sir – We are in a little trouble about a little thing. There are now in

Monday afternoon, just a fortnight after I received Harry Barry's letter, in taking my afternoon walk round the Common, I happened to meet Julia. I always walked in the same direction when I was alone. Julia always preferred to go the other way; it was the only thing in which we differed. When we were together I always went her way of course, and liked it best.

I had told her, long before, all about Harry's letter, and the dear girl in this walk, after a little blushing and sighing, and half faltering and half hesitating and feeling uncertain, yielded to my last and warmest persuasions, and agreed to go to Mrs Pollexfen's ball that evening, ready to leave it with me in my buggy sleigh, for a three hours' ride to Topsham, where we both knew Harry would be waiting for us. I do not know how she managed to get through tea that evening with her lion of a grandfather, for she could not then cover her tearful eyes with a veil as she did through the last half of our walk together.

I know that I got through my tea and such like ordinary affairs by skipping them. I made all my arrangements, bade Gage and Streeter be ready with the sleigh at my lodgings (fortunately only two doors from

---

this city no less than three gentlemen bearing credentials to government as Chargés from the Republic of Oronoco. They are, of course, accredited from three several home governments. The President signified, when the first arrived, that he would receive the Chargé from that government, on the 2nd proximo, but none of us know who the right Chargé is. The newspapers tell nothing satisfactory about it. I suppose you know: can you write me word before the 2nd?

The gentlemen are: Dr Estremadura, accredited from the 'Constitutional Government' – his credentials are dated the 2nd of November; Don Paulo Vibeira, of the 'Friends of the People', 6th of November; M. Antonio de Vesga, 'Constitution of 1823', October 27th. They attach great importance to our decision, each having scrip to sell. In haste, truly yours.

To this letter I returned the following reply –

Sir – Our latest dates from Oronoco are to the 13th ultimo. The 'Constitution of '23' was then in full power. If, however, the policy of our government be to recognize the gentlemen whose principals shall be in office on the 2nd proximo, it is a very different affair.

You may not be acquainted with the formulas for ascertaining the duration of any given modern revolution. I now use the following, which I find almost exactly correct.

Multiply the age of the President by the number of statute miles from the equator, divide by the number of pages in the given Constitution; the result will be the length of the outbreak, in days. This formula includes, as

Mrs Pollexfen's) at half-past nine o'clock, and was the highest spirited of men when, on returning to those lodgings myself at eight o'clock, I found the following missives from the *Argus* office, which had been accumulating through the afternoon.

No. 1

4 o'clock, p.m.

Dear Sir – The southern mail, just in, brings Buenos Aires papers six days later, by the *Medora*, at Baltimore.   In haste, J.C.

(Mr C— was the gentleman who opened the newspapers, and arranged the deaths and marriages; he always kindly sent for me when I was out of the way.)

No. 2

5 o'clock, p.m.

Dear Sir – The US ship *Preble* is in at Portsmouth; latest from Valparaiso. The mail is not sorted.   Yours, J. D.

(Mr D— arranged the ship news for the *Argus*.)

---

you will see, an allowance for the heat of the climate, the zeal of the leader, and the verbosity of the theorists. The Constitution of 1823 was reproclaimed on the 25th of October last. If you will give the above formula into the hands of any of your clerks, the calculation from it will show that that government will go out of power on the 1st of February, at 25 minutes after 1 P.M. Your choice, on the 2nd, must be therefore between Vibeira and Estremadura; here you will have no difficulty. Bobádil (Vibeira's principal) was on the 13th ultimo confined under sentence of death, at such a distance from the capital that he cannot possibly escape and get into power before the 2nd of February. The 'Friends of the People', in Oronoco, have always moved slowly; they never got up an insurrection in less than nineteen days' canvassing; that was in 1839. Generally they are even longer. Of course, Estremadura will be your man.

Believe me, sir, very respectfully, your obedient servant,

GEORGE HACKMATACK.

The Cabinet had the good sense to act on my advice. My information proved nearly correct, the only error being one of seven minutes in the downfall of the 1823 Constitution. This arose from my making no allowance for difference of longitude between Piaut, where their government was established, and Opee, where it was crushed. The difference of time between those places is six minutes and fifty-three seconds, as the reader may see on a globe.

Estremadura was, of course, presented to the President, and sold his scrip.

No. 3.

6 o'clock, p.m.

Dear Sir – I boarded, this morning, off Cape Cod, the *Blunderhead*, from Carthagena, and have a week's later papers.

Truly yours, T. E.

(Mr E— was the enterprising commodore of our news-boats.)

No. 4.

6.15 o'clock, p.m.

Dear Sir – I have just opened accidentally the enclosed letter, from our correspondent at Panama. You will see that it bears a New Orleans post-mark. I hope it may prove exclusive.   Yours, J.F.

(Mr F— was general editor of the *Argus*.)

No. 5.

6.30 o'clock, p.m.

Dear Sir – A seaman, who appears to be an intelligent man, has arrived this morning at New Bedford, and says he has later news of the rebellion in Ecuador than any published. The *Rosina* (his vessel) brought no papers. I bade him call at your room at eight o'clock, which he promised to do.   Truly yours, J. G.

(Mr G— was clerk in the *Argus* counting-room.)

No 6.

7.30 o'clock, p.m.

Dear Sir – The papers by the Ville de Lyon, from Havre, which I have just received, mention the reported escape of M. Bonpland from Paraguay, the presumed death of Dr Francia, the probable overthrow of the government, the possible establishment of a republic, and a great deal more than I understand in the least.

These papers had not come to hand when I wrote you this afternoon. I have left them on your desk at the office.

In haste, J. F.

I was taken all aback by this mass of odd-looking little notes. I had spent the afternoon in drilling Singleton, the kindest of friends, as to what he should do, in any probable contingency of news of the next forty-eight hours, for I did not intend to be absent on a wedding tour even longer than that time; but I felt that Singleton was entirely unequal to such a storm of intelligence as this; and, as I hurried down to the office, my chief sensation was that of gratitude that the cloud had broken before I was out of the way; for I knew I could do a great deal in an hour, and I had faith that I might slur over my digest as quickly as possible, and be at Mrs Pollexfen's within the time arranged.

I rushed into the office in that state of zeal in which a man may do anything in almost no time. But first, I had to go into the conversation-room, and get the oral news from my sailor; then Mr H—, from one of the little news-boats, came to me in high glee, with some Venezuela gazettes, which he had just extorted from a skipper, who, with great plausibility, told him that he knew his vessel had brought no news, for she never had before. (N.B. In this instance she was the only vessel to sail, after a three months' blockade.) And then I had handed to me by Mr J— one of the commercial gentlemen, a private letter from Rio Janeiro, which had been lent him. After these delays, with full materials, I sprang to work – read, read, read; wonder, wonder, wonder; guess, guess guess; scratch, scratch, scratch; and scribble, scribble, scribble, make the only transcript I can give of the operations which followed. At first, several of the other gentlemen in the room sat around me; but soon Mr C—, having settled the deaths and marriages, and the police and municipal reporters immediately after him, screwed out their lamps and went home; then the editor himself, then the legislative reporters, then the commercial editors, then the ship-news conductor, and left me alone.

I envied them that they got through so much earlier than usual, but scratched on, only interrupted by the compositors coming in for the pages of my copy as I finished them; and finally, having made my last translation from the last *Boletin Extraordinario*, sprang up, shouting, 'Now for Mrs P—'s,' and looked at my watch. It was half-past one!* I thought of course it had stopped – no; and my last manuscript page was numbered twenty-eight! Had I been writing there five hours? Yes!

Reader, when you are an editor, with a continent's explosions to describe, you will understand how one may be unconscious of the passage of time.

I walked home, sad at heart. There was no light in all Mr Wentworth's house; there was none in any of Mrs Pollexfen's windows;† and the last carriage of her last relation had left her door. I stumbled upstairs in the dark, and threw myself on my bed. What should I say, what could I say, to Julia? Thus pondering, I fell asleep.

---

* Newspaper men of 1868 will be amused to think that half-past one was late in 1836. At that time the *Great Western Mail* was due in Boston at 6 P.M., and there was no later news except 'local', or an occasional horse express.

† The reader will observe the Arcadian habits of 1836, when the German was yet unknown.

If I were writing a novel, I should say that, at a late hour the next day, I listlessly drew aside the azure curtains of my couch, and languidly rang a silver bell which stood on my dressing-table, and received from a page dressed in an Oriental costume the notes and letters which had been left for me since morning, and the newspapers of the day.

I am not writing a novel.

The next morning, about ten o'clock, I arose and went down to breakfast. As I sat at the littered table which everyone else had left, dreading to attack my cold coffee and toast, I caught sight of the morning papers, and received some little consolation from them. There was the *Argus* with its three columns and a half of 'Important from South America', while none of the other papers had a square of any intelligibility excepting what they had copied from the *Argus* the day before. I felt a grim smile creeping over my face as I observed this signal triumph of our paper, and ventured to take a sip of the black broth as I glanced down my own article to see if there were any glaring misprints in it. Before I took the second sip, however, a loud peal at the door-bell announced a stranger, and, immediately after, a note was brought in for me which I knew was in Julia's handwriting.

> DEAR GEORGE – Don't be angry; it was not my fault, really it was not. Grandfather came home just as I was leaving last night, and was so angry, and said I should not go to the party, and I had to sit with him all the evening. Do write to me or let me see you; do something –

What a load that note took off my mind! And yet, what must the poor girl have suffered! Could the old man suspect? Singleton was true to me as steel, I knew. He could not have whispered – nor Barry; but that Jane, Barry's wife. O woman! woman! what newsmongers they are! Here were Julia and I, made miserable for life, perhaps, merely that Jane Barry might have a good story to tell. What right had Barry to a wife? Not four years out of college, and hardly settled in his parish. To think that I had been fool enough to trust even him with the particulars of my all-important secret! But here I was again interrupted, coffee-cup still full, toast still untasted, by another missive.

> *Tuesday morning*
> SIR – I wish to see you this morning. Will you call upon me, or appoint a time and place where I may meet you?
> Yours,   JEDEDIAH WENTWORTH
>
> Send word by the bearer.

'Tell Mr Wentworth I will call at his house at eleven o'clock.'

The cat was certainly out; Mrs Barry had told, or someone else had, who I did not know and hardly cared. The scene was to come now, and I was almost glad of it. Poor Julia! what a time she must have had with the old bear!

At eleven o'clock I was ushered into Mr Wentworth's sitting-room. Julia was there, but before I had even spoken to her the old gentleman came bustling across the room, with his 'Mr Hackmatack, I suppose'; and then followed a formal introduction between me and her, which both of us bore with the most praiseworthy fortitude and composure, neither evincing, even by a glance, that we had ever seen or heard of each other before. Here was another weight off my mind and Julia's. I had wronged poor Mrs Barry. The secret was not out – what could he want? It very soon appeared.

After a minute's discussion of the weather, the snow, and the thermometer, the old gentleman drew up his chair to mine, with 'I think, sir, you are connected with the *Argus* office?'

'Yes, sir; I am its South American editor.'

'Yes!' roared the old man, in a sudden rage. 'Sir, I wish South America was sunk in the depths of the sea!'

'I am sure I do, sir,' replied I, glancing at Julia, who did not, however, understand me. I had not fully passed out of my last night's distress.

My sympathising zeal soothed the old gentleman a little, and he said more coolly, in an undertone – 'Well, Sir, you are well informed, no doubt; tell me, in strict secrecy, sir, between you and me, do you – do you place full credit – entire confidence in the intelligence in this morning's paper?'

'Excuse me, sir; what paper do you allude to? Ah! the *Argus*, I see. Certainly, sir; I have not the least doubt that it is perfectly correct.'

'No doubt, sir! Do you mean to insult me? – Julia, I told you so; he says there is no doubt it is true. Tell me again there is some mistake, will you?' The poor girl had been trying to soothe him with the constant remark of uninformed people, that the newspapers are always in the wrong. He turned from her, and rose from his chair in a positive rage. She was half crying. I never saw her more distressed. What did all this mean? Were one, two, or all of us crazy?

It soon appeared. After pacing the length of the room once or twice, Wentworth came up to me again, and, attempting to appear cool, said between his closed lips – 'Do you say you have no doubt that Rio Janeiro is strictly blockaded?'

'Not the slightest in the world,' said I, trying to seem unconcerned.

'Not the slightest, sir? What are you so impudent and cool about it for? Do you think you are talking of the opening of a rose-bud or the death of a mosquito? Have you no sympathy with the sufferings of a fellow-creature? Why, sir!' and the old man's teeth chattered as he spoke, 'I have five cargoes of flour on their way to Rio, and their captains will – Damn it, sir, I shall lose the whole venture.'

The secret was out. The old fool had been sending flour to Rio, knowing as little of the state of affairs there as a child.

'And do you really mean, sir,' continued the old man, 'that there is an embargo in force in Montevideo?'

'Certainly, sir; but I'm very sorry for it.'

'Sorry for it! Of course you are – and that all foreigners are sent out of Buenos Aires?'

'Undoubtedly, sir. I wish – '

'Who does not wish so? Why, sir, my corresponding friends there are half across the sea by this time. I wish Rosas was in — and that the Indians have risen near Maranham?'

'Undoubtedly, sir.'

'Undoubtedly! I tell you, sir, I have two vessels waiting for cargoes of india-rubbers there, under a blunder-headed captain, who will do nothing he has not been bidden to – obey his orders if he breaks his owners. You smile, sir? Why, I should have made thirty thousand dollars this winter, sir, by my india-rubbers, if we had not had this devilish mild, open weather, you and Miss Julia there have been praising so. But next winter must be a severe one, and with those india-rubbers I should have made – But now those Indians – pshaw! And a revolution in Chile?'

'Yes, sir.'

'No trade there! And in Venezuela?'

'Yes, sir '

'Yes, sir; yes, sir; yes, sir; yes, sir! Sir, I am ruined. Say "Yes, sir," to that. I have thirteen vessels at this moment in the South American trade, sir; say "Yes, sir," to that. Half of them will be taken by the piratical scoundrels; say "Yes, sir," to that. Their insurance will not cover them; say "Yes, sir," to that. The other half will forfeit their cargoes, or sell them for next to nothing; say "Yes, sir," to that. I tell you I am a ruined man, and I wish South America, and your daily *Argus*, and you – '

Here the old gentleman's old-school breeding got the better of his rage, and he sank down in his armchair, and, bursting into tears, said – 'Excuse me, sir – excuse me, sir – I am too warm.'

We all sat for a few moments in silence, but then I took my share of the conversation. I wish you could have seen the old man's face light up little by little, as I showed him that to a person who understood the politics and condition of the mercurial country with which he had ignorantly attempted to trade, his condition was not near so bad as he thought it; that though one port was blockaded, another was opened; that though one revolution thwarted him, a few weeks would show another which would favour him; that the goods which, as he saw, would be worthless at the port to which he had sent them, would be valuable elsewhere; that the vessels which would fail in securing the cargoes he had ordered could secure others; that the very revolutions and wars which troubled him would require in some instances large government purchases, perhaps large contracts for freight, possibly even for passage – his vessels might be used for transports; that the very excitement of some districts might be made to turn to our advantage; that, in short, there were a thousand chances open to him which skilful agents could readily improve. I reminded him that a quick run in a clipper schooner could carry directions to half these skippers of his, to whom, with an infatuation which I could not and cannot conceive, he had left no discretion, and who indeed were to be pardoned if they could use none, seeing the tumult as they did with only half an eye. I talked to him for half an hour, and went into detail to show that my plans were not impracticable. The old gentleman grew brighter and brighter, and Julia, as I saw, whenever I stole a glance across the room, felt happier and happier. The poor girl had had a hard time since he had first heard this news whispered the evening before.

His difficulties were not over, however; for when I talked to him of the necessity of sending out one or two skilful agents immediately to take the personal superintendence of his complicated affairs, the old man sighed, and said he had no skilful agents to send.

With his customary suspicion, he had no partners, and had never entrusted his clerks with any general insight into his business. Besides, he considered them all, like his captains, blunder-headed to the last degree. I believe it was an idea of Julia's, communicated to me in an eager, entreating glance, which induced me to propose myself as one of these confidential agents, and to be responsible for the other. I thought, as I spoke, of Singleton, to whom I knew I could explain my plans in full, and whose mercantile experience would make him a valuable coadjutor. The old gentleman accepted my offer eagerly. I told him that twenty-four hours were all I wanted to prepare myself. He immediately took measures for the charter of two little clipper schooners which lay in port then; and before two days were past, Singleton and I were on our voyage to South America. Imagine, if you can, how these two days were spent. Then, as now, I could prepare for any journey in twenty minutes, and of course I had no little time at my disposal for last words with Mr and – Miss Wentworth. How I won on the old gentleman's heart in those two days! How he praised me to Julia, and then, in as natural affection, how he praised her to me! And how Julia and I smiled through our tears, when, in the last goodbyes, he said he was too old to write or read any but business letters, and charged me and her to keep up a close correspondence, which on one side should tell all that I saw and did, and on the other hand remind me of all at home.

I have neither time nor room to give the details of that South American expedition. I have no right to. There were revolutions accomplished in those days without any object in the world's eyes; and, even in mine, only serving to sell certain cargoes of long cloths and flour. The details of those outbreaks now told would make some patriotic presidents tremble in their seats; and I have no right to betray confidence at whatever rate I purchased it. Usually, indeed, my feats and Singleton's were only obtaining the best information and communicating the most speedy instructions to Mr Wentworth's vessels, which were made to move from port to port with a rapidity and intricacy of movement which none besides us two understood in the least. It was in that expedition that I travelled almost alone across the continent. I was, I think, the first white man who ever passed through the mountain path of Xamaulipas, now so famous in all the Chilean picturesque annuals. I was carrying directions for some vessels which had gone round the Cape; and what a time Burrows and Wheatland and I had a week after, when we rode into the public square of Valparaiso shouting, 'Muera la Constitucion – Viva Libertad!' by our own unassisted lungs actually raising a rebellion, and, which was of more importance, a prohibition on foreign flour, while Bahamarra and his army were within a hundred miles of us. How those vessels came up the harbour, and how we unloaded them, knowing that at best our revolution could only last five days! But as I said, I must be careful, or I shall be telling other people's secrets.

The result of that expedition was that those thirteen vessels all made good outward voyages, and all but one or two eventually made profitable home voyages.

When I returned home, the old gentleman received me with open arms. I had rescued, as he said, a large share of that fortune which he valued so highly. To say the truth, I felt and feel that he had planned his voyages so blindly, that, without some wiser head than his, they would never have resulted in anything. They were his last, as they were almost his first, South American ventures. He returned to his old course of more methodical trading for the few remaining years of his life. They were, thank Heaven, the only taste of mercantile business which I ever had. Living as I did, in the very sunshine of Mr Wentworth's favour, I went through the amusing farce of paying my addresses to Julia in approved form, and in due time received the old gentleman's cordial assent to our union, and his blessing upon it. In six months after my return, we were married; the old man as happy as a king. He would have preferred a little that the ceremony should have been performed by Mr B—, his friend and pastor, but readily assented to my wishes to call upon a dear and early friend of my own.

Harry Barry came from Topsham and performed the ceremony, 'assisted by Revd Mr B—'.

G.H.
Argus Cottage, 1 April 1842

The Old and the New, Face to Face

A THUMB-NAIL SKETCH

This essay was published in Sartain's Magazine, *in 1852, as 'A Thumb-nail Sketch', having received one of ten premiums which Mr Sartain offered to encourage young writers. It had been written a few years earlier, some time before the studies of St Paul's life by Conybeare and Howson, now so well known, were made public. The chronology of my essay does not precisely agree with that of these distinguished scholars. But I make no attempt now either to recast the essay or to discuss the delicate and complicated questions which belong to the chronology of Paul's life or to that of Nero; for there is no question with regard to the leading facts. At the end of twenty years I may again express the wish that some master competent to the greatest themes might take the trial of Paul as the subject of a picture.*

In a Roman audience-chamber, the old civilisation and the new civilisation brought out, at the very birth of the new, their chosen champions.

In that little scene, as in one of Rembrandt's thumb-nail studies for a great picture, the lights and shades are as distinct as they will ever be in the largest scene of history. The champions were perfect representatives of the parties. And any man, with the soul of a man, looking on, could have prophesied the issue of the great battle from the issue of that contest.

The old civilisation of the Roman Empire, just at that time, had reached a point which, in all those outward forms which strike the eye, would regard our times as mean indeed. It had palaces of marble, where even modern kings would build of brick with a marble front to catch the eye; it counted its armies by thousands, where we count ours by hundreds; it surmounted long colonnades with its exquisite statues, for which modern labour digs deep in ruined cities, because it cannot equal them from its own genius; it had roads, which are almost eternal, and which, for their purposes, show a luxury of wealth and labour that our boasted locomotion cannot rival. These are its works of a larger scale. And if you enter the palaces, you find pictures of matchless worth, rich dresses which modern looms cannot rival, and sumptuous furniture at which modern times can only wonder. The outside of the ancient civilisation is unequalled by the outside of ours, and for centuries will be unequalled by it. We have not surpassed it there. And we see how it attained this distinction, such as it was. It came by the constant concentration of power. Power in few hands is the secret of its display and glory. And thus that form of civilisation attained its very climax in the moment of the greatest unity of the Roman Empire. When the Empire nestled into rest, after the convulsions in which it was born; when a generation had passed away of those who had been Roman citizens; when a generation arose, which, excepting one man, the emperor, was a nation of Roman subjects – then the Empire was at its height of power, its centralisation was complete, the system of its civilisation was at the zenith of its success.

At that moment it was that there dawned at Rome the first grey morning-light of the new civilisation.

At that moment it was that that short scene, in that one chamber, contrasted the two as clearly as they can be contrasted even in long centuries.

There is one man, the emperor, who is a precise type, an exact representative, of the old. That man is brought face to face with another who is a precise type, an exact representative, of the new.

Only look at them as they stand there! The man who best illustrates the old civilisation owes to it the most careful nurture. From his childhood he has been its petted darling. Its principal is concentration under one head. He is that head. When he is a child, men know he will be emperor of the world. The wise men of the world teach him; the poets of the world flatter him; the princes of the world bow to him. He is trained in all elegant accomplishments; he is led forward through a graceful, luxurious society. His bearing is that of an emperor; his face is the face of fine physical beauty. Imagine for yourself the sensual countenance of a young Bacchus, beautiful as Milton's devils; imagine him clad in splendour before which even English luxury is mean; arrayed in jewels, to which even Eastern pomp is tinsel; imagine an expression of tired hate, of low, brutal lust, hanging on those exquisite licentious features, and you have before you the type of Roman civilisation. It is the boy just budding into manhood, whom later times will name as the lowest embodiment of meanness and cruelty! You are looking upon Nero!

Not only is this man an exact type of the ancient civilisation, its central power, its outside beauty, but the precise time of this sketch of ours is the exact climax of the *moral* results of the ancient civilisation. We are to look at Nero just when he has returned to Rome from a Southern journey.* That journey had one object, which succeeded. To his after-life it gives one memory, which never dies. He has travelled to his beautiful country palace, that he might kill his mother!

We can picture to ourselves Agrippina, by knowing that she was Nero's mother, and our picture will not fail in one feature. She has all the beauty of sense, all the attraction of passion. Indeed, she is the Empress of Rome, because she is queen of beauty – and of lust. She is most beautiful among the beautiful of Rome; but what is that beauty of feature in a state of whose matrons not one is virtuous, of whose daughters not one is chaste? It is the beauty of sense alone, fit adornment of that external grandeur, of that old society.

In the infancy of her son, this beautiful Agrippina consulted a troop of fortune-tellers as to his fate; and they told her that he would live to be Emperor of Rome, and to kill his mother. With all the ecstasy of a mother's pride fused so strangely with all the excess of an ambitious woman's love of power, she cried in answer, 'He may kill me, if only he rules Rome!'

She spoke her own fate in these words.

Here is the account of it by Tacitus. Nero had made all the preparations; had arranged a barge, that of a sudden its deck might fall heavily upon those in the cabin, and crush them in an instant. He meant thus to give to the murder which he planned the aspect of an accident. To this fatal vessel he led Agrippina. He talked with her affectionately and gravely on the way; 'and when they parted at the lakeside, with his old boyish familiarity he pressed her closely to his heart, either to conceal his purpose, or because the last sight of a mother, on the eve of death, touched even his cruel nature, and then bade her farewell.'

Just at the point upon the lake where he had directed, as the Empress sat in her cabin talking with her attendants, the treacherous deck was let fall upon them all. But the plot failed. She saw dead at her feet one of her favourites, crushed by the sudden blow. But she had escaped it. She saw that death awaited them all upon the vessel. The men around sprang forward, ready to do their master's bidding in a less clumsy and

* In the year AD 60.

more certain way. But the Empress, with one of her attendants, sprang from the treacherous vessel into the less treacherous waves. And there, this faithful friend of hers, with a woman's wit and a woman's devotion, drew on her own head the blows and stabs of the murderers above, by crying, as if in drowning, 'Save me, I am Nero's mother!' Uttering those words of self-devotion, she was killed by the murderers above, while the Empress, in safer silence, buoyed up by fragments of the wreck, floated to the shore.

Nero had failed thus in secret crime, and yet he knew that he could not stop here. And the next day after his mother's deliverance, he sent a soldier to her palace, with a guard; and there, where she was deserted even by her last attendant, without pretence of secrecy, they put to death the daughter and the mother of a Cæsar. And Nero only waits to look with a laugh upon the beauty of the corpse, before he returns to resume his government at Rome.

That moment was the culminating moment of the ancient civilisation. It is complete in its centralising power; it is complete in its external beauty; it is complete in its crime. Beautiful as Eden to the eye, with luxury, with comfort, with easy indolence to all; but dust and ashes beneath the surface! It is corrupted at the head! It is corrupted at the heart! There is nothing firm!

This is the moment which I take for our little picture At this very moment there is announced the first germ of the new civilisation. In the very midst of this falsehood, there sounds one voice of truth; in the very arms of this giant, there plays the baby boy who is to cleave him to the ground. This Nero slowly returns to the city. He meets the congratulations of a senate, which thank him and the gods that he has murdered his own mother. With the agony of an undying conscience torturing him, he strives to avert care by amusement. He hopes to turn the mob from despising him by the grandeur of their public entertainments. He enlarges for them the circus. He calls unheard-of beasts to be baited and killed for their enjoyment. The finest actors rant, the sweetest musicians sing, that Nero may forget his mother, and that his people may forget him.

At that period, the statesmen who direct the machinery of affairs inform him that his personal attention is required one morning for a state trial, to be argued before the Emperor in person. Must the Emperor be there? May he not waste the hours in the blandishments of lying courtiers, or the honeyed falsehoods of a mistress? If he chooses thus to postpone the audience, be it so; Seneca, Burrhus, and his other counsellors will obey. But the time will come when the worn-out boy will be pleased some morning with the almost forgotten majesty of state. The time comes one day. Worn out by the dissipation of the week, fretted by some blunder of his flatterers, he sends for his wiser counsellors, and bids them lead him to the audience-chamber where he will attend to these cases which need an Emperor's decision. It is at that moment that we are to look upon him.

He sits there, upon that unequalled throne, his face sickly pale with boyish debauchery; his young forehead worn with the premature sensual wrinkles of lust; and his eyes bloodshot with last night's intemperance. He sits there, the Emperor-boy, vainly trying to excite himself, and forget her, in the blazonry of that pomp, and bids them call in the prisoner.

A soldier enters, at whose side the prisoner has been chained for years. This soldier is a tried veteran of the Prætorian cohorts. He was selected, that from him this criminal could not escape; and for that purpose they have been inseparably bound. But, as he leads that other through the hall, he looks at him with a regard and earnestness which say he is no criminal to him. Long since, the criminal has been the guardian of his keeper. Long since, the keeper has cared for the prisoner with all the ardour of a new found son's affection.

They lead that grey-haired captive forward, and with his eagle eye he glances keenly round the hall. That flashing eye has ere now bade monarchs quail and those thin lips have uttered words which shall make the world ring till the last moment of the world shall come. The stately Eastern captive moves unawed through the assembly, till he makes a subject's salutation to the Emperor-judge who is to hear him. And when, then, the grey-haired sage kneels before the sensual boy, you see the prophet of the new civilisation kneel before the monarch of the old! You see Paul make a subject's formal reverence to Nero! Let me do justice to the court which is to try him. In that judgement-hall there are not only the pomp of Rome, and its crime; we have also the best of its wisdom. By the dissolute boy, Nero, there stands the prime minister Seneca, the chief of the philosophers of his time; 'Seneca the saint', cry the Christians of the next century. We will own him to be Seneca the wise, Seneca almost the good. To this sage had been given the education of the monster who was to rule the world. This sage had introduced him into power, had restrained his madness when he could, and with his colleague had conducted the general administration of the Empire with the greatest honour, while the boy was wearing out his life in debauchery in the palace. Seneca dared say more to Nero, to venture more with him, than did any other man. For the young tiger was afraid of his old master long after he had tasted blood. Yet Seneca's system was a cowardly system. It was the best of Roman morality and Greek philosophy, and still it was mean. His daring was the bravest of the men of the old civilisation. He is the type of their excellences, as is Nero the model of their power and their adornments. And yet all that Seneca's daring could venture was to seduce the baby-tyrant into the least injurious of tyrannies. From the plunder of a province he would divert him by the carnage of the circus. From the murder of a senator he could lure him by some new lust at home. From the ruin of the Empire, he could seduce him by diverting him with the ruin of a noble family. And Seneca did this with the best of motives. He said he used all the power in his hands, and he thought he did. He was one of those men of whom all times have their share. The bravest of his time, he satisfied himself with alluring the beardless Emperor by petty crime from public wrong; he could flatter him to the expedient. He dared not order him to the right.

But Seneca knew what was right. Seneca also had a well-trained conscience, which told him of right and of wrong. Seneca's brother, Gallio, had saved Paul's life when a Jewish mob would have dragged him to pieces in Corinth; and the legend is that Seneca and Paul had corresponded with each other before they stood together in Nero's presence, the one as counsel for, the other as the criminal. When Paul arose from that formal salutation, when the apostle of the new civilisation spoke to the tottering monarch of the old, if there had been one man in that assemblage, could he have failed to see that that was a turning point in the world's history? Before him in that little hall, in that little hour, was passing the scene which for centuries would be acted out upon the larger stage.

Faith on the one side, before expediency and cruelty on the other! Paul before Seneca and Nero! He was ready to address Nero, with the eloquence and vehemence which for years had been demanding utterance.

He stood at length before the baby Cæsar, to whose tribunal he had appealed from the provincial court of a doubting Festus and a trembling Agrippa.

And who shall ask what words the vigorous Christian spoke to the dastard boy! Who that knows the eloquence which rung out on the ears of astonished Stoics at Athens, which commanded the incense and the hecatombs of wandering peasants in Asia, which stilled the gabbling clamour of a wild mob at Jerusalem – who will doubt the tone in which Paul spoke to Nero! The boy quailed for the moment before the man! The gilded dotard shrunk back from the home truths of the new, young, vigorous faith: the ruler of a hundred legions was nothing before the God-commissioned prisoner.

No; though at this audience all men forsook Paul as he tells us; though not one of the timid converts were there, but the soldier chained at his side – still he triumphed over Nero and Nero's minister.

From that audience-hall those three men retire. The boy, grown old in lust, goes thence to be an hour alone, to ponder for an hour on this God, this resurrection, and this truth, of which the Jew, in such uncourtly phrase, has harangued him. To be alone, until the spectre of a dying mother rises again to haunt him, to persecute him and drive him forth to his followers and feasters, where he will try to forget Paul and the Saviour and God, where he would be glad to banish them forever. He does not banish them forever! Henceforward, whenever that spectre of a mother comes before him, it must re-echo the words of God and eternity which Paul has spoken. Whenever the chained and bleeding captive of the arena bends suppliant before him, there must return the memory of the only captive who was never suppliant before him, and his words of sturdy power!

And Seneca? Seneca goes home with the mortified feelings of a great man who has detected his own meanness.

We all know the feeling; for all God's children might be great, and it is with miserable mortification that we detect ourselves in one or another pettiness. Seneca goes home to say – 'This wild *Easterner* has rebuked the Emperor as I have so often wanted to rebuke him. He stood there, as I have wanted to stand – a man before a brute.

'He said what I have thought, and have been afraid to say. Downright, straightforward, he told the Emperor truths as to Rome, as to man, and as to his vices, which I have longed to tell him. He has done what I am afraid to do. He has dared this, which I have dallied with, and left undone. *What is the mystery of his power?*'

Seneca did not know. Nero did not know. The 'Eastern mystery' was in presence before them, and they knew it not!

What was the mystery of Paul's power?

Paul leaves them with the triumph of a man who has accomplished the hope of long years. Those solemn words of his, 'After that, I *must* also see Rome', expressed the longing of years, whose object now, in part, at least, is gratified. He must see Rome!

It is God's mission to him that he see Rome and its Emperor. Paul has seen with the spirit's eye what we have seen since in history – that he is to be the living link by which the electric fire of life should pass first from religious Asia to quicken this dead, brutish Europe. He knows that he is God's messenger to bear this mystery of life eternal from the one land to the other, and to unfold it there. And today has made real, in fact, this his inward confidence. Today has put the seal of fact on that vision of his, years since, when he first left his Asiatic home. A prisoner in chains, still he has today seen the accomplishment of the vows, hopes, and resolutions of that field of Troy, most truly famous from the night he spent there. There was another of these hours when God brings into one spot the acts which shall be the *argument* of centuries of history. Paul had come down there in his long Asiatic journeys – Eastern in his lineage, Eastern in his temperament, Eastern in his outward life, and Eastern in his faith – to that narrow Hellespont, which for long ages has separated East from West, tore madly up the chains which would unite them, overwhelmed even love when it sought to intermarry them, and left their cliffs frowning eternal hate from shore to shore. Paul stood upon the Asian shore and looked across upon the Western. There were Macedonia and the hills of Greece, here Troas and the ruins of Ilium. The names speak war. The blue Hellespont has no voice but separation, except to Paul. But to Paul, sleeping, it might be, on the tomb of Achilles, that night the 'man of Macedonia' appears, and bids him come over to avenge Asia, to pay back the debt of Troy.

'Come over *and help us.*' Give us life, for we gave you death. Give us help for we gave you ruin. Paul was not disobedient to the heavenly vision. The Christian Alexander, he crosses to Macedon with the words of peace instead of war – the Christian shepherd of the people, he carries to Greece, from Troy, the tidings of salvation instead of carnage, of Charity instead of licence. And he knows that to Europe it is the beginning of her new civilisation, it is the dawn of her new warfare, of her new poetry, of her reign of heroes who are immortal.

That *faith* of his, now years old, has this day received its crowning victory. This day, when he has faced Nero and Seneca together, may well stand in his mind as undoing centuries of bloodshed and of licence.

And in this effort, and in that spiritual strength which had nerved him in planning it and carrying it through, was the 'Asian mystery'. Ask what was the secret of Paul's power as he bearded the baby Emperor, and abashed the baby Philosopher? What did he give the praise to, as he left that scene? What was the principle in action there, but faith in the new life, faith in the God who gave it!

We do not wonder, as Seneca wondered, that such a man as Paul dared say anything to such a boy as Nero! The absolute courage of the new faith was the motive-power which forced it upon the world. Here were the sternest of morals driven forward with the most ultra bravery.

Perfect faith gave perfect courage to the first witnesses. And there was the 'mystery' of their victories.

And so, in this case, when after a while Seneca again reminded Nero of his captive, poor Nero did not dare but meet him again. Yet, when he met him again in that same judgment-hall, he did not dare hear him long; and we may be sure that there were but few words before, with such affectation of dignity as he could summon, he bade them set the prisoner free.

Paul free! The old had faced the new. Each had named its champion. And the new conquers!

The Dot and Line Alphabet

This sketch was originally published in the Atlantic Monthly *for October 1858, just at the time that the first Atlantic cable, whose first prattle had been welcomed by the acclamations of a continent, gasped its last under the manipulations of De Sauty. It has since been copied by Mr Prescott in his valuable hand-book of the electric telegraph.*

The war, which has taught us all so much, has given a brilliant illustration of the dot and line alphabet, wholly apart from the electric use of it, which will undoubtedly be often repeated. In the movements of our troops under General Foster in North Carolina, Dr J. B. Upham of Boston, the distinguished medical director in that depart-ment, equally distinguished for the success with which he has led forward the musical education of New England, trained a corps of buglers to converse with each other by long and short bugle-notes, and thus to carry information with literal accuracy from point to point at any distance within which the tones of a bugle could be heard. It will readily be seen that there are many occasions in military affairs when such means of conversation might prove of inestimable value. Mr Tuttle, the astronomer, on duty in the same campaign, made a similar arrangement with long and short flashes of light.

Just in the triumph week of that Great Telegraph which takes its name from the *Atlantic Monthly*, I read in the September number of that journal the revelations of an observer who was surprised to find that he had the power of reading, as they run, the revelations of the wire. I had the hope that he was about to explain to the public the more general use of this instrument – which, with a stupid fatuity, the public has as yet failed to grasp. Because its signals have been first applied by means of electro-magnetism, and afterwards by means of the chemical power of electricity, the many-headed people refuses to avail itself, as it might do very easily, of the same signals for the simpler transmission of intelligence, whatever the power employed.

The great invention of Mr Morse is his register and alphabet. He himself eagerly disclaims any pretension to the original conception of the use of electricity as an errand-boy. Hundreds of people had thought of that and suggested it; but Morse was the first to give the errand-boy such a written message, that he could not lose it on the way, nor mistake it when he arrived. The public, eager to thank Morse, as he deserves, thanks him for something he did not invent. For this he probably cares very little; nor do I care more. But the public does not thank him for what he did originate – this invaluable and simple alphabet. Now, as I use it myself in every detail of life, and see every hour how the public might use it, if it chose, I am really sorry for this negligence – both on the score of his fame, and of general convenience.

Please to understand, then, ignorant Reader, that this curious alphabet reduces all the complex machinery of Cadmus and the rest of the writing-masters to characters as simple as can be made by a dot, a space, and a line, variously combined. Thus, the marks · – designate the letter A. The marks – · · · designate the letter B. All the other letters are designated in as simple a manner.

Now I am stripping myself of one of the private comforts of my life, (but what will one not do for mankind?) when I explain that this simple alphabet need not be confined to electrical signals. *Long* and *short* make it all – and wherever long and short can be combined, be it in marks, sounds, sneezes, fainting fits, canes, or children, ideas can be conveyed by this arrangement of the long and short together. Only last night I was talking scandal with Mrs Wilberforce at a summer party at the Hammersmiths. To my amazement, my wife, who scarcely can play 'The Fisher's Hornpipe', interrupted us by asking Mrs Wilberforce if she could give her the idea of an air in 'The Butcher of Turin.' Mrs Wilberforce had never heard that opera – indeed, had never heard of it. My angel-wife was surprised – stood thrumming at the piano – wondered she could not catch this very odd bit of discordant accord at all – but checked herself in her effort, as soon as I observed that her long notes and short notes, in their tum-tee, tee – tee-tee, tee-tum tum, meant, 'He's her brother.' The conversation on her side turned from 'The Butcher of Turin', and I had just time on the hint thus given me by Mrs I. to pass a grateful eulogium on the distinguished statesman whom Mrs Wilberforce, with all a sister's care, had rocked in his baby-cradle – whom but for my wife's long and short notes, I should have clumsily abused among the other statesmen of the day.

You will see, in an instant, awakening Reader, that it is not the business simply of 'operators' in telegraphic dens to know this Morse alphabet, but your business, and that of every man and woman. If our school committees understood the times, it would be taught, even before phonography or physiology, at school. I believe both these sciences now precede the old English alphabet.

As I write these words, the bell of the South Congregational strikes dong, dong, dong – dong, dong, dong, dong – dong. Nobody has unlocked the church-door I know that, for I am locked up in the vestry. The old tin sign, 'In case of fire, the key will be found at the opposite house', has long since been taken down, and made into the nose of a water-pot. Yet there is no Goody-Two-Shoes locked in. No one except me, and certainly I am not ringing the bell. No! But, thanks to Dr Channing's Fire Alarm,* the bell is informing the South End that there is a fire in District Dong-dong-dong – that is to say, District No. 3. Before I have explained to you so far, the 'Eagle' engine, with a good deal of noise, has passed the house on its way to that fated district. An immense improvement this on the old system, when the engines radiated from their houses in every possible direction, and the fire was extinguished by the few machines whose lines of quest happened to cross each other at the particular place where the child had been building cob-houses out of lucifer-matches in a paper warehouse. Yes, it is a very great improvement. All those persons, like you and me, who have no property in District Dong-dong-dong, can now sit at home at ease – and little need we think upon the mud above the knees of those who have property in that district and are running to look after it. But for them the improvement only brings misery. You arrive wet, hot or cold, or both, at the large District No. 2, to find that the lucifer-matches were half a mile away from your store – and that your own private watchman, even, had not been waked by the working of the distant engines. Wet property holder, as you walk home, consider this. When you are next in the Common Council, vote an appropriation for applying Morse's alphabet of long and short to the bells. Then they can be made to sound intelligibly. Daung ding ding – ding ding daung – daung daung daung, and so on, will tell you as you wake in the night that it is Mr B—'s store which is on fire, and not yours, or that it is yours and not his. This is not only a convenience to you and a relief to your wife and family, who will thus be spared your excursions to unavailable and unsatisfactory fires, and your somewhat irritated return

---

*   The Fire Alarm is the invention of Dr William F. Channing:

> Wizard of such dreaded fame,
>   That when in Salamanca's cave,
>   Him listed his magic wand to wave,
>   The bells would ring in Notre Dame.

– it will be a great relief to the Fire Department. How placid the operations of a fire where none attend except on business! The various engines arrive, but no throng of distant citizens, men and boys, fearful of the destruction of their all. They have all roused on their pillows to learn that it is No. 530 Pearl Street which is in flames. All but the owner of No. 530 Pearl Street have dropped back to sleep. He alone has rapidly repaired to the scene. That is he, who stands in the uncrowded street with the Chief Engineer, on the deck of No. 18, as she plays away. His property destroyed, the engines retire – he mentions the amount of his insurance to those persons who represent the daily press, they all retire to their homes – and the whole is finished as simply, almost, as was his private entry in his day-book the afternoon before.*

This is what might be, if the magnetic alarm only struck *long* and *short*, and we had all learned Morse's alphabet. Indeed, there is nothing the bells could not tell, if you would only give them time enough. We have only one chime, for musical purposes, in the town. But, without attempting tunes, only give the bells the Morse alphabet, and every bell in Boston might chant in monotone the words of Hail Columbia at length, every Fourth of July. Indeed, if Mr Barnard should report any day that a discouraged 'prentice-boy had left town for his country home, all the bells could instantly be set to work to speak articulately, in language regarding which the dullest imagination need not be at loss,

> Turn again, Higginbottom,
> Lord Mayor of Boston!

I have suggested the propriety of introducing this alphabet into the primary schools. I need not say I have taught it to my own children – and I have been gratified to see how rapidly it made head, against the more complex alphabet, in the grammar schools. Of course it does; an alphabet of two characters matched against one of twenty-six – or of forty-odd, as the very odd one of the phonotypists employ! On the Franklin-medal day I went to the Johnson School examination. One of the committee asked a nice girl what was the capital of Brazil. The

---

* I am proud to say that such suggestions have had so much weight, that in 1868 the alarm strikes the number of the box which first telegraphs danger, six-four, six-four, &c., six being the district number, and four the box number in that district.

child looked tired and pale, and, for an instant, hesitated. But, before she had time to commit herself, all answering was rendered impossible by an awful turn of whooping-cough which one of my own sons was seized with – who had gone to the examination with me. Hawm, hem hem – hem hem hem – hem, hem – hawm, hem hem – hem hem hem – hem, hem – barked the poor child, who was at the opposite extreme of the school-room. The spectators and the committee looked to see him fall dead with a broken blood-vessel. I confess that I felt no alarm, after I observed that some of his gasps were long and some very *staccato*; nor did pretty little Mabel Warren. She recovered her colour – and, as soon as silence was in the least restored, answered, '*Rio* is the capital of Brazil,' – as modestly and properly as if she had been taught it in her cradle. They are nothing but children, any of them – but that afternoon, after they had done all the singing the city needed for its annual entertainment of the singers, I saw Bob and Mabel start for a long expedition into West Roxbury – and when he came back, I know it was a long featherfew, from her prize school-bouquet, that he pressed in his Greene's *Analysis*, with a short frond of maiden's hair.

I hope nobody will write a letter to the *Atlantic*, to say that these are very trifling uses. The communication of useful information is never trifling. It is as important to save a nice child from mortification on examination day, as it is to tell Mr Fremont that he is not elected President. If, however, the reader is distressed, because these illustrations do not seem to his more benighted observation to belong to the big bow-wow strain of human life, let him consider the arrangement which ought to have been made years since, for lee shores, railroad collisions, and that curious class of maritime accidents where one steamer runs into another under the impression that she is a lighthouse. Imagine the Morse alphabet applied to a steam whistle, which is often heard five miles. It needs only *long* and *short* again. 'Stop *Comet*', for instance, when you send it down the railroad line, by the wire, is expressed thus –

$$\cdots \ — \ \cdot\cdot \ \cdots\cdot\cdot \ \cdots \ \cdot\cdot \ —— \ \cdot —$$

Very good message, if *Comet* happens to be at the telegraph station when it comes! But what if *Comet* has gone by? Much good will your trumpery message do then! If, however, you have the wit to sound your long and short on an engine-whistle, thus – scre scre, scre; screeee; scre scre; scre scre scre scre scre; scre scre scre; scre scre; screeeee screeeee; scre; screeeee – why, then the whole neighbour-hood, for five miles around, will know that *Comet* must stop, if only they understand spoken language – and among others, the engineman of *Comet* will understand it; and *Comet* will not run into that wreck of worlds which gives the order – with the nucleus of hot iron and his tail of five hundred tons of coal. – So, of the signals which fog-bells can give, attached to lighthouses. How excellent to have them proclaim through the darkness, 'I am Wall!' Or of signals for steamship engineers. When our friends were on board the *Arabia* the other day, and she and the *Europa* pitched into each other – as if, on that happy week, all the continents were to kiss and join hands all round – how great the relief to the passengers on each, if, through every night of their passage, collision had been prevented by this simple expedient! One boat would have screamed, '*Europa, Europa, Europa*', from night to morning – and the other, '*Arabia, Arabia, Arabia*' – and neither would have been mistaken, as one unfortunately was, for a lighthouse.

The long and short of it is, that whoever can mark distinctions of time can use this alphabet of long-and-short, however he may mark them. It is therefore within the compass of all intelligent beings, except those who are no longer conscious of the passage of time, having exchanged its limitations for the wide sweep of eternity. The illimitable range of this alphabet, however, is not half disclosed when this has been said. Most articulate language addresses itself to one sense, or at most to two, sight and sound. I see, as I write, that the particular illustrations I have given are all of them confined to signals seen or signals heard. But the dot-and-line alphabet, in the few years of its history, has already shown that it is not restricted to these two senses, but makes itself intelligible to all. Its message, of course, is heard as well as read. Any good operator understands the sounds of its ticks upon the flowing strip of paper, as well as when he sees it. As he lies in his cot at midnight, he will expound the passing message without striking a light to see it. But this is only what may be said of any written language. You can read this article to your wife, or she can read it, as she prefers; that is, she chooses whether it shall address her eye or her ear. But the long-and-short alphabet of Morse and his imitators despises such narrow range. It addresses whichever of the five senses the listener chooses. This fact is illustrated by a curious set of anecdotes – never yet put in print, I think – of that critical despatch which in one night announced General Taylor's death to this whole land. Most of the readers of these lines probably read that despatch in the morning's paper. The compositors and editors had read it. To them it was a despatch to the eye. But half the operators at the stations *heard* it ticked out, by the register stroke, and knew it before they wrote it down for the press. To them it was a despatch to the ear. My good friend Langenzunge had not that resource. He had just been promised, by the General himself (under whom he served at Palo Alto), the office of Superintendent of the Rocky Mountain Lines. He was returning from Washington over the Baltimore and Ohio Railroad, on a freight-train, when he heard of the President's danger. Langenzunge loved Old Rough and Ready – and he felt badly about his own office, too. But his extempore train chose to stop at a forsaken shanty-village on the Potomac, for four mortal hours, at midnight. What does he do, but walk down the line into the darkness, climb a telegraph-post, cut a wire, and applied the two ends to his tongue, to *taste*, at the fatal moment, the words, 'Died at half-past ten.' Poor Langenzunge! he hardly had nerve to solder the wire again. Cogs told me that they had just fitted up the Naguadavick stations with Bain's chemical revolving disk. This disk is charged with a salt of potash, which, when the electric spark passes through it, is changed to Prussian blue. Your despatch is noiselessly written in dark blue dots and lines. Just as the disk started on that fatal despatch, and Cogs bent over it to read, his spirit-lamp blew up – as the dear things will. They were beside themselves in the lonely, dark office; but, while the men were fumbling for matches, which would not go, Cogs's sister, Nydia, a sweet blind girl, who had learned Bain's alphabet from Dr Howe at South Boston, bent over the chemical paper, and *smelt* out the prussiate of potash, as it formed itself in lines and dots to tell the sad story. Almost anybody used to reading the blind books can read the embossed Morse messages with the finger – and so this message was read at all the midnight way-stations where no night-work is expected, and where the companies do not supply fluid or oil. Within my narrow circle of acquaintance, therefore, there were these simultaneous instances, where the same message was seen, heard, smelled, tasted, and felt. So universal is the dot-and-line alphabet – for Bain's is on the same principle as Morse's.

The reader sees, therefore, first, that the dot-and-line alphabet can be employed by any being who has command of any long and short symbols – be they long and short notches, such as Robinson Crusoe kept his accounts with, or long and short waves of electricity, such as these which Valentia is sending across to the Newfoundland bay, so prophetically and appropriately named the Bay of Bulls. Also, I hope the reader sees that the alphabet can be understood by any intelligent being who has any one of the five senses left him – by all rational men, that is, excepting the few eyeless deaf persons who have lost both taste and smell in some complete paralysis. The use of Morse's telegraph is by no means confined to the small clique who possess or who understand electrical batteries. It is not only the torpedo or the *Gymnotus electricus* that can send us messages from the ocean. Whales in the sea can telegraph as well as senators on land, if they will only note the difference between long spoutings and short ones. And they can listen, too. If they will only note the difference between long and short, the eel of Ocean's bottom may feel on his slippery skin the smooth messages of our Presidents, and the catfish, in his darkness, look fearless on the secrets of a Queen. Any beast, bird, fish, or insect which can discriminate between long and short, may use the telegraph alphabet, if he have sense enough. Any creature which can hear, smell, taste, feel, or see, may take note of its signals, if he can understand them. A tired listener at church, by properly varying his long yawns and his short ones, may express his opinion of the sermon to the opposite gallery before the sermon is done. A dumb tobacconist may trade with his customers in an alphabet of short sixes and long nines. A beleaguered Sebastopol may explain its wants to the relieving army beyond the line of the Chernaya by the lispings of its short Paixhans and its long twenty-fours.

The Last Voyage of the Resolute

I had some opportunities, which no other writer for the press had, I believe, of examining the Resolute on her return from that weird voyage which is the most remarkable in the history of the navies of the world. And, as I know of no other printed record of the whole of that voyage than this, which was published in the Boston Daily Advertiser *of 11 June 1856, I reprint it here. Readers should remember that the English government abandoned all claim on the vessel; that the American government then bought her of the salvors, refitted her completely, and sent her to England as a present to the Queen. The Queen visited the ship, and accepted the present in person. The* Resolute *has never since been to sea. I do not load the page with authorities; but I studied the original reports of the Arctic expeditions carefully in preparing the paper, and I believe it to be accurate throughout.*

The voyage from New London to England, when she was thus returned, is strictly her last voyage. But when this article was printed its name was correct.

It was in early spring in 1852, early on the morning of the 21 April, that the stout English discovery ship *Resolute*, manned by a large crew, commanded by a most manly man, Henry Kellett, left her moorings in the great river Thames, a little below the old town of London, was taken in tow by a fussy steam-tug, and proudly started as one of a fine English squadron in the great search of the nations for the lost Sir John Franklin. It was late in the year 1855, on the 24 December, that the same ship, weatherworn, scantily rigged, without her lighter masts, all in the trim of a vessel which has had a hard fight with wind, water, ice, and time, made the lighthouse of *New* London – waited for day and came round to anchor in the other river Thames, of *New* England. Not one man of the English crew was on board. The gallant Captain Kellett was not there; but in his place an American master, who had shown, in his way, equal gallantry. The sixty or seventy men with whom she sailed were all in their homes more than a year ago. The eleven men with whom she returned had had to double parts, and to work hard to make good the places of the sixty. And between the day when the Englishmen left her, and the day the Americans found her, she had spent fifteen months and more alone. She was girt in by the ice of the Arctic seas. No man knows where she went, what narrow scapes she passed through, how low her thermometers marked cold – it is a bit of her history which was never written. Nor what befell her little tender, the *Intrepid*, which was left in her neighbourhood, 'ready for occupation', just as she was left. No man will ever tell of the nip that proved too much for her – of the opening of her seams, and her disappearance beneath the ice. But here is the hardly *Resolute*, which, on 15 May 1854, her brave commander left, as he was ordered, 'ready for occupation' – which the brave Captain Buddington found 10 September 1855, more than a thousand miles from there, and pronounced still 'ready for occupation' – and of what can be known of her history from Old London to New London, from Old England's Thames to New England's Thames, we will try to tell the story; as it is written in the letters of her old officers and told by the lips of her new rescuers.

For Arctic work, if ships are to go into every nook and lane of ice that will yield at all to wind and steam, they must be as nearly indestructible as man can make them. For Arctic work, therefore, and for discovery work, ships built of the teak wood of Malabar and Java are considered most precisely fitted. Ships built of teak are said to be wholly indestructible by time. To this we owe the fact, which now becomes part of a strange coincidence, that one of the old Captain Cook's ships which went round the world with him has been, till within a few years, a-whaling among the American whalers, revisiting, as a familiar thing, the shores which she was first to discover. The English admiralty, eager to fit out for Arctic service a ship of the best build they could find, bought the two teak-built ships *Baboo* and *Ptarmigan* in 1850 – sent them to their own dockyards to be refitted, and the *Baboo* became the *Assistance* – the *Ptarmigan* became the *Resolute*, of their squadrons of Arctic discovery.

Does the reader know that in the desolation of the Arctic shores the ptarmigan is the bird most often found? It is the Arctic grouse or partridge, and often have the ptarmigans of Melville Island furnished sport and even dinners to the hungry officers of the *Resolute*, wholly unconscious that she had ever been their god-child, and had thrown off their name only to take that which she now wears.

Early in May 1850, just at the time we now know that brave Sir John Franklin and the remnant of his crew were dying of starvation at the mouth of Back's River, the *Resolute* sailed first for the Arctic seas, the flag-ship of Commodore Austin, with whose little squadron our own De Haven and his men had such pleasant intercourse near Beechey Island. In the course of that expedition she wintered off Cornwallis Island – and in autumn of the next year returned to England.

Whenever a squadron or a man or an army returns to England, unless in the extreme and exceptional case of complete victory over obstacle invincible, there is always dissatisfaction. This is the English way. And so there was dissatisfaction when Captain Austin returned with his ships and men. There was also still a lingering hope that some trace of Franklin might yet be found, perhaps some of his party. Yet more, there were two of the searching ships which had entered the Polar seas from Behring's Straits on the west, the *Enterprise* and *Investigator*, which might need relief before they came through or returned. Arctic search became a passion by this time, and at once a new squadron was fitted out to take the seas in the spring of 1852. This squadron consisted of the *Assistance* and *Resolute* again, which had been refitted since their return, of the *Intrepid* and *Pioneer*, two steamships used as tenders to the *Assistance* and *Resolute* respectively, and of the *North Star*, which had also been in those regions, and now went as a storeship to the rest of the squadron. To the command of the whole Sir Edward Belcher was appointed, an officer who had served in some of the earlier Arctic expeditions. Officers and men volunteered in full numbers for the service, and these five vessels therefore carried out a body of men who brought more experience of the Northern seas together than any expedition which had ever visited them.

Of these, Captain Henry Kellett had command of the *Resolute*, and was second in seniority to Sir Edward Belcher, who made the *Assistance* the flagship. It shows what sort of man he was, to say that for more than ten years he spent only part of one in England, and was the rest of the time in an antipodean hemisphere or a hyperborean zone. Before brave Sir John Franklin sailed, Captain Kellett was in the Pacific. Just as he was to return home, he was ordered into the Arctic seas to search for Sir John. Three years successively, in his ship the *Herald*, he passed inside Behring's Straits, and far into the Arctic Ocean. He discovered Herald Island, the farthest land known there. He was one of the last men to see McClure in the *Investigator* before she entered the Polar seas from the northwest. He sent three of his men on board that ship to meet them all again, as will be seen, in strange surroundings. After more than seven years of this Pacific and Arctic life, he returned to England, in May or June 1851, and in the next winter volunteered to try the eastern approach to the same Arctic seas in our ship, the *Resolute*. Some of his old officers sailed with him.

We know nothing of Captain Kellett but what his own letters, despatches, and instructions show, as they are now printed in enormous parliamentary blue-books, and what the despatches and letters of his officers and of his commander show. But these papers present the picture of a vigorous, hearty man, kind to his crew and a great favourite with them, brave in whatever trial, always considerate, generous to his officers, reposing confidence in their integrity; a man, in short, of whom the world will be apt to hear more. His commander, Sir Edward Belcher, tried by the same standard, appears a brave and ready man, apt to talk of himself, not very considerate of his inferiors, confident in his own opinion; in short, a man with whom one would not care to spend three Arctic winters. With him, as we trace the *Resolute*'s fortunes, we shall have much to do. Of Captain Kellett we shall see something all along till the day when he sadly left her, as bidden by Sir Edward Belcher, 'ready for occupation.'

With such a captain, and with sixty-odd men, the *Resolute* cast off her moorings in the grey of the morning on 21 April 1852, to go in search of Sir John Franklin. The brave Sir John had died two years before, but no one knew that, nor whispered it. The river steam-tug *Monkey* took her in tow, other steamers took the *Assistance* and the *North Star*; the *Intrepid* and *Pioneer* got up their own steam, and to the cheers of the little company gathered at Greenhithe to see them off, they went down the Thames. At the Nore, the steamship *Desperate* took the *Resolute* in charge, Sir Edward Belcher made the signal 'Orkneys' as the place of rendezvous, and in four days she was there, in Stromness outer harbour. Here there was a little shifting of provisions and coal-bags, those of the men who could get on shore squandered their spending-money, and then, on 28 April, she and hers bade goodbye to British soil. And, though they have welcomed it again long since, she has not seen it from then till now.

The *Desperate* steamer took her in tow, she sent her own tow-lines to the *North Star*, and for three days in this procession of so wild and weird a name, they three forged on westward toward Greenland – a train which would have startled any old Viking had he fallen in with it, with a fresh gale blowing all the time and 'a nasty sea'. On the fourth day all the tow-lines broke or were cast off however, Neptune and the winds claimed their own, and the *Resolute* tried her own resources. The towing steamers were sent home in a few days more, and the squadron left to itself.

We have too much to tell in this short article to be able to dwell on the details of her visits to the hospitable Danes of Greenland, or of her passage through the ice of Baffin's Bay. But here is one incident, which, as the event has proved, is part of a singular coincidence. On the 6th of July all the squadron, tangled in the ice, joined a fleet of whalers beset in it by a temporary opening between the gigantic masses. Caught at the head of a bight in the ice, with the *Assistance* and the *Pioneer*, the *Resolute* was, for the emergency, docked there, and, by the ice closing behind her, was, for a while, detained. Meanwhile the rest of the fleet, whalers and discovery ships, passed on by a little lane of water, the American whaler *McLellan* leading. This *McLellan* was one of the ships of the spirited New London merchants, Messrs Perkins & Smith, another of whose vessels has now found the *Resolute* and befriended her in her need in those seas. The *McLellan* was their pioneer vessel there.

The *North Star* of the English squadron followed the *McLellan*. A long train stretched out behind. Whalers and government ships, as they happened to fall into line – a long three quarters of a mile. It was lovely weather, and, though the long lane closed up so that they could neither go back nor forward – nobody apprehended injury till it was announced on the morning of the 7th that the poor *McLellan* was nipped in the ice and her crew were deserting her. Sir Edward Belcher was then in condition to befriend her, sent his carpenters to examine her – put a few charges of powder into the ice to relieve the pressure upon her – and by the end of the day it was agreed that her injuries could be repaired, and her crew went on board again. But there is no saying what ice will do next. The next morning there was a fresh wind, the *McLellan* was caught again, and the water poured into her, a steady stream. She drifted about unmanageable, now into one ship, now into another, and the English whalemen began to pour on board, to help themselves to such plunder as they chose. At the Captain's request, Sir Edward Belcher put an end to this, sent sentries on board, and working parties, to clear her as far as might be, and keep account of what her stores were and where they went to. In a day or two more she sank to the water's edge and a friendly charge or two of powder put her out of the way of harm to the rest of the fleet. After such a week spent together it will easily be understood that the New London whalemen did not feel strangers on board one of Sir Edward's vessels when they found her 'ready for occupation' three years and more afterwards.

In this tussle with the ice, the *Resolute* was nipped once or twice, but she has known harder nips than that since. As July wore away, she made her way across Baffin's Bay, and on 10 August made Beechey Island – known now as the headquarters for years of the searching squadrons, because, as it happened, the place where the last traces of Franklin's ships were found – the wintering place of his first winter. But Captain Kellett was on what is called the 'western search', and he only stayed at Beechey Island to complete his provisions from the storeships and in the few days which this took, to see for himself the sad memorials of Franklin's party – and then the *Resolute* and *Intrepid* were away, through Barrow's Straits – on the track which Parry ran along with such success thirty-three years before – and which no one had followed with as good fortune as he, until now.

On 15 August Captain Kellett was off; bade goodbye to the party at Beechey Island, and was try his fortune in independent command. He had not the best of luck at starting. The reader must remember that one great object of these Arctic expeditions was to leave provisions for starving men. For such a purpose, and for travelling parties of his own over the ice, Captain Kellett was to leave a depot at Assistance Bay, some thirty miles only from Beechey Island. In nearing for that purpose the *Resolute* grounded, was left with but seven feet of water, the ice threw her over on her starboard bilge, and she was almost lost. Not quite lost, however, or we should not be telling her story. At midnight she was got off, leaving sixty feet of her false keel behind. Captain Kellett forged on in her – left a depot here and another there – and at the end of the short Arctic summer had come as far westward as Sir Edward Parry came. Here is the most westerly point the reader will find on most maps far north in America – the Melville Island of Captain Parry. Captain Kellett's associate, Captain McClintock of the *Intrepid*, had commanded the only party which had been here since Parry. In 1851 he came over from Austin's squadron with a sledge party. So confident is everyone there that nobody has visited those parts unless he was sent, that McClintock encouraged his men one day by telling them that if they got on well, they should have an old cart Parry had left thirty-odd years before, to make a fire of. Sure enough; they came to the place, and there was the wreck of the cart just as Parry left it. They even found the ruts the old cart left in the ground as if they had not been left a week.

Captain Kellett came into harbour, and with great spirit he and his officers began to prepare for the extended searching parties of the next spring. The *Resolute* and her tender came to anchor off Dealy Island, and there she spent the next eleven months of her life, with great news around her in that time.

There is not much time for travelling in autumn. The days grow very short and very cold. But what days there were were spent in sending out carts and sledges with depots of provisions, which the parties of the next spring could use. Different officers were already assigned to different lines of search in spring. On their journeys they would be gone three months and more, with a party of some eight men – dragging a sled very like a Yankee wood-sled with their instruments and provisions, over ice and snow. To extend those searches as much as possible, and to prepare the men for that work when it should come, advanced depots were now sent forward in the autumn, under the charge of the gentlemen who would have to use them in the spring.

One of these parties, the 'South line of Melville Island' party, was under a spirited young officer Mr Mecham, who had tried such service in the last expedition. He had two of 'Her Majesty's sledges', the *Discovery* and the *Fearless*, a depot of twenty days' provision to be used in the spring, and enough for twenty-five days' present use. All the sledges had little flags, made by some young lady friends of Sir Edward Belcher's. Mr Mecham's bore an armed hand and sword on a white ground, with the motto, '*Per mare, per terram, per glaciem.*' Over mud, land, snow, and ice they carried their depot, and were nearly back, when, on 12 October 1852, Mr Mecham made the great discovery of the expedition.

On the shore of Melville Island, above Winter Harbour, is a great sandstone boulder, ten feet high, seven or eight broad, and twenty and more long, which is known to all those who have anything to do with those regions as 'Parry's sandstone', for it stood near Parry's observatory the winter he spent here, and Mr Fisher, his surgeon, cut on a flat face of it this inscription –

HIS BRITANNIC MAJESTY'S SHIPS
HECLA and GRIPER,
COMMANDED BY
W. E. Parry and Mr Liddon,
WINTERED IN THE ADJACENT
HARBOUR
1819–20
A. FISHER, SCULPT.

It was a sort of God Terminus put up to mark the end of that expedition, as the Danish gentlemen tell us our Dighton rock is the last point of Thorfinn's expedition to these parts. Nobody came to read Mr Fisher's inscription for thirty years and more – a little Arctic hare took up her home under the great rock, and saw the face of man for the first time when, on 5 June 1851, Mr McClintock, on his first expedition this way, had stopped to see whether possibly any of Franklin's men had ever visited it. He found no signs of them, had not so much time as Mr Fisher for stone-cutting, but carved the figures 1851 on the stone, and left it and the hare. To this stone, on his way back to the *Resolute*, Mr Mecham came again (as we said) on 12 October, one memorable Tuesday morning, having been bidden to leave a record there. He went on in advance of his party, meaning to cut 1852 on the stone. On top of it was a small cairn of stones built by Mr McClintock the year before. Mecham examined this, and to his surprise a copper cylinder rolled out from under a spirit tin. 'On opening it, I drew out a roll folded in a bladder, which, being frozen, broke and crumbled. From its dilapidated appearance, I thought at the moment it must be some record of Sir Edward Parry, and, fearing I might damage it, laid it down with the intention of lighting a fire to thaw it. My curiosity, however, overcame my prudence, and on opening it carefully with my knife, I came to a roll of cartridge paper with the impression fresh upon the seals. My astonishment may be conceived on finding it contained an account of the proceedings of HM ship *Investigator* since parting company with the *Herald* [Captain Kellett's old ship] in August 1850, in Behring's Straits. Also a chart which disclosed to view not only the long-sought Northwest Passage, but the completion of the survey of Banks and Wollaston lands. Opened and indorsed Commander McClintock's dispatch; found it contained the following additions –

Opened and copied by his old friend and messmate upon this date, 28 April 1852.   ROBERT MCCLURE.
    Party all well and return to *Investigator* today.

A great discovery indeed to flash across one in a minute. The *Investigator* had not been heard from for more than two years. Here was news of her not yet six months old. The Northwest Passage had been dreamed of for three centuries and more. Here was news of its discovery – news that had been known to Captain McClure for two years. McClure and McClintock were lieutenants together in the *Enterprise* when she was sent after Sir John Franklin in 1848, and wintered together at Port Leopold the next winter. Now, from different hemispheres, they had come so near meeting at this old block of sandstone. Mr Mecham bade his mate build a new cairn, to put the record of the story in, and hurried on to the *Resolute* with his great news – news of almost everybody but Sir John Franklin. Strangely enough, the other expedition, Captain Collinson's, had had a party in that neighbourhood, between the other two, under Mr Parks; but it was his extreme point possible, and he could not reach the Sandstone, though he saw the ruts of McClure's sleigh. This was not known till long afterwards.

The *Investigator*, as it appeared from this despatch of Captain McClure's, had been frozen up in the Bay of Mercy of Banks Land: Banks Land having been for thirty years at once an Ultima Thule and Terra Incognita, put down on the maps where Captain Parry saw it across thirty miles of ice and water in 1819. Perhaps she was still in that same bay: these old friends wintering there, while the *Resolute* and *Intrepid* were lying under Dealy Island, and only one hundred and seventy miles between. It must have been tantalising to all parties to wait the winter through, and not even get a message across. But until winter made it too cold and dark to travel, the ice in the strait was so broken up that it was impossible to attempt to traverse it, even with a light boat, for the lanes of water. So the different autumn parties came in, the last on the last of October, and the officers and men entered on their winter's work and play, to push off the winter days as quickly as they could.

The winter was very severe; and it proved that, as the *Resolute* lay, they were a good deal exposed to the wind. But they kept themselves busy – exercised freely – found game quite abundant within reasonable distances on shore, whenever the light served – kept schools for the men – delivered scientific lectures to whoever would listen – established the theatre for which the ship had been provided at home – and gave juggler's exhibitions by way of variety. The recent system of travelling in the fall and spring cuts in materially to the length of the Arctic winters as Ross, Parry, and Back used to experience it, and it was only from 1 November to 10 March that they were left to their own resources. Late in October one of the *Resolute*'s men died, and in December one of the *Intrepid*'s, but, excepting these cases, they had little sickness, for weeks no one on the sick-list; indeed, Captain Kellett says cheerfully that a sufficiency of good provisions, with plenty of work in the open air, will ensure good health in that climate.

As early in the spring as he dared risk a travelling party, namely, on 10 March 1858, he sent what they all called a forlorn hope across to the Bay of Mercy, to find any traces of the *Investigator*; for they scarcely ventured to hope that she was still there. This start was earlier by thirty-five days than the early parties had started on the preceding expedition. But it was every way essential that, if Captain McClure had wintered in the Bay of Mercy, the messenger should reach him before he sent off any or all his men, in travelling parties, in the spring. The little forlorn hope consisted of ten men under the command of Lieutenant Pim, an officer who had been with Captain Kellett in the *Herald* on the Pacific side, had spent a winter in the *Plover* up Behring's Straits, and had been one of the last men whom the *Investigator* had seen before they put into the Arctic Ocean, to discover, as it proved, the Northwest Passage.

Here we must stop a moment, to tell what one of these sledge parties is by whose efforts so much has been added to our knowledge of Arctic geography, in journeys which could never have been achieved in ships or boats. In the work of the *Resolute*'s parties, in this spring of 1852, Commander McClintock travelled 1,325 miles with his sledge, and Lieutenant Mecham 1,163 miles with his, through regions before wholly unexplored. The sledge, as we have said, is in general contour not unlike a Yankee wood-sled, about eleven feet long. The runners are curved at each end. The sled is fitted with a light canvas trough, so adjusted that, in case of necessity, all the stores, &c., can be ferried over any narrow lane of water in the ice. There are packed on this sled a tent for eight or ten men; five or six pikes, one or more of which is fitted as an ice-chisel; two large buffalo-skins, a water-tight floor-cloth, which contrives ' . . . a double debt to pay, A floor by night, the sledge's sail by day' (and it must be remembered that 'day' and 'night' in those regions are very equivocal terms). There are, besides, a cooking-apparatus, of which the fire is made in spirit or tallow lamps, one or two guns, a pick and shovel, instruments for observation, pannikins, spoons, and a little magazine of such necessaries with the extra clothing of the party. Then the provision, the supply of which measures the length of the expedition, consists of about a pound of bread and a pound of pemmican per man per day, six ounces of pork, and a little preserved potato, rum, lime-juice, tea, chocolate, sugar, tobacco, or other such creature comforts. The sled is fitted with two drag-ropes, at which the men haul. The officer goes ahead to find the best way among hummocks of ice or masses of snow. Sometimes on a smooth floe, before the wind, the floor-cloth is set for a sail, and she runs off merrily, perhaps with several of the crew on board, and the rest running to keep up. But sometimes over broken ice it is a constant task to get her on at all. You hear, 'One, two, three, *haul*,' all day long, as she is worked out of one ice 'cradle-hole' over a hummock into another. Different parties select different hours for travelling. Captain Kellett finally considered that the best division of time, when, as usual, they had constant daylight, was to start at four in the afternoon, travel till ten P.M., *breakfast* then, tent and rest four hours; travel four more, tent, dine, and sleep nine hours. This secured sleep, when the sun was the highest and most trying to the eyes. The distances accomplished with this equipment are truly surprising.

Each man, of course, is dressed as warmly as flannel, woollen cloth, leather, and seal-skin will dress him. For such long journeying, the study of boots becomes a science, and our authorities are full of discussions as to canvas or woollen, or carpet or leather boots, of strings and of buckles. When the time 'to tent' comes, the pikes are fitted for tent-poles, and the tent set up, its door to leeward, on the ice or snow. The floor-cloth is laid for the carpet. At an hour fixed, all talking must stop. There is just room enough for the party to lie side by side on the floor-cloth. Each man gets into a long felt bag, made of heavy felting literally nearly half an inch thick. He brings this up wholly over his head, and buttons himself in. He has a little hole in it to breathe through. Over the felt is sometimes a brown holland bag, meant to keep out moisture. The officer lies farthest in the tent, as being next the wind, the point of hardship and so of honour. The cook for the day lies next the doorway, as being first to be called. Side by side the others lie between. Over them all Mackintosh blankets with the buffalo-robes are drawn, by what power this deponent sayeth not, not knowing. No watch is kept, for there is little danger of intrusion. Once a whole party was startled by a white bear smelling at them, who waked one of their dogs, and a droll time they bad of it, springing to their arms while enveloped in their sacks. But we remember no other instance where a sentinel was needed. And occasionally in the journals the officer notes that he overslept in the morning, and did not 'call the cook' early enough. What a passion is sleep, to be sure, that one should oversleep with such comforts round him!

Some thirty or forty parties, thus equipped, set out from the *Resolute* while she was under Captain Kellett's charge, on various expeditions. As the journey of Lieutenant Pim to the *Investigator* at Banks Land was that on which turned the great victory of her voyage, we will let that stand as a specimen of all. None of the others, however, were undertaken at so early a period of the year, and, on the other hand, several others were much longer – some of them, as has been said, occupying three months and more.

Lieutenant Pim had been appointed in the autumn to the 'Banks Land search', and had carried out his depots of provisions when the other officers took theirs. Captain McClure's chart and despatch made it no longer necessary to have that coast surveyed, but made it all the more necessary to have someone go and see if he was still there. The chances were against this, as a whole summer had intervened since he was heard from. Lieutenant Pim proposed, however, to travel all round Banks Land, which is an island about the size and shape of Ireland, in search of him, Collinson, Franklin, or anybody. Captain Kellett, however, told him not to attempt this with his force, but to return to the ship by the route he went. First he was to go to the Bay of Mercy; if the *Investigator* was gone, he was to follow any traces of her, and, if possible, communicate with her or her consort, the *Enterprise*.

Lieutenant Pim started with a sledge and seven men, and a dog-sledge with two under Dr Domville, the surgeon, who was to bring back the earliest news from the Bay of Mercy to the captain. There was a relief sledge to go part way and return. For the intense cold of this early season they had even more careful arrangements than those we have described. Their tent was doubled. They had extra Mackintoshes, and whatever else could be devised. They had bad luck at starting – broke down one sledge and had to send back for another; had bad weather, and must encamp, once for three days. 'Fortunately,' says the lieutenant of this encampment, 'the temperature arose from fifty-one below zero to thirty-six below, and there remained,' while the drift accumulated to such a degree around the tents, that within them the thermometer was only twenty below, and, when they cooked, rose to zero. A pleasant time of it they must have had there on the ice, for those three days, in their bags smoking and sleeping! No wonder that on the fourth day they found they moved slowly, so cramped and benumbed were they. This morning a new sledge came to them from the ship; they got out of their bags, packed, and got under way again. They were still running along shore, but soon sent back the relief party which had brought the new sled, and in a few days more set out to cross the strait, some twenty-five to thirty miles wide, which, when it is open, as no man has ever seen it, is one of the Northwest Passages discovered by these expeditions.

Horrible work it was! Foggy and dark, so they could not choose the road, and, as it happened, lit on the very worst mass of broken ice in the channel. Just as they entered on it, one black raven must needs appear. 'Bad luck,' said the men. And when Mr Pim shot a musk-ox, their first, and the wounded creature got away, 'So much for the raven,' they croaked again. Only three miles the first day, four miles the second day, two and a half the third, and half a mile the fourth; this was all they gained by most laborious hauling over the broken ice, dragging one sledge at a time, and sometimes carrying forward the stores separately and going back for the sledges. Two days more gave them eight miles more, but on the seventh day on this narrow strait, the dragging being a little better, the great sledge slipped off a smooth hummock, broke one runner to smash, and 'there they were'.

If the two officers had a little bit of a 'tiff' out there on the ice, with the thermometer at eighteen below, only a little dog-sledge to get them anywhere, their ship a hundred miles off, fourteen days' travel as they had come, nobody ever knew it; they kept their secret from us, it is nobody's business, and it is not to be wondered at. Certainly they did not agree. The Doctor, whose sled, the *James Fitzjames*, was still sound, thought they had best leave the stores and all go back; but the Lieutenant, who had the command, did not like to give it up, so he took the dogs and the *James Fitzjames* and its two men and went on, leaving the Doctor on the floe, but giving him directions to go back to land with the wounded sledge and wait for him to return. And the Doctor did it, like a spirited fellow, travelling back and forth for what he could not take in one journey, as the man did in the story who had a peck of corn, a goose, and a wolf to get across the river. Over ice, over hummock the Lieutenant went on his way with his dogs, not a bear nor a seal nor a hare nor a wolf to feed them with; preserved meats, which had been put up with dainty care for men and women, all he had for the ravenous, tasteless creatures, who would have been more pleased with blubber, came to Banks Land at last, but no game there; awful drifts; shut up in the tent for a whole day, and he himself so sick he could scarcely stand! There were but three of them in all; and the captain of the sledge not unnaturally asked poor Pim, when he was at the worst, 'What shall I do, sir, if you die?' Not a very comforting question!

He did not die. He got a few hours' sleep, felt better and started again, but had the discouragement of finding such tokens of an open strait the last year that he felt sure that the ship he was going to look for would be gone. One morning, he had been off for game for the dogs unsuccessfully, and, when he came back to his men, learned that they had seen seventeen deer. After them goes Pim; he finds them to be *three hares*, magnified by fog and mirage, and their long ears answering for horns. This same day they got upon the Bay of Mercy. No ship in sight! Right across it goes the Lieutenant to look for records; when, at two in the afternoon, Robert Hoile sees something black up the bay. Through the glass the Lieutenant makes it out to be a ship. They change their direction at once. Over the ice towards her! He leaves the sledge at three and goes on. How far it seems! At four he can see people walking about, and a pile of stones and flag-staff on the beach. Keep on, Pim; shall one never get there? At five he is within a hundred yards of her, and no one has seen him. But just then the very persons see him who ought to! Pim beckons, waves his arms as the Esquimaux do in sign of friendship. Captain McClure and his lieutenant Haswell are 'taking their exercise,' the chief business of those winters, and at last see him! Pim is black as Erebus from the smoke of cooking in the little tent. McClure owns, not to surprise only, but to a twinge of dismay. 'I paused in my advance,' says he, 'doubting who or what it could be, a denizen of this or the other world.' But this only lasts a moment. Pim speaks. Brave man that he can. How his voice must have choked, as if he were in a dream. 'I am Lieutenant Pim, late of *Herald*. Captain Kellett is at Melville Island.' Well-chosen words, Pim, to be sent in advance over the hundred yards of floe! Nothing about the *Resolute* – that would have confused them. But 'Pim', 'Herald', and 'Kellett' were among the last signs of England they had seen – all this was intelligible. An excellent little speech, which the brave man had been getting ready, perhaps, as one does a telegraphic despatch, for the hours that he had been walking over the floe to her. Then such shaking hands, such a greeting. Poor McClure could not speak at first. One of the men at work got the news on board; and up through the hatches poured everybody, sick and well, to see the black stranger, and to hear his news from England. It was nearly three years since they had seen any civilised man but themselves.

The 28th July, three years before, Commander McClure had sent his last despatch to the Admiralty. He had then prophesied just what in three years he had almost accomplished. In the winter of 1850 he had discovered the Northwest Passage. He had come round into one branch of it, Banks Straits, in the next summer; had gladly taken refuge on the Bay of Mercy in a gale; and his ship had never left it since. Let it be said, in passing, that most likely she is there now. In his last despatches he had told the Admiralty not to be anxious about him if he did not arrive home before the autumn of 1854. As it proved, that autumn he did come with all his men, except those whom he had sent home before, and those who had died. When Pim found them, all the crew but thirty were under orders for marching, some to Baffin's Bay, some to the Mackenzie River, on their return to England. McClure was going to stay with the rest, and come home with the ship, if they could; if not, by sledges to Port Leopold, and so by a steam-launch which he had seen left there for Franklin in 1849. But the arrival of Mr

Pim put an end to all these plans. We have his long despatch to the Admiralty explaining them, finished only the day before Pim arrived. It gives the history of his three years' exile from the world – an exile crowded full of effective work – in a record which gives a noble picture of the man. The Queen has made him Sir Robert Le Mesurier McClure since, in honour of his great discovery.

Banks Land, or Baring Island, the two names belong to the same island, on the shores of which McClure and his men had spent most of these two years or more, is an island on which they were first of civilised men to land. For people who are not very particular, the measurement of it which we gave before, namely, that it is about the size and shape of Ireland, is precise enough. There is high land in the interior probably, as the winds from in shore are cold. The crew found coal and dwarf willow which they could burn; lemmings, ptarmigan, hares, reindeer, and musk-oxen, which they could eat.

> Farewell to the land where I often have wended
> My way o'er its mountains and valleys of snow;
>   Farewell to the rocks and the hills I've ascended,
> The bleak Arctic homes of the buck and the doe;
>   Farewell to the deep glens where oft has resounded
> The snow-bunting's song, as she carolled her lay
>   To hillside and plain, by the green sorrel bounded,
> Till struck by the blast of a cold winter's day.

There is a bit of description of Banks Land, from the anthology of that country, which, so far as we know, consists of two poems by a seaman named Nelson, one of Captain McClure's crew. The highest temperature ever observed on this 'gem of the sea' was 53° in midsummer. The lowest was 65° below zero in January 1853; that day the thermometer did not rise to 60° below, that month was never warmer than 16° below, and the average of the month was 43° below. A pleasant climate to spend three years in!

One day for talk was all that could be allowed, after Mr Pim's amazing appearance. On 8 April, he and his dogs, and Captain McClure and a party, were ready to return to our friend the *Resolute*. They picked up Dr Domville on the way; he had got the broken sledge mended, and killed five musk-oxen, against they came along. He went on in the dog-sledge to tell the news, but McClure and his men kept pace with them; and he and Dr Domville had the telling of the news together.

It was decided that the *Investigator* should be abandoned, and the

Intrepid and *Resolute* made room for her men. Glad greeting they gave them too, as British seamen can give. More than half the crews were away when the *Investigator*'s parties came in, but by July everybody had returned. They had found islands where the charts had guessed there was sea, and sea where they had guessed there was land; had changed peninsulas into islands and islands into peninsulas. Away off beyond the seventy-eighth parallel, Mr McClintock had christened the farthest dot of land 'Ireland's Eye', as if his native island were peering off into the unknown there; a great island, which will be our farthest now, for years to come, had been named 'Prince Patrick's Land', in honour of the baby prince who was the youngest when they left home. Will he not be tempted, when he is a man, to take a crew, like another Madoc, and, as younger sons of queens should, go and settle upon this tempting god-child? They had heard from Sir Edward Belcher's part of the squadron; they had heard from England; had heard of everything but Sir John Franklin. They had even found an ale-bottle of Captain Collinson's expedition – but not a stick nor straw to show where Franklin or his men had lived or died. Two officers of the *Investigator* were sent home to England this summer by a ship from Beechey Island, the headquarters; and thus we heard, in October 1853, of the discovery of the Northwest Passage.

After their crews were on board again, and the *Investigator*'s sixty stowed away also, the *Resolute* and *Intrepid* had a dreary summer of it. The ice would not break up. They had hunting-parties on shore and races on the floe; but the captain could not send the 'Investigators' home as he wanted to, in his steam tender. All his plans were made, and made on a manly scale – if only the ice would open. He built a storehouse on the island for Collinson's people, or for you, reader, and us, if we should happen there, and stored it well, and left this record –

'This is a house which I have named the "Sailor's Home", under the especial patronage of my Lords Commissioners of the Admiralty.

'*Here* royal sailors and marines are fed, clothed, and receive double pay for inhabiting it.'

In that house is a little of everything, and a good deal of victuals and drink; but nobody has been there since the last of the *Resolute*'s men came away.

At last, the 17 August, a day of foot-racing and jumping in bags and wrestling, all hands present, as at a sort of 'Isthmian games', ended with a gale, a cracking up of ice, and the 'Investigators' thought they were on their way home, and Kellett thought he was to have a month of summer yet. But no; 'there is nothing certain in this navigation from one hour to the next.' The *Resolute* and *Intrepid* were never really free of ice all that autumn; drove and drifted to and fro in Barrow's Straits till the 12 November; and then froze up, without anchoring, off Cape Cockburn, perhaps one hundred and forty miles from their harbour of the last winter. The log-book of that winter is a curious record; the ingenuity of the officer in charge was well tasked to make one day differ from another. Each day has the first entry for 'ship's position' thus – 'In the floe off Cape Cockburn.' And the blank for the second entry, thus – 'In the same position.' Lectures, theatricals, schools, &c., whiled away the time; but there could be no autumn travelling parties, and not much hope for discovery in the summer.

Spring came. The captain went over ice in his little dog-sled to Beechey Island, and received his directions to abandon his ships. It appears that he would rather have sent most of his men forward, and with a small crew brought the *Resolute* home that autumn or the next. But Sir Edward Belcher considered his orders peremptory 'that the safety of the crews must preclude any idea of extricating the ships.' Both ships were to be abandoned. Two distant travelling parties were away, one at the *Investigator*, one looking for traces of Collinson, which they found. Word was left for them, at a proper point, not to seek the ship again, but to come on to Beechey Island. And at last, having fitted the *Intrepid*'s engines so that she could be under steam in two hours, having stored both ships with equal proportions of provisions, and made both vessels 'ready for occupation', the captain calked down the hatches, and with all the crew he had not sent on before – forty-two persons in all – left her Monday, 15 May 1854, and started with the sledges for Beechey Island.

Poor old *Resolute*! All this gay company is gone who have made her sides split with their laughter. Here is Harlequin's dress, lying in one of the wardrooms, but there is nobody to dance Harlequin's dances. 'Here is a lovely clear day – surely today they will come on deck and take a meridian!' No, nobody comes. The sun grows hot on the decks; but it is all one, nobody looks at the thermometer! 'And so the poor ship was left all alone.' Such gay times she has had with all these brave young men on board! Such merry winters, such a lightsome summer! So much fun, so much nonsense! So much science and wisdom, and now it is all so still! Is the poor *Resolute* conscious of the change? Does she miss the races on the ice, the scientific lecture every Tuesday, the occasional racket and bustle of the theatre, and the worship of every Sunday? Has not she shared the hope of Captain Kellett, of McClure, and of the crew, that she may *break out well!* – She sees the last sledge leave her. The captain drives off his six dogs – vanishes over the ice, and they are all gone. 'Will they not come back again?' says the poor ship. And she looks wistfully across the ice to her little friend the steam tender *Intrepid*, and she – sees there is no one there. '*Intrepid! Intrepid!* have they really deserted us? We have served them well, and have they really left us alone? A great many were away travelling last year, but they came home. Will not any of these come home now?' No, poor *Resolute*! Not one of them ever came back again! Not one of them meant to. Summer came. August came. No one can tell how soon, but some day or other this her icy prison broke up, and the good ship found herself on her own element again; shook herself proudly, we cannot doubt, nodded joyfully across to the *Intrepid*, and was free. But alas! there was no master to take latitude and longitude, no helmsman at the wheel. In clear letters cast in brass over her helm there are these words, 'England expects each man to do his duty.' But here is no man to heed the warning, and the rudder flaps this way and that way, no longer directing her course, but stupidly swinging to and fro. And she drifts here and there – drifts out of sight of her little consort – strands on a bit of ice floe now, and then is swept off from it – and finds herself, without even the *Intrepid*'s company, alone on these blue seas with those white shores. But what utter loneliness! Poor *Resolute*! She longed for freedom – but what is freedom where there is no law? What is freedom without a helmsman! And the *Resolute* looks back so sadly to the old days when she had a master. And the short bright summer passes. And again she sees the sun set from her decks. And now even her topmasts see it set. And now it does not rise to her deck. And the next day it does not rise to her topmast. Winter and night together! She has known them before! But now it is winter and night and loneliness all together. This horrid ice closes up round her again. And there is no one to bring her into harbour – she is out in the open sound. If the ice-drifts west, she must go west. If it goes east, she must go east. Her seeming freedom is over, and for that long winter she is chained again. But her heart is true to old England. And when she can go east, she is so happy! and when she must go west, she is so sad! Eastward she does go! Southward she does go! True to the instinct which sends us all home, she tracks undirected and without a sail fifteen hundred miles of that sea, without a beacon, which separates her from her own. And so goes a dismal year. 'Perhaps another spring they will come and find me out, and fix things below. It is getting dreadfully damp down there; and I cannot keep the guns bright and the floors dry.' No, good old *Resolute*. May and June pass off the next year, and nobody comes; and here you are all alone out in the bay, drifting in this dismal pack. July and August – the days are growing shorter again. 'Will nobody come and take care of me, and cut off these horrid blocks of ice, and see to these sides of bacon in the hold, and all these mouldy sails, and this powder, and the bread and the spirit that I have kept for them so well? It is September, and the sun begins to set again. And here is another of those awful gales. Will it be my very last? I all alone here – who have done so much – and if they would only take care of me I can do so much more. Will nobody come? Nobody? . . . What! Is it ice blink – are my poor old lookouts blind? Is not there the *Intrepid*? Dear *Intrepid*, I will never look down on you again! No! there is no smoke-stack, it is not the *Intrepid*. But it is somebody. Pray see me, good somebody. Are you a Yankee whaler? I am glad to see the Yankee whalers. I remember the Yankee whalers very pleasantly. We had a happy summer together once . . . It will be dreadful if they do not see me! But this ice, this wretched ice! They do see me – I know they see me, but they cannot get at me. Do not go away, good Yankees; pray come and help me. I know I can get out, if you will help a little . . . But now it is a whole week and they do not come! Are there any Yankees, or am I getting crazy? I have heard them talk of crazy old ships, in my young days . . . No! I am not crazy. They are coming! they are coming. Brave Yankees! over the hummocks, down into the sludge. Do not give it up for the cold. There is coal below, and we will have a fire in the Sylvester, and in the captain's cabin . . . There is a horrid lane of water. They have not got a Halkett. O, if one of these boats of mine would only start for them, instead of lying so stupidly on my deck here! But the men are not afraid of water! See them ferry over on that ice block! Come on, good friends! Welcome, whoever you be – Dane, Dutch, French, or Yankee, come on! come on! It is coming up a gale, but I can bear a gale. Up the side, men. I wish I could let down the gangway alone. But here are all these blocks of ice piled up – you can scramble over them! Why do you stop? Do not be afraid. I will make you very comfortable and jolly. Do not stay talking there. Pray come in. There is port in the captain's cabin, and a little preserved meat in the pantry. You must be hungry; pray come in! O, he is coming, and now all four are coming. It would be dreadful if they had gone back! They are on deck. Now I shall go home! How lonely it has been!'

It was true enough that when Mr Quail, the brother of the captain of the *McLellan*, whom the *Resolute* had befriended, the mate of the *George Henry*, whaler, whose master, Captain Buddington, had discovered the *Resolute* in the ice, came to her after a hard day's journey with his men, the men faltered with a little superstitious feeling, and hesitated for a minute about going on board. But the poor lonely ship wooed them too lovingly, and they climbed over the broke ice and came on deck. She was lying over on her larboard side, with a heavy weight of ice holding her down. Hatches and companion were made fast, as Captain Kellett had left them. But, knocking open the companion, groping down stairs to the after cabin they found their way to the captain's table; somebody put his hand on a box of lucifers, struck a light, and revealed – books scattered in confusion, a candle standing, which he lighted at once, the glasses and the decanters from which Kellett and his officers had drunk goodbye to the vessel. The whalemen filled them again, and undoubtedly felt less discouraged. Meanwhile night came on, and a gale arose. So hard did it blow, that for two days these four were the whole crew of the *Resolute*, and it was not till 19 September that they returned to their own ship, and reported what their prize was.

All these ten days, since Captain Buddington had first seen her, the vessels had been nearing each other. On the 19th he boarded her himself; found that in her hold, on the larboard side, was a good deal of ice; on the starboard side there seemed to be water. In fact, her tanks had burst from the extreme cold; and she was full of water, nearly to her lower deck. Everything that could move from its place had moved; everything was wet; everything that would mould was mouldy. 'A sort of perspiration' settled on the beams above. Clothes were wringing wet. The captain's party made a fire in Captain Kellett's stove, and soon started a sort of shower from the vapour with which it filled the air. The *Resolute* has, however, four fine force-pumps. For three days the captain and six men worked fourteen hours a day on one of these, and had the pleasure of finding that they freed her of water – that she was tight still. They cut away upon the masses of ice; and on 23 September, in the evening, she freed herself from her encumbrances, and took an even keel. This was off the west shore of Baffin's Bay, in latitude 67°. On the shortest tack she was twelve hundred miles from where Captain Kellett left her.

There was work enough still to be done. The rudder was to be shipped, the rigging to be made taut, sail to be set; and it proved, by the way, that the sail on the yards was much of it still serviceable, while a suit of new linen sails below were greatly injured by moisture. In a week more they had her ready to make sail. The pack of ice still drifted with both ships; but on 21 October, after a long northwest gale, the *Resolute* was free – more free than she had been for more than two years.

Her 'last voyage' is almost told. Captain Buddington had resolved to bring her home. He had picked ten men from the *George Henry*, leaving her fifteen, and with a rough tracing of the American coast drawn on a sheet of foolscap, with his lever watch and a quadrant for his instruments, he squared off for New London. A rough, hard passage they had of it. The ship's ballast was gone, by the bursting of the tanks; she was top-heavy and under-manned. He spoke a British whaling bark, and by her sent to Captain Kellett his epaulettes, and to his own owners news that he was coming. They had heavy gales and head winds, were driven as far down as the Bermudas; the water left in the ship's tanks was brackish, and it needed all the seasoning which the ship's chocolate would give to make it drinkable. 'For sixty hours at a time,' says the spirited captain, 'I frequently had no sleep'; but his perseverance was crowned with success at last, and on the night of 23–24 December he made the light off the magnificent harbour from which he sailed; and on Sunday morning, the 24th, dropped anchor in the Thames, opposite *New* London, ran up the royal ensign on the shorn masts of the *Resolute*, and the good people of the town knew that he and his were safe, and that one of the victories of peace was won.

As the fine ship lies opposite the piers of that beautiful town, she attracts visitors from everywhere, and is, indeed, a very remarkable curiosity. Seals were at once placed, and very properly, on the captain's book-cases, lockers, and drawers, and wherever private property might be injured by wanton curiosity, and two keepers are on duty on the vessel, till her destination is decided. But nothing is changed from what she was when she came into harbour. And, from stem to stern, every detail of her equipment is a curiosity, to the sailor or to the landsman. The candlestick in the cabin is not like a Yankee candlestick. The hawse hole for the chain cable is fitted as has not been seen before. And so of everything between. There is the aspect of wet over everything now, after months of ventilation; the rifles, which were last fired at musk-oxen in Melville Island, are red with rust, as if they had lain in the bottom of the sea; the volume of Shakespeare, which you find in an officer's berth, has a damp feel, as if you had been reading it in the open air in a March north-easter. The old seamen look with most amazement, perhaps, on the preparations for amusement – the juggler's cups and balls, or Harlequin's spangled dress; the quiet landsman wonders at the gigantic ice-saws, at the cast-off canvas boots, the long thick Arctic stockings. It seems almost wrong to go into Mr Hamilton's wardroom, and see how he arranged his soap-cup and his toothbrush; and one does not tell of it, if he finds on a blank leaf the secret prayer a sister wrote down for the brother to whom she gave a prayer-book. There is a good deal of disorder now – thanks to her sudden abandonment, and perhaps to her three months' voyage home. A little union-jack lies over a heap of unmended and unwashed underclothes; when Kellett left the ship, he left his country's flag over his armchair as if to keep possession. Two officers' swords and a pair of epaulettes were on the cabin table. Indeed, what is there not there – which should make an Arctic winter endurable – make a long night into day – or while long days away?

The ship is stanch and sound. The 'last voyage' which we have described will not, let us hope, be the last voyage of her career. But wherever she goes, under the English flag or under our own, she will scarcely ever crowd more adventure into one cruise than into that which sealed the discovery of the Northwest Passage; which gave new lands to England, nearest to the pole of all she has; which spent more than a year, no man knows where, self-governed and unguided; and which, having begun under the strict regime of the English navy, ended under the remarkable mutual rules, adopted by common consent, in the business of American whalemen.

Is it not worth noting that in this chivalry of Arctic adventure, the ships which have been wrecked have been those of the fight or horror? They are the *Fury*, the *Victory*, the *Erebus*, the *Terror*. But the ships which never failed their crews – which, for all that man knows, are as sound now as ever – bear the names of peaceful adventure; the *Hecla*, the *Enterprise* and *Investigator*, the *Assistance* and *Resolute*, the *Pioneer* and *Intrepid*, and our *Advance* and *Rescue* and *Arctic*, never threatened any one, even in their names. And they never failed the men who commanded them or who sailed in them.

My Double, and How He Undid Me

ONE OF THE INGHAM PAPERS

A Boston journal, in noticing this story, called it improbable. I think it is. But I think the moral important. It was first published in the Atlantic Monthly *for September 1859.*

It is not often that I trouble the readers of the *Atlantic Monthly*. I should not trouble them now, but for the importunities of my wife, who 'feels to insist' that a duty to society is unfulfilled till I have told why I had to have a double, and how he undid me. She is sure, she says, that intelligent persons cannot understand that pressure upon public servants which alone drives any man into the employment of a double. And while I fear she thinks, at the bottom of her heart, that my fortunes will never be remade, she has a faint hope that, as another Rasselas, I may teach a lesson to future publics, from which they may profit, though we die. Owing to the behaviour of my double, or, if you please, to that public pressure which compelled me to employ him, I have plenty of leisure to write this communication.

I am, or rather was, a minister, of the Sandemanian connection. I was settled in the active, wide-awake town of Naguadavick, on one of the finest water-powers in Maine. We used to call it a Western town in the heart of the civilisation of New England. A charming place it was and is. A spirited, brave young parish had I; and it seemed as if we might have all 'the joy of eventful living' to our heart's content.

Alas! how little we knew on the day of my ordination and in those halcyon moments of our first housekeeping. To be the confidential friend in a hundred families in the town – cutting the social trifle, as my friend Haliburton says, 'from the top of the whipped syllabub to the bottom of the sponge-cake, which is the foundation' – to keep abreast of the thought of the age in one's study, and to do one's best on Sunday to interweave that thought with the active life of an active town, and to inspirit both and make both infinite by glimpses of the Eternal Glory, seemed such an exquisite forelook into one's life! Enough to do, and all so real and so grand! If this vision could only have lasted!

The truth is, that this vision was not in itself a delusion, nor, indeed, half bright enough. If one could only have been left to do his own business, the vision would have accomplished itself and brought out new paraheliacal visions, each as bright as the original. The misery was and is, as we found out, I and Polly, before long, that besides the vision, and besides the usual human and finite failures in life (such as breaking the old pitcher that came over in the *Mayflower*, and putting into the fire the Alpenstock with which her father climbed Mont Blanc) – besides these, I say (imitating the style of Robinson Crusoe), there were pitchforked in on us a great rowen-heap of humbugs, handed down from some unknown seed-time, in which we were expected, and I chiefly, to fulfil certain public functions before the community, of the character of those fulfilled by the third row of supernumeraries who stand behind the Sepoys in the spectacle of the 'Cataract of the Ganges'. They were the duties, in a word, which one performs as member of one or another social class or subdivision, wholly distinct from what one does as A. by himself A. What invisible power put these functions on me, it would be very hard to tell. But such power there was and is. And I had not been at work a year before I found I was living two lives, one real and one merely functional, for two sets of people, one my parish, whom I loved, and the other a vague public, for whom I did not care two straws. All this was in a vague notion, which everybody had and has, that this second life would eventually bring out some great results, unknown at present, to somebody somewhere.

Crazed by this duality of life, I first read Dr Wigan on the 'Duality of the Brain', hoping that I could train one side of my head to do these outside jobs, and the other to do my intimate and real duties. For Richard Greenough once told me, that, in studying for the statue of Franklin, he found that the left side of the great man's face was philosophic and reflective, and the right side funny and smiling. If you will go and look at the bronze statue, you will find he has repeated this observation there for posterity. The eastern profile is the portrait of the statesman Franklin, the western of poor Richard. But Dr Wigan does not go into these niceties of this subject, and I failed. It was then that, on my wife's suggestion, I resolved to look out for a Double.

I was, at first, singularly successful. We happened to be recreating at Stafford Springs that summer. We rode out one day, for one of the relaxations of that watering-place, to the great Monson Poorhouse.

We were passing through one of the large halls, when my destiny was fulfilled!

He was not shaven. He had on no spectacles. He was dressed in a green baize roundabout and faded blue overalls, worn sadly at the knee. But I saw at once that he was of my height, five feet four and a half. He had black hair, worn off by his hat. So have and have not I. He stooped in walking. So do I. His hands were large, and mine. And – choicest gift of Fate in all – he had not 'a strawberry-mark on his left arm', but a cut from a juvenile brickbat over his right eye, slightly affecting the play of that eyebrow. Reader, so have I! My fate was sealed!

A word with Mr Holley, one of the inspectors, settled the whole thing. It proved that this Dennis Shea was a harmless, amiable fellow, of the class know as shiftless, who had sealed his fate by marrying a dumb wife, who was at that moment ironing in the laundry. Before I left Stafford, I had hired both for five years. We had applied to Judge Pynchon, then the probate judge at Springfield, to change the name of Dennis Shea to Frederic Ingham. We had explained to the Judge, what was the precise truth, that an eccentric gentleman wished to adopt Dennis, under this new name, into his family. It never occurred to him that Dennis might be more than fourteen years old. And thus, to shorten this preface, when we returned at night to my parsonage at Naguadavick, there entered Mrs Ingham, her new dumb laundress, myself, who am Mr Frederic Ingham, and my double, who was Mr Frederic Ingham by as good right as I.

O the fun we had the next morning in shaving his beard to my pattern, cutting his hair to match mine, and teaching him how to wear and how to take off gold-bowed spectacles! Really, they were electro-plate, and the glass was plain (for the poor fellow's eyes were excellent). Then in four successive afternoons I taught him four speeches. I had found these would be quite enough for the supernumerary-Sepoy line of life, and it was well for me they were; for though he was good-natured, he was very shiftless, and it was, as our national proverb says, 'like pulling teeth' to teach him. But at the end of the next week he could say, with quite my easy and frisky air –

1 *Very well, thank you. And you?* This for an answer to casual salutations.
2 *I am very glad you liked it.*
3 *There has been so much said, and, on the whole, so well said, that I will not occupy the time.*
4 *I agree, in general, with my friend the other side of the room.*

At first I had a feeling that I was going to be at great cost for clothing him. But it proved, of course, at once, that, whenever he was out, I should be at home. And I went, during the bright period of his success, to so few of those awful pageants which require a black dress-coat and what the ungodly call, after Mr Dickens, a white choker, that in the happy retreat of my own dressing-gowns and jackets my days went by as happily and cheaply as those of another Thalaba. And Polly declares there was never a year when the tailoring cost so little. He lived (Dennis, not Thalaba) in his wife's room over the kitchen. He had orders never to show himself at that window. When he appeared in the front of the house, I retired to my sanctissimum and my dressing-gown. In short, the Dutchman and his wife, in the old weather-box, had not less to do with each other than he and I. He made the furnace-fire and split the wood before daylight; then he went to sleep again, and slept late; then came for orders, with a red silk bandanna tied round his head, with his overalls on, and his dress-coat and spectacles off. If we happened to be interrupted, no one guessed that he was Frederic Ingham as well as I; and, in the neighbourhood, there grew up an impression that the minister's Irishman worked day times in the factory-village at New Coventry. After I had given him his orders, I never saw him till the next day.

I launched him by sending him to a meeting of the Enlightenment Board. The Enlightenment Board consists of seventy-four members, of whom sixty-seven are necessary to form a quorum. One becomes a member under the regulations laid down in old Judge Dudley's will. I became one by being ordained pastor of a church in Naguadavick. You see you cannot help yourself, if you would. At this particular time we had had four successive meetings, averaging four hours each – wholly occupied in whipping in a quorum. At the first only eleven men were present; at the next, by force of three circulars, twenty-seven; at the third, thanks to two days' canvassing by Auchmuty and myself, begging men to come, we had sixty. Half the others were in Europe. But without a quorum we could do nothing. All the rest of us waited grimly for our four hours, and adjourned without any action. At the fourth meeting we had flagged, and only got fifty-nine together. But on the first appearance of my double – whom I sent on this fatal Monday to the fifth meeting – he was the *sixty-seventh* man who entered the room. He was greeted with a storm of applause! The poor fellow had missed his way – read the street signs ill through his spectacles (very ill, in fact, without them) – and had not dared to inquire. He entered the room – finding the president and secretary holding to their chairs two judges of the Supreme Court, who were also members *ex officio*, and were begging leave to go away. On his entrance all was changed. *Presto*, the by-laws were suspended, and the Western property was given away. Nobody stopped to converse with him. He voted, as I had charged him to do, in every instance, with the minority. I won new laurels as a man of sense, though a little unpunctual – and Dennis, *alias* Ingham, returned to the parsonage, astonished to see with how little wisdom the world is governed. He cut a few of my parishioners in the street; but he had his glasses off, and I am known to be near-sighted. Eventually he recognised them more readily than I.

I 'set him again' at the exhibition of the New Coventry Academy; and here he undertook a 'speaking part', – as, in my boyish, worldly days, I remember the bills used to say of Mlle Celeste. We are all trustees of the New Coventry Academy; and there has lately been 'a good deal of feeling' because the Sandemanian trustees did not regularly attend the exhibitions. It has been intimated, indeed, that the Sandemanians are leaning towards Free Will, and that we have, therefore, neglected these semi-annual exhibitions, while there is no doubt that Auchmuty last year went to Commencement at Waterville. Now the headmaster at New Coventry is a real good fellow, who knows a Sanskrit root when he sees it, and often cracks etymologies with me – so that, in strictness, I ought to go to their exhibitions. But think, reader, of sitting through three long July days in that Academy chapel, following the programme from *Tuesday morning, English composition*: "*Sunshine*", *Miss Jones*, round to *Trio on three pianos: duet from the opera of* Midshipman Easy, *Marryat*, coming in at nine, Thursday evening! Think of this, reader, for men who know the world is trying to go backward, and who would give their lives if they could help it on! Well! The double had succeeded so well at the Board, that I sent him to the Academy. (Shade of Plato, pardon!) He arrived early on Tuesday, when, indeed, few but mothers and clergymen are generally expected, and returned in the evening to us, covered with honours. He had dined at the right hand of the chairman, and he spoke in high terms of the repast. The chairman had expressed his interest in the French conversation. 'I am very glad you liked it,' said Dennis; and the poor chairman, abashed, supposed the accent had been wrong. At the end of the day, the gentlemen present had been called upon for speeches – the Revd Frederic Ingham first, as it happened; upon which Dennis had risen, and had said, 'There has been so much said, and, on the whole, so well said, that I will not occupy the time.' The girls were delighted, because Dr Dabney, the year before, had given them at this occasion a scolding on impropriety of behaviour at lyceum lectures. They all declared Mr Ingham was a love – and *so* handsome! (Dennis is good-looking.) Three of them, with arms behind the others' waists, followed him up to the wagon he rode home in; and a little girl with a blue sash had been sent to give him a rosebud. After this *début* in speaking, he went to the exhibition for two days more, to the mutual satisfaction of all concerned. Indeed, Polly reported that he had pronounced the trustees' dinners of a higher grade than those of the parsonage. When the next term began, I found six of the Academy girls had obtained permission to come across the river and attend our church. But this arrangement did not long continue.

After this he went to several Commencements for me, and ate the dinners provided; he sat through three of our Quarterly Conventions for me – always voting judiciously, by the simple rule mentioned above, of siding with the minority. And I, meanwhile, who had before been losing caste among my friends, as holding myself aloof from the associations of the body, began to rise in everybody's favour. 'Ingham's a good fellow – always on hand'; 'never talks much, but does the right thing at the right time'; 'is not as unpunctual as he used to be – he comes early, and sits through to the end'. 'He has got over his old talkative habit, too. I spoke to a friend of his about it once; and I think Ingham took it kindly,' etc., etc.

This voting power of Dennis was particularly valuable at the quarterly meetings of the proprietors of the Naguadavick Ferry. My wife inherited from her father some shares in that enterprise, which is not yet fully developed, though it doubtless will become a very valuable property. The law of Maine then forbade stockholders to appear by proxy at such meetings. Polly disliked to go, not being, in fact, a 'hens'-rights hen', transferred her stock to me. I, after going once, disliked it more than she. But Dennis went to the next meeting, and liked it very much. He said the armchairs were good, the collation good, and the free rides to stockholders pleasant. He was a little frightened when they first took him upon one of the ferry-boats, but after two or three quarterly meetings he became quite brave.

Thus far I never had any difficulty with him. Indeed, being, as I implied, of that type which is called shiftless, he was only too happy to be told daily what to do, and to be charged not to be forthputting or in any way original in his discharge of that duty. He learned, however, to discriminate between the lines of his life, and very much preferred these stockholders' meetings and trustees' dinners and Commencement collations to another set of occasions, from which he used to beg off most piteously. Our excellent brother, Dr Fillmore, had taken a notion at this time that our Sandemanian churches needed more expression of mutual sympathy. He insisted upon it that we were remiss. He said, that, if the Bishop came to preach at Naguadavick, all the Episcopal clergy of the neighbourhood were present; if Dr Pond came, all the Congregational clergymen turned out to hear him; if Dr Nichols, all the Unitarians; and he thought we owed it to each other, that, whenever there was an occasional service at a Sandemanian church, the other brethren should all, if possible, attend. 'It looked well,' if nothing more. Now this really meant that I had not been to hear one of Dr Fillmore's lectures on the Ethnology of Religion. He forgot that he did not hear one of my course on the 'Sandemanianism of Anselm'. But I felt badly when he said it; and afterwards I always made Dennis go to hear all the brethren preach, when I was not preaching myself. This was what he took exceptions to – the only thing, as I said, which he ever did except to. Now came the advantage of his long morning-nap, and of the green tea with which Polly supplied the kitchen. But he would plead, so humbly, to be let off, only from one or two! I never excepted him, however. I knew the lectures were of value, and I thought it best he should be able to keep the connection.

Polly is more rash than I am, as the reader has observed in the outset of this memoir. She risked Dennis one night under the eyes of her own sex. Governor Gorges had always been very kind to us, and, when he gave his great annual party to the town, asked us. I confess I hated to go. I was deep in the new volume of Pfeiffer's *Mystics*, which Haliburton had just sent me from Boston. 'But how rude,' said Polly, 'not to return the Governor's civility and Mrs Gorges's, when they will be sure to ask why you are away!' Still I demurred, and at last she, with the wit of Eve and of Semiramis conjoined, let me off by saying that, if I would go in with her, and sustain the initial conversations with the Governor and the ladies staying there, she would risk Dennis for the rest of the evening. And that was just what we did. She took Dennis in training all that afternoon, instructed him in fashionable conversation, cautioned him against the temptations of the supper-table – and at nine in the evening he drove us all down in the carryall. I made the grand star-*entrée* with Polly and the pretty Walton girls, who were staying with us. We had put Dennis into a great rough top-coat, without his glasses; and the girls never dreamed, in the darkness, of looking at him. He sat in the carriage, at the door, while we entered. I did the agreeable to Mrs Gorges, was introduced to her niece, Miss Fernanda; I complimented Judge Jeffries on his decision in the great case of D'Aulnay *vs*. Laconia Mining Company; I stepped into the dressing-room for a moment, stepped out for another, walked home after a nod with Dennis and tying the horse to a pump; and while I walked home, Mr Frederic Ingham, my double, stepped in through the library into the Gorges's grand saloon.

Oh! Polly died of laughing as she told me of it at midnight! And even here, where I have to teach my hands to hew the beech for stakes to fence our cave, she dies of laughing as she recalls it – and says that single occasion was worth all we have paid for it. Gallant Eve that she is! She joined Dennis at the library-door, and in an instant presented him to Dr Ochterlony, from Baltimore, who was on a visit in town, and was talking with her as Dennis came in. 'Mr Ingham would like to hear what you were telling us about your success among the German population.' And Dennis bowed and said, in spite of a scowl from Polly, 'I'm very glad you liked it.' But Dr Ochterlony did not observe, and plunged into the tide of explanation; Dennis listened like a prime-minister, and bowing like a mandarin, which is, I suppose, the same thing. Polly declared it was just like Haliburton's Latin conversation with the Hungarian minister, of which he is very fond of telling. '*Quæne sit historia Reformationis in Ungaria?*' quoth Haliburton, after some thought. And his *confrère* replied gallantly, '*In seculo decimo tertio,*' etc., etc., etc.; and from *decimo tertio** to the nineteenth century and a half lasted till the oysters came. So was it that before Dr Ochterlony came to the 'success', or near it, Governor Gorges came to Dennis, and asked him to hand Mrs Jeffries down to supper, a request which he heard with great joy.

Polly was skipping round the room, I guess, gay as a lark. Auchmuty came to her 'in pity for poor Ingham', who was so bored by the stupid pundit – and Auchmuty could not understand why I stood it so long. But when Dennis took Mrs Jeffries down, Polly could not resist standing near them. He was a little flustered, till the sight of the eatables and drinkables gave him the same Mercian courage which it gave Diggory. A little excited then, he attempted one or two of his speeches to the Judge's lady. But little he knew how hard it was to get in even a *promptu* there edgewise. 'Very well, I thank you,' said he, after the eating elements were adjusted; 'and you?' And then did not he have

---

* Which means, 'In the thirteenth century', my dear little bell-and-coral reader. You have rightly guessed that the question means, 'What is the history of the Reformation in Hungary?'

to hear about the mumps, and the measles, and arnica, and belladonna, and camomile-flower, and dodecatheon, till she changed oysters for salad; and then about the old practice and the new, and what her sister said, and what her sister's friend said, and what the physician to her sister's friend said, and then what was said by the brother of the sister of the physician of the friend of her sister, exactly as if it had been in Ollendorff? There was a moment's pause, as she declined Champagne. 'I am very glad you liked it,' said Dennis again, which he never should have said but to one who complimented a sermon. 'Oh! you are so sharp, Mr Ingham! No! I never drink any wine at all, – except sometimes in summer a little currant shrub – from our own currants, you know. My own mother – that is, I call her my own mother, because, you know, I do not remember,' etc., etc., etc.; till they came to the candied orange at the end of the feast, when Dennis, rather confused, thought he must say something, and tried No. 4 – 'I agree, in general, with my friend the other side of the room,' – which he never should have said but at a public meeting. But Mrs Jeffries, who never listens expecting to understand, caught him up instantly with 'Well, I'm sure my husband returns the compliment; he always agrees with you – though we do worship with the Methodists; but you know, Mr Ingham,' etc., etc., etc., till the move upstairs; and as Dennis led her through the hall, he was scarcely understood by any but Polly, as he said, 'There has been so much said, and, on the whole, so well said, that I will not occupy the time.'

His great resource the rest of the evening was standing in the library, carrying on animated conversations with one and another in much the same way. Polly had initiated him in the mysteries of a discovery of mine, that it is not necessary to finish your sentences in a crowd, but by a sort of mumble, omitting sibilants and dentals. This, indeed, if your words fail you, answers even in public extempore speech, but better where other talking is going on. Thus – 'We missed you at the Natural History Society, Ingham.' Ingham replies, 'I am very gligloglum, that is, that you were mmmmm.' By gradually dropping the voice, the interlocutor is compelled to supply the answer. 'Mrs Ingham, I hope your friend Augusta is better.' Augusta has not been ill. Polly cannot think of explaining, however, and answers, 'Thank you, Ma'am; she is very rearason wewahweoh,' in lower and lower tones. And Mrs Throckmorton, who forgot the subject of which she spoke as soon as she asked the question, is quite satisfied. Dennis could see into the card-room, and came to Polly to ask if he might not go and play all-fours. But, of course, she sternly refused. At midnight they came home delighted – Polly, as I said, wild to tell me the story of the victory; only both the pretty Walton girls said, 'Cousin Frederic, you did not come near me all the evening.'

We always called him Dennis at home, for convenience, though his real name was Frederic Ingham, as I have explained. When the election-day came round, however, I found that by some accident there was only one Frederic Ingham's name on the voting-list; and as I was quite busy that day in writing some foreign letters to Halle, I thought I would forego my privilege of suffrage, and stay quietly at home, telling Dennis that he might use the record on the voting-list and vote. I gave him a ticket, which I told him he might use, if he liked to. That was that very sharp election in Maine which the readers of the *Atlantic* so well remember, and it had been intimated in public that the ministers would do well not to appear at the polls. Of course, after that, we had to appear by self or proxy. Still, Naguadavick was not then a city, and this standing in a double queue at town-meeting several hours to vote was a bore of the first water; and so when I found that there was but one Frederic Ingham on the list, and that one of us must give up, I stayed at home and finished the letters (which, indeed, procured for Fothergill his coveted appointment of Professor of Astronomy at Leavenworth), and I gave Dennis, as we called him, the chance. Something in the matter gave a good deal of popularity to the Frederic Ingham name; and at the adjourned election, next week, Frederic Ingham was chosen to the legislature. Whether this was I or Dennis I never really knew. My friends seemed to think it was I; but I felt that as Dennis had done the popular thing, he was entitled to the honour; so I sent him to Augusta when the time came, and he took the oaths. And a very valuable member he made. They appointed him on the Committee on Parishes; but I wrote a letter for him, resigning, on the ground that he took an interest in our claim to the stumpage in the minister's sixteenths of Gore A, next No. 7, in the 10th Range. He never made any speeches, and always voted with the minority, which was what he was sent to do. He made me and himself a great many good friends, some of whom I did not afterwards recognise as quickly as Dennis did my parishioners. On one or two occasions, when there was wood to saw at home, I kept him at home; but I took those occasions to go to Augusta myself. Finding myself often in his vacant seat at these times, I watched the proceedings with a good deal of care; and once was so much excited that I delivered my somewhat celebrated speech on the Central School District question, a speech of which the 'State of Maine' printed some extra copies. I believe there is no formal rule permitting strangers to speak; but no one objected.

Dennis himself, as I said, never spoke at all. But our experience this session led me to think that if, by some such 'general understanding' as the reports speak of in legislation daily, every member of Congress might leave a double to sit through those deadly sessions and answer to roll-calls and do the legitimate party-voting, which appears stereotyped in the regular list of Ashe, Bocock, Black, etc., we should gain decidedly in working-power. As things stand, the saddest State prison I ever visit is that Representatives' Chamber in Washington. If a man leaves for an hour, twenty 'correspondents' may be howling, 'Where was Mr Pendergrast when the Oregon bill passed?' And if poor Pendergrast stays there! Certainly the worst use you can make of a man is to put him in prison!

I know, indeed, that public men of the highest rank have resorted to this expedient long ago. Dumas's novel of the 'Iron Mask' turns on the brutal imprisonment of Louis the Fourteenth's double. There seems little doubt, in our own history, that it was the real General Pierce who shed tears when the delegate from Lawrence explained to him the sufferings of the people there, and only General Pierce's double who had given the orders for the assault on that town, which was invaded the next day. My charming friend, George Withers, has, I am almost sure, a double, who preaches his afternoon sermons for him. This is the reason that the theology often varies so from that of the forenoon. But that double is almost as charming as the original. Some of the most well-defined men, who stand out most prominently on the background of history, are in this way stereoscopic men, who owe their distinct relief to the slight differences between the doubles. All this I know. My present suggestion is simply the great extension of the system, so that all public machine-work may be done by it.

But I see I loiter on my story, which is rushing to the plunge. Let me stop an instant more, however, to recall, were it only to myself, that charming year while all was yet well. After the double had become a matter of course, for nearly twelve months before he undid me, what a year it was! Full of active life, full of happy love, of the hardest work, of the sweetest sleep, and the fulfilment of so many of the fresh aspirations and dreams of boyhood! Dennis went to every school-committee meeting, and sat through all those late wranglings which used to keep me up till midnight and awake till morning. He attended all the lectures to which foreign exiles sent me tickets begging me to come for the love of Heaven and of Bohemia. He accepted and used all the tickets for charity concerts which were sent to me. He appeared everywhere where it was specially desirable that 'our denomination', or 'our party', or 'our class', or 'our family', or 'our street', or 'our town', or 'our country', or 'our State', should be fully represented. And I fell back to that charming life which in boyhood one dreams of, when he supposes he shall do his own duty and make his own sacrifices, without being tied up with those of other people. My rusty Sanskrit, Arabic, Hebrew, Greek, Latin, French, Italian, Spanish, German, and English began to take polish. Heavens! how little I had done with them while I attended to my *public* duties! My calls on my parishioners became the friendly, frequent, homelike sociabilities they were meant to be, instead of the hard work of a man goaded to desperation by the sight of his lists of arrears. And preaching! what a luxury preaching was when I had on Sunday the whole result of an individual, personal week, from which to speak to a people whom all that week I had been meeting as hand-to-hand friend; I, never tired on Sunday, and in condition to leave the sermon at home if I chose, and preach it extempore, as all men should do always. Indeed, I wonder, when I think that a sensible people, like ours – really more attached to their clergy than they were in the lost days, when the Mathers and Nortons were noblemen – should choose to neutralise so much of their ministers' lives, and destroy so much of their early training, by this undefined passion for seeing them in public. It springs from our balancing of sects. If a spirited Episcopalian takes an interest in the almshouse, and is put on the Poor Board, every other denomination must have a minister there, lest the poorhouse be changed into St Paul's Cathedral. If a Sandemanian is chosen president of the Young Men's Library, there must be a Methodist vice-president and a Baptist secretary. And if a Universalist Sunday School Convention collects five hundred delegates, the next Congregationalist Sabbath School Conference must be as large, 'lest "they" – whoever *they* may be – should think "we" – whoever *we* may be – are going down'.

Freed from these necessities, that happy year I began to know my wife by sight. We saw each other sometimes. In those long mornings, when Dennis was in the study explaining to map-peddlers that I had eleven maps of Jerusalem already, and to schoolbook agents that I would see them hanged before I would be bribed to introduce their textbooks into the schools – she and I were at work together, as in those old dreamy days – and in these of our log-cabin again. But all this could not last – and at length poor Dennis, my double, overtasked in turn, undid me.

It was thus it happened. There is an excellent fellow, once a minister –

I will call him Isaacs – who deserves well of the world till he dies, and after, because he once, in a real exigency, did the right thing, in the right way, at the right time, as no other man could do it. In the world's great football match, the ball by chance found him loitering on the outside of the field; he closed with it, 'camped' it, charged it home – yes, right through the other side – not disturbed, not frightened by his own success – and breathless found himself a great man, as the Great Delta rang applause. But he did not find himself a rich man; and the football has never come in his way again. From that moment to this moment he has been of no use, that one can see at all. Still, for that great act we speak of Isaacs gratefully and remember him kindly; and he forges on, hoping to meet the football somewhere again. In that vague hope, he had arranged a 'movement' for a general organisation of the human family into Debating-Clubs, County Societies, State Unions, etc., etc., with a view of inducing all children to take hold of the handles of their knives and forks, instead of the metal. Children have bad habits in that way. The movement, of course, was absurd; but we all did our best to forward not it, but him. It came time for the annual county-meeting on this subject to be held at Naguadavick. Isaacs came round, good fellow! to arrange for it – got the town-hall, got the Governor to preside (the saint! – he ought to have triplet doubles provided him by law), and then came to get me to speak. 'No,' I said, 'I would not speak, if ten Governors presided. I do not believe in the enterprise. If I spoke, it should be to say children should take hold of the prongs of the forks and the blades of the knives. I would subscribe ten dollars, but I would not speak a mill.' So poor Isaacs went his way sadly, to coax Auchmuty to speak, and Delafield. I went out. Not long after he came back, and told Polly that they had promised to speak, the Governor would speak, and he himself would close with the quarterly report, and some interesting anecdotes regarding Miss Biffin's way of handling her knife and Mr Nellis's way of footing his fork. 'Now if Mr Ingham will only come and sit on the platform, he need not say one word; but it will show well in the paper – it will show that the Sandemanians take as much interest in the movement as the Armenians or the Mesopotamians, and will be a great favour to me.' Polly, good soul! was tempted, and she promised. She knew Mrs Isaacs was starving, and the babies – she knew Dennis was at home – and she promised! Night came, and I returned. I heard her story. I was sorry. I doubted. But Polly had promised to beg me, and I dared all! I told Dennis to hold his peace, under all circumstances, and sent him down.

It was not half an hour more before he returned, wild with

excitement – in a perfect Irish fury – which it was long before I understood. But I knew at once that he had undone me!

What happened was this. The audience got together, attracted by Governor Gorges's name. There were a thousand people. Poor Gorges was late from Augusta. They became impatient. He came in direct from the train at last, really ignorant of the object of the meeting. He opened it in the fewest possible words, and said other gentlemen were present who would entertain them better than he. The audience were disappointed, but waited. The Governor, prompted by Isaacs, said, 'The Honourable Mr Delafield will address you.' Delafield had forgotten the knives and forks, and was playing the Ruy Lopez opening at the chess-club. 'The Revd Mr Auchmuty will address you.' Auchmuty had promised to speak late, and was at the school committee. 'I see Dr Stearns in the hall; perhaps he will say a word.' Dr Stearns said he had come to listen and not to speak. The Governor and Isaacs whispered. The Governor looked at Dennis, who was resplendent on the platform; but Isaacs, to give him his due, shook his head. But the look was enough. A miserable lad, ill-bred, who had once been in Boston, thought it would sound well to call for me, and peeped out, 'Ingham!' A few more wretches cried, 'Ingham! Ingham!' Still Isaacs was firm; but the Governor, anxious, indeed, to prevent a row, knew I would say something, and said, 'Our friend Mr Ingham is always prepared; and, though we had not relied upon him, he will say a word perhaps.' Applause followed, which turned Dennis's head. He rose, fluttered, and tried No. 3 – 'There has been so much said, and, on the whole, so well said, that I will not longer occupy the time!' and sat down, looking for his hat; for things seemed squally. But the people cried, 'Go on! go on!' and some applauded. Dennis, still confused, but flattered by the applause, to which neither he nor I are used, rose again, and this time tried No. 2 – 'I am very glad you liked it!' in a sonorous, clear delivery. My best friends stared. All the people who did not know me personally yelled with delight at the aspect of the evening; the Governor was beside himself, and poor Isaacs thought he was undone! Alas, it was I! A boy in the gallery cried in a loud tone, 'It's all an infernal humbug,' just as Dennis, waving his hand, commanded silence, and tried No. 4 – 'I agree, in general, with my friend the other side of the room.' The poor Governor doubted his senses and crossed to stop him – not in time, however. The same gallery-boy shouted, 'How's your mother?' and Dennis, now completely lost, tried, as his last shot, No. 1, vainly – 'Very well, thank you; and you?'

I think I must have been undone already. But Dennis, like another

Lockhard, chose 'to make sicker'. The audience rose in a whirl of amazement, rage, and sorrow. Some other impertinence, aimed at Dennis, broke all restraint, and, in pure Irish, he delivered himself of an address to the gallery, inviting any person who wished to fight to come down and do so – stating, that they were all dogs and cowards and the sons of dogs and cowards – that he would take any five of them single-handed. 'Shure, I have said all his Riverence and the Misthress bade me say,' cried he, in defiance; and, seizing the Governor's cane from his hand, brandished it, quarter-staff fashion, above his head. He was, indeed, got from the hall only with the greatest difficulty by the Governor, the City Marshal, who had been called in, and the Superintendent of my Sunday School.

The universal impression, of course, was, that the Revd Frederic Ingham had lost all command of himself, in some of those haunts of intoxication which for fifteen years I have been labouring to destroy. Till this moment, indeed, that is the impression in Naguadavick. This number of the *Atlantic* will relieve from it a hundred friends of mine who have been sadly wounded by that notion now for years; but I shall not be likely ever to show my head there again.

No! My double has undone me.

We left town at seven the next morning. I came to No. 9, in the Third Range, and settled on the Minister's Lot. In the new towns in Maine, the first settled minister has a gift of a hundred acres of land. I am the first settled minister in No. 9. My wife and little Paulina are my parish. We raise corn enough to live on in summer. We kill bear's meat enough to carbonise it in winter. I work on steadily on my *Traces of Sandemanianism in the Sixth and Seventh Centuries*, which I hope to persuade Phillips, Sampson, & Co. to publish next year. We are very happy, but the world thinks we are undone.

The Children of the Public

This story originated in the advertisement of the humbug which it describes. Some fifteen or twenty years since, when gift enterprises rose to one of their climaxes, a gift of a large sum of money, I think $10,000, was offered in New York to the most successful ticket-holder in some scheme, and one of $5,000 to the second. It was arranged that one of these parties should be a man and the other a woman; and the amiable suggestion was added, on the part of the undertaker of the enterprise, that if the gentleman and lady who drew these prizes liked each other sufficiently well when the distribution was made, they might regard the decision as a match made for them in Heaven, and take the money as the dowry of the bride. This thoroughly practical, and, at the same time, thoroughly absurd suggestion, arrested the attention of a distinguished storyteller, a dear friend of mine, who proposed to me that we should each of us write the history of one of the two successful parties, to be woven together by their union at the end. The plan, however, lay latent for years – the gift enterprise of course blew up – and it was not until the summer of 1862 that I wrote my half of the proposed story, with the hope of eliciting the other half. My friend's more important engagements, however, have thus far kept Fausta's detailed biography from the light. I sent my half to Mr Frank Leslie, in competition for a premium offered by him, as is stated in the second chapter of the story. And the story found such favour in the eyes of the judges, that it received one of his second premiums. The first was very properly awarded to Miss Louisa Alcott, for a story of great spirit and power. 'The Children of the Public' was printed in Frank Leslie's Illustrated Newspaper *for 24 January and 31 January 1863. The moral which it tried to illustrate, which is, I believe, an important one, was thus commended to the attention of the very large circle of the readers of that journal – a journal to which I am eager to say I think this nation has been very largely indebted for the loyalty, the good sense, and the high tone which seem always to characterise it. During the war, the pictorial journals had immense influence in the army, and they used this influence with an undeviating regard to the true honour of the country.*

CHAPTER I

The Pork Barrel

'Felix,' said my wife to me, as I came home tonight, 'you will have to go to the pork-barrel.'

'Are you quite sure,' said I – 'quite sure? "Woe to him," says the oracle, "who goes to the pork-barrel before the moment of his need." '

'And woe to him, say I,' replied my brave wife – 'woe and disaster to him; but the moment of our need has come. The figures are here, and you shall see. I have it all in black and in white.'

And so it proved, indeed, that when Miss Sampson, the nurse, was paid for her month's service, and when the boys had their winter boots, and when my life-insurance assessment was provided for, and the new payment for the insurance on the house – when the taxes were settled with the collector (and my wife had to lay aside double for the war) – when the pew-rent was paid for the year, and the water-rate – we must have to start with, on 1 January, one hundred dollars. This, as we live, would pay, in cash, the butcher, and the grocer, and the baker, and all the dealers in things that perish, and would buy the omnibus tickets, and recompense Bridget till 1 April. And at my house, if we can see forward three months we are satisfied. But, at my house, we are never satisfied if there is a credit at any store for us. We are sworn to pay as we go. We owe no man anything.

So it was that my wife said – 'Felix, you will have to go to the pork-barrel.'

This is the story of the pork-barrel.

It happened once, in a little parish in the Green Mountains, that the deacon reported to Parson Plunkett, that, as he rode to meeting by Chung-a-baug Pond, he saw Michael Stowers fishing for pickerel through a hole in the ice on the Sabbath day. The parson made note of the complaint, and that afternoon drove over to the pond in his 'one-horse shay'. He made his visit, not unacceptable, on the poor Stowers household, and then crossed lots to the place where he saw poor Michael hoeing. He told Michael that he was charged with Sabbath-breaking, and bade him plead to the charge. And poor Mike, like a man, pleaded guilty; but, in extenuation, he said that there was nothing to eat in the house, and rather than see wife and children faint, he had cut a hole in the ice, had put in his hook again and again, and yet again, and coming home had delighted the waiting family with an unexpected breakfast. The good parson made no rebuke, nodded pensive, and drove straightway to the deacon's door.

'Deacon,' said he, 'what meat did you eat for breakfast yesterday?'

The deacon's family had eaten salt pork, fried.

'And where did you get the pork, Deacon?'

The Deacon stared, but said he had taken it from his pork-barrel.

'Yes, Deacon,' said the old man; 'I supposed so. I have been to see Brother Stowers, to talk to him about his Sabbath-breaking; and, Deacon, I find the pond is his pork-barrel.'

The story is a favourite with me and with Fausta. But 'woe,' says the oracle, 'to him who goes to the pork-barrel before the moment of his need.' And to that 'woe' both Fausta and I say 'amen'. For we know that there is no fish in our pond for spendthrifts or for lazy-bones; none for people who wear gold chains or Attleborough jewellery; none for people who are ashamed of cheap carpets or wooden mantelpieces. Not for those who run in debt will the fish bite; nor for those who pretend to be richer or better or wiser than they are. No! But we have found, in our lives, that in a great democracy there reigns a great and gracious sovereign. We have found that this sovereign, in a reckless and unconscious way, is, all the time, making the most profuse provision for all the citizens. We have found that those who are not too grand to trust him fare as well as they deserve. We have found, on the other hand, that those who lick his feet or flatter his follies fare worst of living men. We find that those who work honestly, and only seek a man's fair average of life, or a woman's, get that average, though sometimes by the most singular experiences in the long run. And thus we find that, when an extraordinary contingency arises in life, as just now in ours, we have only to go to our pork-barrel, and the fish rises to our hook or spear.

The sovereign brings this about in all sorts of ways, but he does not fail, if, without flattering him, you trust him. Of this sovereign the name is – 'the Public'. Fausta and I are apt to call ourselves his children, and so I name this story of our lives, 'The Children of the Public'.

CHAPTER II

Where is the Barrel?

'Where is the barrel this time, Fausta?' said I, after I had added and subtracted her figures three times, to be sure she had carried her tens and hundreds rightly. For the units, in such accounts, in face of Dr Franklin, I confess I do not care.

'The barrel,' said she, 'is in Frank Leslie's office. Here is the mark!' and she handed me *Frank Leslie's Newspaper*, with a mark at this announcement –

$100

offered for the best Short Tale of from one to
two pages by *Frank Leslie's Illustrated Newspaper*,
to be sent in on or before 1 November 1862.

'There is another barrel,' she said, 'with $5,000 in it, and another with $1,000. But we do not want $5,000 or $1,000. There is a little barrel with $50 in it. But see here, with all this figuring, I cannot make it do. I have stopped the gas now, and I have turned the children's coats – I wish you would see how well Robert's looks – and I have had a new tile put in the cook-stove, instead of buying that lovely new "Banner". But all will not do. We must go to this barrel.'

'And what is to be the hook, darling, this time?' said I.

'I have been thinking of it all day. I hope you will not hate it – I know you will not like it exactly; but why not write down just the whole story of what it is to be "Children of the Public"; how we came to live here, you know; how we built the house, and – all about it?'

'How Felix knew Fausta,' said I; 'and how Fausta first met Felix, perhaps; and when they first kissed each other; and what she said to him when they did so.'

'Tell that, if you dare,' said Fausta; 'but perhaps – the oracle says we must not be proud – perhaps you might tell just a little. You know – really almost everybody is named Carter now; and I do not believe the neighbours will notice – perhaps they won't read the paper. And if they do notice it, I don't care! There!'

'It will not be so bad as – '

But I never finished the sentence. An imperative gesture closed my lips physically as well as metaphorically, and I was glad to turn the subject enough to sit down to tea with the children. After the bread and butter we agreed what we might and what we might not tell, and then I wrote what the reader is now to see.

CHAPTER III

My Life to its Crisis

New Yorkers of today see so many processions, and live through so many sensations, and hurrah for so many heroes in every year, that it is only the oldest of fogies who tells you of the triumphant procession of steamboats which, in the year 1824, welcomed General Lafayette on his arrival from his tour through the country he had so nobly served.

But, if the reader wishes to lengthen out this story he may button the next silver-grey friend he meets, and ask him to tell of the broken English and broken French of the Marquis, of Levasseur, and the rest of them; of the enthusiasm of the people and the readiness of the visitors, and he will please bear in mind that of all that am I.

For it so happened that on the morning when, for want of better lions to show, the mayor and governor and the rest of them took the Marquis and his secretary, and the rest of them, to see the orphan asylum in Deering Street – as they passed into the first ward, after having had 'a little refreshment' in the managers' room, Sally Eaton, the head nurse, dropped the first courtesy to them, and Sally Eaton, as it happened, held me screaming in her arms. I had been sent to the asylum that morning with a paper pinned to my bib, which said my name was Felix Carter.

'Eet ees verra fine,' said the Marquis, smiling blandly.

'*Ravissant!*' said Levasseur, and he dropped a five-franc piece into Sally Eaton's hand. And so the procession of exhibiting managers talking bad French, and of exhibited Frenchmen talking bad English, passed on; all but good old Elkanah Ogden – God bless him! – who happened to have come there with the governor's party, and who loitered a minute to talk with Sally Eaton about me.

Years afterwards she told me how the old man kissed me, how his eyes watered when he asked my story, how she told again of the moment when I was heard screaming on the doorstep, and how she offered to go and bring the paper which had been pinned to my bib. But the old man said it was no matter – 'only we would have called him Marquis,' said he, 'if his name was not provided for him. We must not leave him here,' he said; 'he shall grow up a farmer's lad, and not a little cockney.' And so, instead of going the grand round of infirmaries, kitchens, bakeries, and dormitories with the rest, the good old soul went back into the managers' room, and wrote at the moment a letter to John Myers, who took care of his wild land in St Lawrence County for him, to ask him if Mrs Myers would not bring up an orphan baby by hand for him; and if, both together, they would not train this baby till he said 'stop'; if, on the other hand, he allowed them, in the yearly account, a hundred dollars each year for the charge.

Anybody who knows how far a hundred dollars goes in the backwoods, in St Lawrence County, will know that any settler would be glad to take a ward so recommended. Anybody who knew Betsy Myers as well as old Elkanah Ogden did, would know she would have taken any orphan brought to her door, even if he were not recommended at all.

So it happened, thanks to Lafayette and the city council! that I had not been a 'Child of the Public' a day, before, in its great, clumsy, liberal way, it had provided for me. I owed my healthy, happy home of the next fourteen years in the wilderness to those marvellous habits, which I should else call absurd, with which we lionise strangers. Because our hospitals and poorhouses are the largest buildings we have, we entertain the Prince of Wales and Jenny Lind alike, by showing them crazy people and paupers. Easy enough to laugh at is the display; but if, dear Public, it happen, that by such a habit you ventilate your Bridewell or your Bedlam, is not the ventilation, perhaps, a compensation for the absurdity? I do not know if Lafayette was any the better for his seeing the Deering Street Asylum; but I do know I was.

This is no history of my life. It is only an illustration of one of its principles. I have no anecdotes of wilderness life to tell, and no sketch of the lovely rugged traits of John and Betsy Myers – my real father and mother. I have no quest for the pretended parents, who threw me away in my babyhood, to record. They closed accounts with me when they left me on the asylum steps, and I with them. I grew up with such schooling as the public gave – ten weeks in winter always, and ten in summer, till I was big enough to work on the farm – better periods of schools, I hold, than on the modern systems. Mr Ogden I never saw. Regularly he allowed for me the hundred a year till I was nine years old, and then suddenly he died, as the reader perhaps knows. But John

Myers kept me as his son, none the less. I knew no change until, when I was fourteen, he thought it time for me to see the world, and sent me to what, in those days, was called a 'Manual-Labour School'.

There was a theory coming up in those days, wholly unfounded in physiology, that if a man worked five hours with his hands, he could study better in the next five. It is all nonsense. Exhaustion is exhaustion; and if you exhaust a vessel by one stopcock, nothing is gained or saved by closing that and opening another. The old up-country theory is the true one. Study ten weeks and chop wood fifteen; study ten more and harvest fifteen. But the 'Manual Labour School' offered itself for really no pay, only John Myers and I carried over, I remember, a dozen barrels of potatoes when I went there with my books. The school was kept at Roscius, and if I would work in the carpenter's shop and on the school farm five hours, why they would feed me and teach me all they knew in what I had of the day beside.

'Felix,' said John, as he left me, 'I do not suppose this is the best school in the world, unless you make it so. But I do suppose you can make it so. If you and I went whining about, looking for the best school in the world, and for somebody to pay your way through it, I should die, and you would lose your voice with whining, and we should not find one after all. This is what the public happens to provide for you and me. We won't look a gift-horse in mouth. Get on his back, Felix; groom him well as you can when you stop, feed him when you can, and at all events water him well and take care of him well. My last advice to you, Felix, is to take what is offered you, and never complain because nobody offers more.'

Those words are to be cut on my seal-ring, if I ever have one, and if Dr Anthon or Professor Webster will put them into short enough Latin for me. That is the motto of the 'Children of the Public'.

John Myers died before that term was out. And my more than mother, Betsy, went back to her friends in Maine. After the funeral I never saw them more. How I lived from that moment to what Fausta and I call 'The Crisis' is nobody's concern. I worked in the shop at the school, or on the farm. Afterwards I taught school in neighbouring districts. I never bought a ticket in a lottery or a raffle. But whenever there was a chance to do an honest stroke of work, I did it. I have walked fifteen miles at night to carry an election return to the *Tribune*'s agent at Gouverneur. I have turned out in the snow to break open the road when the supervisor could not find another man in the township.

When Sartain started his magazine, I wrote an essay in competition for his premiums, and the essay earned its hundred dollars. When the managers of the Orphan Home, in Baltimore, offered their prizes for papers on bad boys, I wrote for one of them, and that helped me on four hard months. There was no luck in those things. I needed the money, and I put my hook into the pork-barrel – that is, I trusted the Public. I never had but one stroke of luck in my life. I wanted a new pair of boots badly. I was going to walk to Albany, to work in the State library on the history of the Six Nations, which had an interest for me. I did not have a dollar. Just then there passed Congress the bill dividing the surplus revenue. The State of New York received two or three millions, and divided it among the counties. The county of St Lawrence divided it among the townships, and the township of Roscius divided it among the voters. Two dollars and sixty cents of Uncle Sam's money came to me, and with that money on my feet I walked to Albany. That I call luck! How many fools had to assent in an absurdity before I could study the history of the Six Nations!

But one instance told in detail is better than a thousand told in general, for the illustration of a principle. So I will detain you no longer from the history of what Fausta and I call 'The Crisis'.

CHAPTER IV

The Crisis

I was at work as a veneerer in a pianoforte factory at Attica, when some tariff or other was passed or repealed; there came a great financial explosion, and our boss, among the rest, failed. He owed us all six months' wages, and we were all very poor and very blue. Jonathan Whittemore – a real good fellow, who used to cover the hammers with leather – came to me the day the shop was closed, and told me he was going to take the chance to go to Europe. He was going to the Musical Conservatory at Leipsic, if he could. He would work his passage out as a stoker. He would wash himself for three or four days at Bremen, and then get work, if he could, with Voightlander or Von Hammer till he could enter the Conservatory. By way of preparation for this he wanted me to sell him my Adler's German Dictionary.

'I've nothing to give you for it, Felix, but this foolish thing – it is one of Burrham's tickets – which I bought in a frolic the night of our sleigh-ride. I'll transfer it to you.'

I told Jonathan he might have the dictionary and welcome. He was doing a sensible thing, and he would use it twenty times as much as I should. As for the ticket, he had better keep it. I did not want it. But I saw he would feel better if I took it – so he indorsed it to me.

Now the reader must know that this Burrham was a man who had got hold of one corner of the idea of what the Public could do for its children. He had found out that there were a thousand people who would be glad to make the tour of the mountains and the lakes every summer if they could do it for half-price. He found out that the railroad companies were glad enough to put the price down if they could be sure of the thousand people. He mediated between the two, and so 'cheap excursions' came into being. They are one of the gifts the Public gives its children. Rising from step to step, Burrham had, just before the great financial crisis, conceived the idea of a great cheap combination, in which everybody was to receive a magazine for a year and a cyclopædia, both at half-price; and not only so, but the money that was gained in the combination was to be given by lot to two ticket-holders, one a man and one a woman, for their dowry in marriage. I dare say the reader remembers the prospectus. It savours too much of the modern 'Gift Enterprise' to be reprinted in full; but it had this honest element, that everybody got more than he could get for his money in retail. I have my magazine, the old *Boston Miscellany*, to this day, and I just now looked out Levasseur's name my cyclopædia; and, as you will see, I have reason to know that all the other subscribers got theirs.

One of the tickets for these books, for which Whittemore had given five good dollars, was what he gave to me for my dictionary. And so we parted. I loitered at Attica, hoping for a place where I could put in my oar. But my hand was out at teaching, and in a time when all the world's veneers of different kinds were ripping off, nobody wanted me to put on more of my kind – so that my cash ran low. I would not go in debt – that is a thing I never did. More honest, I say, to go to the poorhouse, and make the Public care for its child there, than to borrow what you cannot pay. But I did not come quite to that, as you shall see.

I was counting up my money one night – and it was easily done – when I observed that the date on this Burrham order was 15 October, and it occurred to me that it was not quite a fortnight before those books were to be delivered. They were to be delivered at Castle Garden, at New York; and the thought struck me that I might go to New York, try my chance there for work, and at least see the city, which I had never seen, and get my cyclopædia and magazine. It was the least offer the Public ever made to me; but just then the Public was in a collapse, and the least was better than nothing. The plan of so long a journey was Quixotic enough, and I hesitated about it a good deal. Finally I came to this resolve: I would start in the morning to walk to the lock-station at Brockport on the canal. If a boat passed that night where they would give me my fare for any work I could do for them, I would go to Albany. If not, I would walk back to Lockport the next day, and try my fortune there. This gave me, for my first day's enterprise, a foot journey of about twenty-five miles. It was out of the question, with my finances, for me to think of compassing the train.

Every point of life is a pivot on which turns the whole action of our after-lives; and so, indeed, of the after-lives of the whole world. But we are so purblind that we only see this of certain special enterprises and endeavours, which we therefore call critical. I am sure I see it of that twenty-five miles of fresh autumnal walking. I was in tiptop spirits. I found the air all oxygen, and everything 'all right'. I did not loiter, and I did not hurry. I swung along with the feeling that every nerve and muscle drew, as in the trades a sailor feels of every rope and sail. And so I was not tired, not thirsty, till the brook appeared where I was to drink, nor hungry till twelve o'clock came, when I was to dine. I called myself as I walked 'The Child of Good Fortune', because the sun was on my right quarter, as the sun should be when you walk, because the rain of yesterday had laid the dust for me, and the frost of yesterday had painted the hills for me, and the northwest wind cooled the air for me. I came to Wilkie's Crossroads just in time to meet the Claremont baker and buy my dinner loaf of him. And when my walk was nearly done, I came out on the low bridge at Sewell's, which is a drawbridge, just before they raised it for a passing boat instead of the moment after. Because I was all right I felt myself and called myself 'The Child of Good Fortune'. Dear reader, in a world made by a loving Father, we are all of us children of good fortune, if we only have wit enough to find it out, as we stroll along.

The last stroke of good fortune which that day had for me was the solution of my question whether or no I would go to Babylon. I was to go if any good-natured boatman would take me. This is a question, Mr Millionnaire, more doubtful to those who have not drawn their dividends than to those who have. As I came down the village street at Brockport, I could see the horses of a boat bound eastward, led along from level to level at the last lock; and, in spite of my determination not to hurry, I put myself on the long, loping trot which the St Regis Indians taught me, that I might overhaul this boat before she got under way at her new speed. I came out on the upper gate of the last lock just as she passed out from the lower gate. The horses were just put on, and a reckless boy gave them their first blow after two hours of rest and corn. As the heavy boat started off under the new motion, I saw, and her skipper saw at the same instant, that a long new tow-rope of his, which had lain coiled on deck, was suddenly flying out to its full length. The outer end of it had been carried upon the lock-side by some chance or blunder, and there some idle loafer had thrown the looped bight of it over a hawser-post. The loafers on the lock saw, as I did, that the rope was running out, and at the call of the skipper one of them condescended to throw the loop overboard, but he did it so carelessly that the lazy rope rolled over into the lock, and the loop caught on one of the valve-irons of the upper gate. The whole was the business of an instant, of course. But the poor skipper saw, what we did not, that the coil of the rope on deck was foul, and so entangled round his long tiller, that ten seconds would do one of three things – they would snap his new rope in two, which was a trifle, or they would wrench his tiller-head off the rudder, which would cost him an hour to mend, or they would upset those two horses, at this instant on a trot, and put into the canal the rowdy youngster who had started them. It was this complex certainty which gave fire to the double cries which he addressed aft to us on the lock, and forward to the magnet boy, whose indifferent intelligence at that moment drew him along.

I was stepping upon the gate-head to walk across it. It took but an instant, not nearly all the ten seconds, to swing down by my arms into the lock, keeping myself hanging by my hands, to catch with my right foot the bight of the rope and lift it off the treacherous iron, to kick the whole into the water, and then to scramble up the wet lock-side again. I got a little wet, but that was nothing. I ran down the tow-path, beckoned to the skipper, who sheered his boat up to the shore, and I jumped on board.

At that moment, reader, Fausta was sitting in a yellow chair on the deck of that musty old boat, crocheting from a pattern in *Godey's Lady's Book*. I remember it as I remember my breakfast of this morning. Not that I fell in love with her, nor did I fall in love with my breakfast; but I knew she was there. And that was the first time I ever saw her. It is many years since, and I have seen her every day from that evening to this evening. But I had then no business with her. My affair was with him whom I have called the skipper, by way of adapting this fresh-water narrative to ears accustomed to Marryat and Tom Cringle. I told him that I had to go to New York; that I had not time to walk, and had not money to pay; that I should like to work my passage to Troy, if there were any way in which I could; and to ask him this I had come on board.

'Waal,' said the skipper, ' 'taint much that is to be done, and Zekiel and I calc'late to do most of that, and there's that blamed boy beside – '

This adjective 'blamed' is the virtuous oath by which simple people, who are improving their habits, cure themselves of a stronger epithet, as men take to flagroot who are abandoning tobacco.

'He ain't good for nothin', as you see,' continued the skipper meditatively, 'and you air, anybody can see that,' he added. 'Ef you've mind to come to Albany, you can have your vittles, poor enough they are too; and ef you are willing to ride sometimes, you can ride. I guess where there's room for three in the bunks there's room for four. 'Taint everybody would have cast off that blamed hawser-rope as neat as you did.'

From which last remark I inferred, what I learned as a certainty as we travelled farther, that but for the timely assistance I had rendered him I should have pleaded for my passage in vain.

This was my introduction to Fausta. That is to say, she heard the whole of the conversation. The formal introduction, which is omitted in no circle of American life to which I have ever been admitted, took place at tea half an hour after, when Mrs Grills, who always voyaged with her husband, brought in the flapjacks from the kitchen. 'Miss Jones,' said Grills, as I came into the meal, leaving Zekiel at the tiller – 'Miss Jones, this is a young man who is going to Albany. I don't rightly know how to call your name, sir.' I said my name was Carter. Then he said, 'Mr Carter, this is Miss Jones. Mrs Grills, Mr Carter. Mr Carter, Mrs Grills. She is my wife.' And so our *partie carrée* was established for the voyage.

In these days there are few people who know that a journey on a canal is the pleasantest journey in the world. A canal has to go through fine scenery. It cannot exist unless it follow through the valley of a stream. The movement is so easy that, with your eyes shut, you do not know you move. The route is so direct, that when you are once shielded from the sun, you're safe for hours. You draw, you read, you write, or you sew, crochet, or knit. You play on your flute or your guitar, without one hint of inconvenience. At a 'low bridge' you duck your head lest you lose your hat – and that reminder teaches you that you are human. You are glad to know this, and you laugh at the memento. For the rest of the time you journey, if you are 'all right' within, in elysium.

I rode one of those horses perhaps two or three hours a day. At locks I made myself generally useful. At night I walked the deck till one o'clock, with my pipe or without it, to keep guard against the lock-thieves. The skipper asked me sometimes, after he found I could 'cipher', to disentangle some of the knots in his bills of lading for him. But all this made but a little inroad in those lovely autumn days, and for the eight days that we glided along – there is one blessed level which is seventy miles long – I spent most of my time with Fausta. We walked together on the tow-path to get our appetites for dinner and for supper. At sunrise I always made a cruise inland, and collected the gentians and black alder-berries and coloured leaves, with which she dressed Mrs Grills's table. She took an interest in my wretched sketchbook, and though she did not and does not draw well, she did show me how to spread an even tint, which I never knew before. I was working up my French. She knew about as much and as little as I did, and we read Mme Reybaud's *Clementine* together, guessing at the hard words, because we had no dictionary.

Dear old Grills offered to talk French at table, and we tried it for a few days. But it proved he picked up his pronunciation at St Catherine's, among the boatmen there, and he would say *shwo* for 'horses', where the book said *chevaux*. Our talk, on the other hand, was not Parisian – but it was not Catherinian – and we subsided into English again.

So sped along these blessed eight days. I told Fausta thus much of my story, that I was going to seek my fortune in New York. She, of course, knew nothing of me but what she saw, and she told me nothing of her story.

But I was very sorry when we came into the basin at Troy, for I knew then that in all reason I must take the steamboat down. And I was very glad – I have seldom in my life been so glad – when I found that she also was going to New York immediately. She accepted, very pleasantly, my offer to carry her trunk to the *Isaac Newton* for her, and to act as her escort to the city. For me, my trunk,

> . . . in danger tried,
> Swung in my hand – nor left my side.

My earthly possessions were few anyway. I had left at Attica most of what they were. Through the voyage I had been man enough to keep on a working-gear fit for a workman's duty. And old Grills had not yet grace enough to keep his boat still on Sunday. How one remembers little things! I can remember each touch of the toilet, as, in that corner of a dark cuddy where I had shared Zekiel's bunk with him, I dressed myself with one of my two white shirts, and with the change of raiment which had been tight squeezed in my portmanteau. The old overcoat was the best part of it, as in a finite world it often is. I sold my felt hat to Zekiel, and appeared with a light travelling-cap. I do not know how Fausta liked my metamorphosis. I only know that, like butterflies, for a day or two after they go through theirs, I felt decidedly cold.

As Carter, the canal man, I had carried Fausta's trunk on board. As Mr Carter, I gave her my arm, led her to the gangway of the *Newton*, took her passage and mine, and afterwards walked and sat through the splendid moonlight of the first four hours down the river.

Miss Jones determined that evening to breakfast on the boat. Be it observed that I did not then know her by any other name. She was to go to an aunt's house, and she knew that if she left the boat on its early arrival in New York, she would disturb that lady by a premature ringing at her bell. I had no reason for haste, as the reader knows. The distribution of the cyclopædias was not to take place till the next day, and that absurd trifle was the only distinct excuse I had to myself for being in New York at all. I asked Miss Jones, therefore, if I might not be her escort still to her aunt's house. I had said it would be hard to break off our pleasant journey before I had seen where she lived, and I thought she seemed relieved to know that she should not be wholly a stranger on her arrival. It was clear enough that her aunt would send no one to meet her.

These preliminaries adjusted, we parted to our respective cabins. And when, the next morning, at that unearthly hour demanded by Philadelphia trains and other exigencies, the *Newton* made her dock, I rejoiced that breakfast was not till seven o'clock, that I had two hours more of the berth, which was luxury compared to Zekiel's bunk – I turned upon my other side and slept on.

Sorry enough for that morning nap was I for the next thirty-six hours. For when I went on deck, and sent in the stewardess to tell Miss Jones that I was waiting for her, and then took from her the check for her trunk, I woke to the misery of finding that, in that treacherous two hours, some pirate from the pier had stepped on board, had seized the waiting trunk, left almost alone, while the baggage-master's back was turned, and that, to a certainty, it was lost. I did not return to Fausta with this story till the breakfast-bell had long passed and the breakfast was very cold. I did not then tell it to her till I had seen her eat her breakfast with an appetite much better than mine. I had already offered upstairs the largest reward to anybody who would bring it back which my scanty purse would pay. I had spoken to the clerk, who had sent for a policeman. I could do nothing more, and I did not choose to ruin her chop and coffee by ill-timed news. The officer came before breakfast was over, and called me from table.

On the whole, his business-like way encouraged one. He had some clues which I had not thought possible. It was not unlikely that they should pounce on the trunk before it was broken open. I gave him a written description of its marks; and when he civilly asked if 'my lady' would give some description of any books or other articles within, I readily promised that I would call with such a description at the police station. Somewhat encouraged, I returned to Miss Jones, and, when I led her from the breakfast-table, told her of her misfortune. I took all shame to myself for my own carelessness, to which I attributed the loss. But I told her all that the officer had said to me, and that I hoped to bring her the trunk at her aunt's before the day was over.

Fausta took my news, however, with a start which frightened me. All her money, but a shilling or two, was in the trunk. To place money in trunks is a weakness of the female mind which I have nowhere seen accounted for. Worse than this, though – as appeared after a moment's examination of her travelling *sac* – her portfolio in the trunk contained the letter of the aunt whom she came to visit, giving her her address in the city. To this address she had no other clue but that her aunt was Mrs Mary Mason, had married a few years before a merchant named Mason, whom Miss Jones had never seen, and whose name and business this was all she knew. They lived in a numbered street, but whether it was Fourth Street, or Fifty-fourth, or One Hundred and Twenty-fourth, or whether it was something between, the poor child had no idea. She had put up the letter carefully, but had never thought of the importance of the address. Besides this aunt, she knew no human being in New York.

'Child of the Public,' I said to myself, 'what do you do now?' I had appealed to my great patron in sending for the officer, and on the whole I felt that my sovereign had been gracious to me, if not yet hopeful. But now I must rub my lamp again, and ask the genie where the unknown Mason lived. The genie of course suggested the Directory, and I ran for it to the clerk's office. But as we were toiling down the pages of 'Masons', and had written off thirteen or fourteen who lived in numbered streets, Fausta started, looked back at the preface and its date, flung down her pencil in the only abandonment of dismay in which I ever saw her, and cried, 'First of May! They were abroad until May. They have been abroad since the day they were married!' So that genie had to put his glories into his pocket, and carry his Directory back to the office again.

The natural thing to propose was, that I should find for Miss Jones a respectable boarding-house, and that she should remain there until her trunk was found, or till she could write to friends who had this fatal address, and receive an answer. But here she hesitated. She hardly liked to explain why – did not explain wholly. But she did not say that she had no friends who knew this address. She had but few relations in the world, and her aunt had communicated with her alone since she came from Europe. As for the boarding-house, 'I had rather look for work,' she said bravely. 'I have never promised to pay money when I did not know how to obtain it; and that' – and here she took out fifty or sixty cents from her purse – 'and that is all now. In respectable boarding-houses, when people come without luggage, they are apt to ask for an advance. Or, at least,' she added, with some pride, 'I am apt to offer it.'

I hastened to ask her to take all my little store; but I had to own that I had not two dollars. I was sure, however, that my overcoat and the dress-suit I wore would avail me something, if I thrust them boldly up some spout. I was sure that I should be at work within a day or two. At all events, I was certain of the cyclopædia the next day. That should go to old Gowan's – in Fulton Street it was then – 'the moral centre of the intellectual world', in the hour I got it. And at this moment, for the first time, the thought crossed me, 'If mine could only be the name drawn, so that that foolish $5,000 should fall to me.' In that case I felt that Fausta might live in 'a respectable boarding-house' till she died. Of this, of course, I said nothing, only that she was welcome to my poor dollar and a half, and that I should receive the next day some more money that was due me.

'You forget, Mr Carter,' replied Fausta, as proudly as before – 'you forget that I cannot borrow of you any more than of a boarding-house-keeper. I never borrow. Please God, I never will. It must be,' she added, 'that in a Christian city like this there is some respectable and fit arrangement made for travellers who find themselves where I am. What that provision is I do not know; but I will find out what it is before this sun goes down.'

I paused a moment before I replied. If I had been fascinated by this lovely girl before, I now bowed in respect before her dignity and resolution; and, with my sympathy, there was a delicious throb of self-respect united, when I heard her lay down so simply, as principles of her life, two principles on which I had always myself tried to live. The half-expressed habit of my boyhood and youth were now uttered for me as axioms by lips which I knew could speak nothing but right and truth.

I paused a moment. I stumbled a little as I expressed my regret that she would not let me help here – joined with my certainty that she was in the right in refusing – and then, in the only stiff speech I ever made to her, I said –

'I am the "Child of the Public". If you ever hear my story, you will say so too. At the least, I can claim this, that I have a right to help you in your quest as to the way in which the public will help you. Thus far I am clearly the officer in his suite to whom he has entrusted you. Are you ready, then, to go on shore?'

Fausta looked around on that forlorn ladies' saloon, as if it were the last link holding her to her old safe world.

> Looked upon skylight, lamp, and chain,
> As what she ne'er might see again.

Then she looked right through me; and if there had been one mean thought in me at that minute, she would have seen the viper. Then she said, sadly –

'I have perfect confidence in you, though people would say we were strangers. Let us go.'

And we left the boat together. We declined the invitations of the noisy hackmen, and walked slowly to Broadway.

We stopped at the station-house for that district, and to the attentive chief Fausta herself described those contents of her trunk which she thought would be most easily detected, if offered for sale. Her mother's Bible, at which the chief shook his head; Bibles, alas! brought nothing at the shops; a soldier's medal, such as were given as target prizes by the Montgomery regiment; and a little silver canteen, marked with the device of the same regiment, seemed to him better worthy of note. Her portfolio was wrought with a cipher, and she explained to him that she was most eager that this should be recovered. The pocketbook contained more than one hundred dollars, which she described, but he shook his head here, and gave her but little hope of that, if the trunk were once opened. His chief hope was for this morning.

'And where shall we send to you then, madam?' said he.

I had been proud, as if it were my merit, of the impression Fausta had made upon the officer, in her quiet, simple, ladylike dress and manner. For myself, I thought that one slip of pretence in my dress or bearing, a scrap of gold or of pinchbeck, would have ruined both of us in our appeal. But, fortunately, I did not disgrace her, and the man looked at her as if he expected her to say 'Fourteenth Street'. What would she say?

'That depends upon what the time will be. Mr Carter will call at noon, and will let you know.'

We bowed, and were gone. In an instant more she begged my pardon, almost with tears; but I told her that if she also had been a 'Child of the Public', she could not more fitly have spoken to one of her father's officers. I begged her to use me as her protector, and not to apologise again. Then we laid out the plans which we followed out that day.

The officer's manner had reassured her, and I succeeded in persuading her that it was certain we should have the trunk at noon. How much better to wait, at least so far, before she entered on any of the enterprises of which she talked so coolly, as of offering herself as a nursery-girl, or as a milliner, to whoever would employ her, if only she could thus secure an honest home till money or till aunt were found. Once persuaded that we were safe from this Quixotism, I told her that we must go on, as we did on the canal, and first we must take our constitutional walk for two hours.

'At least,' she said, 'our good papa, the Public, gives us wonderful sights to see, and good walking to our feet, as a better Father has given us this heavenly sky and this bracing air.'

And with those words the last heaviness of despondency left her face for that day. And we plunged into the delicious adventure of exploring a new city, staring into windows as only strangers can, revelling in print-shops as only they do, really seeing the fine buildings as residents always forget to do, and laying up, in short, with those streets, nearly all the associations which to this day we have with them.

Two hours of this tired us with walking, of course. I do not know what she meant to do next; but at ten I said, 'Time for French, Miss Jones.' '*Ah oui*,' said she, '*mais où*?' and I had calculated my distances, and led her at once into Lafayette Place; and, in a moment, pushed open the door of the Astor library, led her up the main stairway, and said, 'This is what the Public provides for his children when they have to study.'

'This is the Astor,' said she, delighted. 'And we are all right, as you say, here?' Then she saw that our entrance excited no surprise among the few readers, men and women, who were beginning to assemble.

We took our seats at an unoccupied table, and began to revel in the luxuries for which we had only to ask that we might enjoy. I had a little memorandum of books which I had been waiting to see. She needed none; but looked for one and another, and yet another, and between us we kept the attendant well in motion. A pleasant thing to me to be finding out her thoroughbred tastes and lines of work, and I was happy enough to interest her in some of my pet readings; and, of course, for she was a woman, to get quick hints which had never dawned on me before. A very short hour and a half we spent there before I went to the station-house again. I went very quickly. I returned to her very slowly.

The trunk was not found. But they were now quite sure they were on its track. They felt certain it had been carried from pier to pier and taken back up the river. Nor was it hopeless to follow it. The particular rascal who was supposed to have it would certainly stop either at Piermont or at Newburg. They had telegraphed to both places, and were in time for both. 'The day boat, sir, will bring your lady's trunk, and will bring me Rowdy Rob, too, I hope,' said the officer. But at the same moment, as he rang his bell, he learned that no despatch had yet been received from either of the places named. I did not feel so certain as he did.

But Fausta showed no discomfort as I told my news. 'Thus far,' said she, 'the Public serves me well. I will borrow no trouble by want of faith.' And I – as Dante would say – and I, to her, 'will you let me remind you, then, that at one we dine; that Mrs Grills is now placing the salt-pork upon the cabin table, and Mr Grills asking the blessing; and, as this is the only day when I can have the honour of your company, will you let me show you how a Child of the Public dines, when his finances are low?'

Fausta laughed, and said again, less tragically than before, 'I have perfect confidence in you,' – little thinking how she started my blood with the words; but this time, as if in token, she let me take her hand upon my arm, as we walked down the street together.

If we had been snobs, or even if I had been one, I should have taken her to Taylor's, and have spent all the money I had on such a luncheon as neither of us had ever eaten before. Whatever else I am, I am not a snob of that sort. I show my colours. I led her into a little cross-street which I had noticed in our erratic morning pilgrimage. We stopped at a German baker's. I bade her sit down at the neat marble table, and I bought two rolls. She declined lager, which I offered her in fun. We took water instead, and we had dined, and had paid two cents for our meal, and had had a very merry dinner, too, when the clock struck two.

'And now, Mr Carter,' said she, 'I will steal no more of your day. You did not come to New York to escort lone damsels to the Astor Library or to dinner. Nor did I come only to see the lions or to read French. I insist on your going to your affairs, and leaving me to mine. If you will meet me at the Library half an hour before it closes, I will thank you; till then,' with a tragedy shake of the hand, and a merry laugh, 'adieu!'

I knew very well that no harm could happen to her in two hours of an autumn afternoon. I was not sorry for her *congé*, for it gave me an opportunity to follow my own plans. I stopped at one or two cabinet-makers, and talked with the 'jours' about work, that I might tell her with truth that I had been in search of it; then I sedulously began on calling upon every man I could reach named Mason. O, how often I went through one phase or another of this colloquy –

'Is Mr Mason in?'

'That's my name, sir.'

'Can you give me the address of Mr Mason when returned from Europe last May?'

'Know no such person, sir.'

The reader can imagine how many forms this dialogue could be repeated in, before, as I wrought my way through a long line of dry-goods cases to a distant counting-room, I heard someone in it say, 'No, madam, I know no such person as you describe'; and from the recess Fausta emerged and met me. Her plan for the afternoon had been the same with mine. We laughed as we detected each other; then I told her she had had quite enough of this, that it was time she should rest, and took her, *nolens volens*, into the ladies' parlour of the St Nicholas, and bade her wait there through the twilight, with my copy of *Clementine*, till I should return from the police-station. If the reader has ever waited in such a place for someone to come and attend to him, he will understand that nobody will be apt to molest him when he has not asked for attention.

Two hours I left Fausta in the rocking-chair, which there the Public had provided for her. Then I returned, sadly enough. No tidings of Rowdy Rob, none of trunk, Bible, money, letter, medal, or anything. Still was my district sergeant hopeful, and, as always, respectful. But I was hopeless this time, and I knew that the next day Fausta would be plunging into the war with intelligence-houses and advertisements. For the night, I was determined that she should spend it in my ideal 'respectable boarding-house'. On my way down town, I stopped in at one or two shops to make inquiries, and satisfied myself where I would take her. Still I thought it wisest that we should go after tea; and another cross-street baker, and another pair of rolls, and another tap at the Croton, provided that repast for us. Then I told Fausta of the respectable boarding-house, and that she must go there. She did not say no. But she did say she would rather not spend the evening there. 'There must be some place open for us,' said she. 'There! there is a church-bell! The church is always home. Let us come there.'

So to 'evening meeting' we went, startling the sexton by arriving an hour early. If there were any who wondered what was the use of that Wednesday-evening service, we did not. In a dark gallery pew we sat, she at one end, I at the other; and, if the whole truth be told, each of us fell asleep at once, and slept till the heavy organ tones taught us that the service had begun. A hundred or more people had straggled in then, and the preacher, good soul, he took for his text, 'Doth not God care for the ravens?' I cannot describe the ineffable feeling of home that came over me in that dark pew of that old church. I had never been in so lárge a church before. I had never heard so heavy an organ before. Perhaps I had heard better preaching, but never any that came to my occasions more. But it was none of these things which moved me. It was the fact that we were just where we had a right to be. No impudent waiter could ask us why we were sitting there, nor any petulant policeman propose that we should push on. It was God's house, and, because his, it was his children's.

All this feeling of repose grew upon me, and, as it proved, upon Fausta also. For when the service was ended, and I ventured to ask her whether she also had this sense of home and rest, she assented so eagerly, that I proposed, though with hesitation, a notion which had crossed me, that I should leave her there.

'I cannot think,' I said, 'of any possible harm that could come to you before morning.'

'Do you know, I had thought of that very same thing, but I did not dare tell you,' she said.

Was not I glad that she had considered me her keeper! But I only said, 'At the "respectable boarding-house" you might be annoyed by questions.'

'And no one will speak to me here. I know that from Goody-Two-Shoes.'

'I will be here,' said I, 'at sunrise in the morning.' And so I bade her goodbye, insisting on leaving in the pew my own greatcoat. I knew she might need it before morning. I walked out as the sexton closed the door below on the last of the downstairs worshippers. He passed along the aisles below, with his long poker which screwed down the gas. I saw at once that he had no intent of exploring the galleries. But I loitered outside till I saw him lock the doors and depart; and then, happy in the thought that Miss Jones was in the safest place in New York – as comfortable as she was the night before, and much more comfortable than she had been any night upon the canal, I went in search of my own lodging.

'To the respectable boarding-house?'

Not a bit, reader. I had no shillings for respectable or disrespectable boarding-houses. I asked the first policeman where his district station was. I went into its office, and told the captain that I was green in the city; had got no work and no money. In truth, I had left my purse in Miss Jones's charge, and a five-cent piece, which I showed the chief, was all I had. He said no word but to bid me go up two flights and turn into the first bunk I found. I did so; and in five minutes was asleep in a better bed than I had slept in for nine days.

That was what the Public did for me that night. I, too, was safe!

I am making this story too long. But with that night and its anxieties the end has come. At sunrise I rose and made my easy toilet. I bought and ate my roll – varying the brand from yesterday's. I bought another, with a lump of butter, and an orange, for Fausta. I left my portmanteau at the station, while I rushed to the sexton's house, told his wife I had left my gloves in church the night before – as was the truth – and easily obtained from her the keys. In a moment I was in the vestibule – locked in – was in the gallery, and there found Fausta, just awake, as she declared, from a comfortable night, reading her morning lesson in the Bible, and sure, she said, that I should soon appear. Nor ghost, nor wraith, had visited her. I spread for her a brown paper tablecloth on the table in the vestibule. I laid out her breakfast for her, called her, and wondered at her toilet. How is it that women always make themselves appear as neat and finished as if there were no conflict, dust, or wrinkle in the world.

[Here Fausta adds, in this manuscript, a parenthesis, to say that she folded her undersleeves neatly, and her collar, before she slept, and put them between the cushions, upon which she slept. In the morning they had been pressed – without a sad-iron.]

She finished her repast. I opened the church door for five minutes. She passed out when she had enough examined the monuments, and at a respectable distance I followed her. We joined each other, and took our accustomed morning walk; but then she resolutely said, 'Goodbye,' for the day. She would find work before night – work and a home. And I must do the same. Only when I pressed her to let me know of her success, she said she would meet me at the Astor Library just before it closed. No, she would not take my money. Enough, that for twenty-four hours she had been my guest. When she had found her aunt and told her the story, they should insist on repaying this hospitality. Hospitality, dear reader, which I had dispensed at the charge of six cents. Have you ever treated Miranda for a day and found the charge so low? When I urged other assistance she said resolutely, 'No.' In fact, she had already made an appointment at two, she said, and she must not waste the day.

I also had an appointment at two; for it was at that hour that Burrham was to distribute the cyclopædias at Castle Garden. The Emigrant Commission had not yet seized it for their own. I spent the morning in asking vainly for Masons fresh from Europe, and for work in cabinet-shops. I found neither, and so wrought my way to the appointed place, where, instead of such wretched birds in the bush, I was to get one so contemptible in my hand.

Those who remember Jenny Lind's first triumph night at Castle Garden have some idea of the crowd as it filled gallery and floor of that immense hall when I entered. I had given no thought to the machinery of this folly. I only know that my ticket bade me be there at two P.M. this day. But as I drew near, the throng, the bands of policemen, the long queues of persons entering, reminded me that here was an affair of ten thousand persons, and also that Mr Burrham was not unwilling to make it as showy, perhaps as noisy, an affair as was respectable, by way of advertising future excursions and distributions. I was led to seat No. 3,671 with a good deal of parade, and when I came there I found I was very much of a prisoner. I was late, or rather on the stroke of two. Immediately, almost, Mr Burrham arose in the front and made a long speech about his liberality, and the public's liberality, and everybody's liberality in general, and the method of the distribution in particular. The mayor and four or five other well-known and respectable gentlemen were kind enough to be present to guarantee the fairness of the arrangements. At the suggestion of the mayor and the police, the doors would now be closed, that no persons might interrupt the ceremony till it was ended. And the distribution of the cyclopædias would at once go forward, in the order in which the lots were drawn – earliest numbers securing the earliest impressions; which, as Mr Burrham almost regretted to say, were a little better than the latest. After these had been distributed two figures would be drawn – one green and one red, to indicate the fortunate lady and gentleman who would receive respectively the profits which had arisen from this method of selling the cyclopædias, after the expenses of printing and distribution had been covered, and after the magazines had been ordered.

Great cheering followed this announcement from all but me. Here I had shut myself up in this humbug hall, for Heaven knew how long, on the most important day of my life. I would have given up willingly my cyclopædia and my chance at the 'profits', for the certainty of seeing Fausta at five o'clock. If I did not see her then, what might befall her, and when might I see her again. An hour before this certainty was my own, now it was only mine by my liberating myself from this prison. Still I was encouraged by seeing that everything was conducted like clockwork. From literally a hundred stations they were distributing the books. We formed ourselves into queues as we pleased, drew our numbers, and then presented ourselves at the bureau, ordered our magazines, and took our cyclopædias. It would be done, at that rate, by half-past four. An omnibus might bring me to the Park, and a Bowery car do the rest in time. After a vain discussion for the right of exit with one or two of the attendants, I abandoned myself to this hope, and began studying my cyclopædia.

It was sufficiently amusing to see ten thousand people resign themselves to the same task, and affect to be unconcerned about the green and red figures which were to divide the 'profits'. I tried to make out who were as anxious to get out of that tawdry den as I was. Four o'clock struck, and the distribution was not done. I began to be very impatient. What if Fausta fell into trouble? I knew, or hoped I knew, that she would struggle to the Astor Library, as to her only place of rescue and refuge – her asylum. What if I failed her there? I who had pretended to be her protector! 'Protector, indeed!' she would say, if she knew I was at a theatre witnessing the greatest folly of the age. And if I did not meet her today, when should I meet her? If she found her aunt, how should I find her? If she did not find her – good God? that was worse – where might she not be before twelve hours were over? Then the fatal trunk! I had told the police agent he might send it to the St Nicholas, because I had to give him some address. But Fausta did not know this, and the St Nicholas people knew nothing of us. I grew more and more excited, and when at last my next neighbour told me that it was half-past four, I rose and insisted on leaving my seat. Two ushers with blue sashes almost held me down; they showed me the whole assembly sinking into quiet. In fact, at that moment Mr Burrham was begging everyone to be seated. I would not be seated. I would go to the door. I would go out. 'Go, if you please!' said the usher next it, contemptuously. And I looked, and there was no handle! Yet this was not a dream. It is the way they arrange the doors in halls where they choose to keep people in their places. I could have collared that grinning blue sash. I did tell him I would wring his precious neck for him, if he did not let me out. I said I would sue him for false imprisonment; I would have a writ *of habeas corpus*.

'*Habeas corpus* be damned!' said the officer, with an irreverent disrespect to the palladium. 'If you are not more civil, sir, I will call the police, of whom we have plenty. You say you want to go out; you are keeping everybody in.'

And, in fact, at that moment the clear voice of the mayor was announcing that they would not go on until there was perfect quiet; and I felt that I was imprisoning all these people, not they me.

'Child of the Public,' said my mourning genius; 'are you better than other men?' So I sneaked back to seat No. 3,671, amid the contemptuous and reproachful looks and sneers of my more respectable neighbours, who had sat where they were told to do. We must be through in a moment, and perhaps Fausta would be late also. If only the Astor would keep open after sunset! How often have I wished that since, and for less reasons!

Silence thus restored, Mr A—, the mayor, led forward his little daughter, blindfolded her, and bade her put her hand into a green box, from which she drew out a green ticket. He took it from her, and read, in his clear voice again, 'No. 2,973!' By this time we all knew where the 'two thousands' sat. Then 'nine hundreds' were not far from the front, so that it was not far that that frightened girl, dressed all in black, and heavily veiled, had to walk, who answered to this call. Mr A— met her, helped her up the stair upon the stage, took from her her ticket, and read, 'Jerusha Stillingfleet, of Yellow Springs, who, at her death, as it seems, transferred this right to the bearer.'

The disappointed nine thousand nine hundred and ninety-nine joined in a rapturous cheer, each man and woman, to show that he or she was not disappointed. The bearer spoke with Mr Burrham, in answer to his questions, and, with a good deal of ostentation, he opened a cheque-book, filled a cheque and passed it to her, she signing a receipt as she took it, and transferring to him her ticket. So far, in dumb show, all was well. What was more to my purpose, it was rapid, for we should have been done in five minutes more, but that some devil tempted some loafer in a gallery to cry, 'Face! face!' Miss Stillingfleet's legatee was still heavily veiled.

In one horrid minute that whole amphitheatre, which seemed to me then more cruel than the Coliseum ever was, rang out with a cry of 'Face, face!' I tried the counter-cry of 'Shame! shame!' but I was in disgrace among my neighbours, and a counter-cry never takes as its prototype does, either. At first, on the stage, they affected not to hear or understand; then there was a courtly whisper between Mr Burrham and the lady; but Mr A—, the mayor, and the respectable gentlemen, instantly interfered. It was evident that she would not unveil, and that they were prepared to indorse her refusal. In a moment more she courtesied to the assembly; the mayor gave her his arm, and led her out through a side-door.

O, the yell that rose up then! The whole assembly stood up, and, as if they had lost some vested right, hooted and shrieked, 'Back! back! Face! face!' Mr A— returned, made as if he would speak, came forward to the very front, and got a moment's silence.

'It is not in the bond, gentlemen,' said he. 'The young lady is unwilling to unveil, and we must not compel her.'

'Face! face!' was the only answer, and oranges from upstairs flew about his head and struck upon the table – an omen only fearful from what it prophesied. Then there was such a row for five minutes as I hope I may never see or hear again. People kept their places fortunately, under a vague impression that they should forfeit some magic rights if they left those numbered seats. But when, for a moment, a file of policemen appeared in the orchestra, a whole volley of cyclopædias fell like rain upon their chief, with a renewed cry of 'Face! face!'

At this juncture, with a good deal of knowledge of popular feeling, Mr A— led forward his child again. Frightened to death the poor thing was, and crying; he tied his handkerchief round her eyes hastily, and took her to the red box. For a minute the house was hushed. A cry of 'Down! down!' and everyone took his place as the child gave the red ticket to her father. He read it as before, 'No. 3,671!' I heard the words as if he did not speak them. All excited by the delay and the row, by the injustice to the stranger and the personal injustice of everybody to me, I did not know, for a dozen seconds, that everyone was looking towards our side of the house, nor was it till my next neighbour with the watch said, 'Go, you fool,' that I was aware that 3,671 was I! Even then, as I stepped down the passage and up the steps, my only feeling was, that I should get out of this horrid trap, and possibly find Miss Jones lingering near the Astor – not by any means that I was invited to take a cheque for $5,000.

There was not much cheering. Women never mean to cheer, of course. The men had cheered the green ticket, but they were mad with the red one. I gave up my ticket, signed my receipt, and took my cheque, shook hands with Mr A— and Mr Burrham, and turned to bow to the mob – for mob I must call it now. But the cheers died away. A few people tried to go out perhaps, but there was nothing now to retain any in their seats as before, and the generality rose, pressed down the passages, and howled, 'Face! face!' I thought for a moment that I ought to say something, but they would not hear me, and, after a moment's pause, my passion to depart overwhelmed me. I muttered some apology to the gentlemen, and left the stage by the stage door.

I had forgotten that to Castle Garden there can be no back entrance. I came to door after door, which were all locked. It was growing dark. Evidently the sun was set, and I knew the library door would be shut at sunset. The passages were very obscure. All around me rang this horrid yell of the mob, in which all that I could discern was the cry, 'Face, face!' At last, as I groped round, I came to a practicable door. I entered a room where the western sunset glare dazzled me. I was not alone. The veiled lady in black was there. But the instant she saw me she sprang towards me, flung herself into my arms, and cried –

'Felix, is it you? – you are indeed my protector!'

It was Miss Jones! It was Fausta! She was the legatee of Miss Stillingfleet. My first thought was, 'O, if that beggarly usher had let me go! Will I ever, ever think I have better rights than the Public again?'

I took her in my arms. I carried her to the sofa. I could hardly speak for excitement Then I did say that I had been wild with terror; that I had feared I had lost her, and lost her forever; that to have lost that interview would have been worse to me than death; for unless she knew that I loved her better than any man ever loved woman, I could not face a lonely night, and another lonely day.

'My dear, dear child,' I said, 'you may think me wild; but I must say this – it has been pent up too long.'

'Say what you will,' she said after a moment, in which still I held her in my arms; she was trembling so that she could not have sat upright alone – 'say what you will, if only you do not tell me to spend another day alone.'

And I kissed her, and I kissed her, and I kissed her, and I said, 'Never, darling, God helping me, till I die.'

How long we sat there I do not know. Neither of us spoke again. For one, I looked out on the sunset and the bay. We had but just time to rearrange ourselves in positions more independent, when Mr A— came in, this time in alarm, to say –

'Miss Jones, we must get you out of this place, or we must hide you somewhere. I believe, before God, they will storm this passage, and pull the house about our ears.'

He said this, not conscious as he began that I was there. At that moment, however, I felt as if I could have met a million men. I started forward and passed him, saying, 'Let me speak to them.' I rushed upon the stage, fairly pushing back two or three bullies who were already upon it. I sprang upon the table, kicking down the red box as I did so, so that the red tickets fell on the floor and on the people below. One stuck in an old man's spectacles in a way which made the people in the galleries laugh. A laugh is a great blessing at such a moment. Curiosity is another. Three loud words spoken like thunder do a good deal more. And after three words the house was hushed to hear me. I said –

'Be fair to the girl. She has no father nor mother. She has no brother nor sister. She is alone in the world, with nobody to help her but the Public – and me!'

The audacity of the speech brought out a cheer and we should have come off in triumph, when some rowdy – the original 'Face' man, I suppose – said –

'And who are you?'

If the laugh went against me now I was lost, of course. Fortunately I had no time to think. I said without thinking –

'I am the Child of the Public, and her betrothed husband!'

O Heavens! what a yell of laughter, of hurrahings, of satisfaction with a *dénouement*, rang through the house, and showed that all was well. Burrham caught the moment, and started his band, this time successfully – I believe with 'See the Conquering Hero'. The doors, of course, had been open long before. Well-disposed people saw they need stay no longer; ill-disposed people dared not stay; the blue-coated men with buttons sauntered on the stage in groups, and I suppose the worst rowdies disappeared as they saw them. I had made my single speech, and for the moment I was a hero.

I believe the major would have liked to kiss me. Burrham almost did. They overwhelmed me with thanks and congratulations. All these I received as well as I could – somehow I did not feel at all surprised – everything was as it should be. I scarcely thought of leaving the stage myself, till, to my surprise, the mayor asked me to go home with him to dinner.

Then I remembered that we were not to spend the rest of our lives in Castle Garden. I blundered out something about Miss Jones, that she had no escort except me, and pressed into her room to find her. A group of gentlemen was around her. Her veil was back now. She was very pale, but very lovely. Have I said that she was beautiful as heaven? She was the queen of the room, modestly and pleasantly receiving their felicitations that the danger was over, and owning that she had been very much frightened. 'Until,' she said, 'my friend, Mr Carter, was fortunate enough to guess that I was here. How he did it,' she said, turning to me, 'is yet an utter mystery to me.'

She did not know till then that it was I who had shared with her the profits of the cyclopædias.

As soon as we could excuse ourselves, I asked someone to order a carriage. I sent to the ticket-office for my valise, and we rode to the St Nicholas. I fairly laughed as I gave the hackman at the hotel door what would have been my last dollar and a half only two hours before. I entered Miss Jones's name and my own. The clerk looked, and said, inquiringly –

'Is it Miss Jones's trunk which came this afternoon?'

I followed his finger to see the trunk on the marble floor. Rowdy Rob had deserted it, having seen, perhaps, a detective when he reached Piermont. The trunk had gone to Albany, had found no owner, and had returned by the day boat of that day.

Fausta went to her room, and I sent her supper after her. One kiss and 'Good-night' was all that I got from her then.

'In the morning,' said she, 'you shall explain.'

It was not yet seven. I went to my own room and dressed, and tendered myself at the mayor's just before his gay party sat down to dine. I met, for the first time in my life, men whose books I had read, and whose speeches I had by heart, and women whom I have since known to honour; and, in the midst of this brilliant group, so excited had Mr A— been in telling the strange story of the day, I was, for the hour, the lion.

I led Mrs A— to the table; I made her laugh very heartily by telling her of the usher's threats to me, and mine to him, and of the disgrace into which I fell among the three thousand six hundreds. I had never been at any such party before. But I found it was only rather simpler and more quiet than most parties I had seen, that its good breeding was exactly that of dear Betsy Myers.

As the party broke up, Mrs A— said to me –

'Mr Carter, I am sure you are tired, with all this excitement. You say you are a stranger here. Let me send round for your trunk to the St Nicholas, and you shall spend the night here. I know I can make you a better bed than they.'

I thought as much myself, and assented. In half an hour more I was in bed in Mrs A—'s 'best room'.

'I shall not sleep better,' said I to myself, 'than I did last night.'

That was what the Public did for me that night. I was safe again!

CHAPTER THE LAST

Fausta's Story

Fausta slept late, poor child. I called for her before breakfast. I waited for her after. About ten she appeared, so radiant, so beautiful, and so kind! The trunk had revealed a dress I never saw before, and the sense of rest, and eternal security, and unbroken love had revealed a charm which was never there to see before. She was dressed for walking, and, as she met me, said –

'Time for constitutional, Mr Millionaire.'

So we walked again, quite up town, almost to the region of pig-pens and cabbage-gardens which is now the Central Park. And after just the first gush of my enthusiasm, Fausta said, very seriously –

'I must teach you to be grave. You do not know whom you are asking to be your wife. Excepting Mrs Mason, No. 27 Thirty-fourth Street, sir, there is no one in the world who is of kin to me, and she does not care for me one straw, Felix,' she said, almost sadly now. 'You call yourself "Child of the Public." I started when you first said so, for that is just what I am.

'I am twenty-two years old. My father died before I was born. My mother, a poor woman, disliked by his relatives and avoided by them, went to live in Hoboken over there, with me. How she lived, God knows! but it happened that of a strange death she died, I in her arms.'

After a pause, the poor girl went on –

'There was a great military review, an encampment. She was tempted out to see it. Of a sudden by some mistake, a ramrod was fired from a careless soldier's gun, and it pierced her through her heart. I tell you, Felix, it pinned my baby frock into the wound, so that they could not part me from her till it was cut away.

'Of course everyone was filled with horror. Nobody claimed poor me, the baby. But the battalion, the Montgomery Battalion, it was, which had, by mischance, killed my mother, adopted me as their child. I was voted "Fille du Regiment". They paid an assessment annually, which the colonel expended for me. A kind old woman nursed me.'

'She was your Betsy Myers,' interrupted I.

'And when I was old enough I was sent into Connecticut, to the best of schools. This lasted till I was sixteen. Fortunately for me, perhaps, the Montgomery Battalion then dissolved. I was finding it hard to answer the colonel's annual letters. I had my living to earn – it was best I should earn it. I declined a proposal to go out as a missionary. I had no call. I answered one of Miss Beecher's appeals for Western teachers. Most of my life since has been a schoolma'am's. It has had ups and downs. But I have always been proud that the Public was my godfather; and, as you know,' she said, 'I have trusted the Public well. I have never been lonely, wherever I went. I tried to make myself of use. Where I was of use I found society. The ministers have been kind to me. I always offered my services in the Sunday schools and sewing-rooms. The school committees have been kind to me. They are the Public's high chamberlains for poor girls. I have written for the journals. I won one of Sartain's hundred-dollar prizes – '

'And I another,' interrupted I.

'When I was very poor, I won the first prize for an essay on bad boys.'

'And I the second,' answered I.

'I think I know one bad boy better than he knows himself,' said she. But she went on. 'I watched with this poor Miss Stillingfleet the night she died. This absurd "distribution" had got hold of her, and she would not be satisfied till she had transferred that strange ticket, No. 2,973, to me, writing the indorsement which you have heard. I had had a longing to visit New York and Hoboken again. This ticket seemed to me to beckon me. I had money enough to come, if I would come cheaply. I wrote to my father's business partner, and enclosed a note to his only sister. She is Mrs Mason. She asked me, coldly enough, to her house. Old Mr Grills always liked me – he offered me escort and passage as far as Troy or Albany. I accepted his proposal, and you know the rest.'

When I told Fausta my story, she declared I made it up as I went along. When she believed it – as she does believe it now – she agreed with me in declaring that it was not fit that two people thus joined should ever be parted. Nor have we been, ever!

She made a hurried visit at Mrs Mason's. She prepared there for her wedding. On 1 November we went into that same church which was our first home in New York; and that dear old raven-man made us 'one'!

The Skeleton in the Closet

BY J. THOMAS DARRAGH (LATE C.C.S.)

This paper was first published in the Galaxy, *in 1866.*

I see that an old chum of mine is publishing bits of confidential Confederate history in *Harper's Magazine*. It would seem to be time, then, for the pivots to be disclosed on which some of the wheelwork of the last six years has been moving. The science of history, as I understand it, depends on the timely disclosure of such pivots, which are apt to be kept out of view while things are moving.

I was in the Civil Service at Richmond. Why I was there, or what I did, is nobody's affair. And I do not in this paper propose to tell how it happened that I was in New York in October 1864, on confidential business. Enough that I was there, and that it was honest business. That business done, as far as it could be with the resources entrusted to me, I prepared to return home. And thereby hangs this tale, and, as it proved, the fate of the Confederacy.

For, of course, I wanted to take presents home to my family. Very little question was there what these presents should be – for I had no boys nor brothers. The women of the Confederacy had one want, which overtopped all others. They could make coffee out of beans; pins they had from Columbus; straw hats they braided quite well with their own fair hands; snuff we could get better than you could in 'the old concern'. But we had no hoop-skirts – skeletons, we used to call them. No ingenuity had made them. No bounties had forced them. The *Bat*, the *Greyhound*, the *Deer*, the *Flora*, the *J. C. Cobb*, the *Varuna* and the *Fore-and-Aft* all took in cargoes of them for us in England. But the *Bat* and the *Deer* and the *Flora* were seized by the blockaders, the *J. C. Cobb* sunk at sea, the *Fore-and-Aft* and the *Greyhound* were set fire to by their own crews, and the *Varuna* (our *Varuna*) was never heard of. Then the State of Arkansas offered sixteen townships of swamp land to the first manufacturer who would exhibit five gross of a home-manufactured article. But no one ever competed. The first attempts, indeed, were put to an end, when Schofield crossed the Blue Lick, and destroyed the dams on Yellow Branch. The consequence was, that people's crinoline collapsed faster than the Confederacy did, of which that brute of a Grierson said there was never anything of it but the outside.

Of course, then, I put in the bottom of my new large trunk in New York, not a 'duplex elliptic', for none were then made, but a 'Belmonte', of thirty Springs, for my wife. I bought, for her more common wear, a good 'Belle-Fontaine'. For Sarah and Susy each, I got two 'Dumb-Belles'. For Aunt Eunice and Aunt Clara, maiden sisters of my wife, who lived with us after Winchester fell the fourth time, I got the 'Scotch Harebell', two of each. For my own mother I got one 'Belle of the Prairies' and one 'Invisible Combination Gossamer'. I did not forget good old Mamma Chloe and Mamma Jane. For them I got substantial `cages, without names. With these, tied in the shapes of figure eights in the bottom of my trunk, as I said, I put in an assorted cargo of dry-goods above, and, favoured by a pass, and Major Mulford's courtesy on the flag-of-truce boat, I arrived safely at Richmond before the autumn closed.

I was received at home with rapture. But when, the next morning, I opened my stores, this became rapture doubly enraptured. Words cannot tell the silent delight with which old and young, black and white, surveyed these fairy-like structures, yet unbroken and unmended.

Perennial summer reigned that autumn day in that reunited family. It reigned the next day, and the next. It would have reigned till now if the Belmontes and the other things would last as long as the advertisements declare; and, what is more, the Confederacy would have reigned till now, President Davis and General Lee! but for that great misery, which all families understand, which culminated in our great misfortune.

I was up in the cedar closet one day, looking for an old parade cap of mine, which I thought, though it was my third best, might look better than my second best, which I had worn ever since my best was lost at the Seven Pines. I say I was standing on the lower shelf of the cedar closet, when, as I stepped along in the darkness, my right foot caught in a bit of wire, my left did not give way in time, and I fell, with a small wooden hat-box in my hand, full on the floor. The corner of the hat-box struck me just below the second frontal sinus, and I fainted away.

When I came to myself I was in the blue chamber; I had vinegar on a brown paper on my forehead; the room was dark, and I found mother sitting by me, glad enough indeed to hear my voice, and to know that I knew her. It was some time before I fully understood what had happened. Then she brought me a cup of tea, and I, quite refreshed, said I must go to the office.

'Office, my child!' said she. 'Your leg is broken above the ankle; you will not move these six weeks. Where do you suppose you are?'

Till then I had no notion that it was five minutes since I went into the closet. When she told me the time, five in the afternoon, I groaned in the lowest depths. For, in my breast pocket in that innocent coat, which I could now see lying on the window-seat, were the duplicate despatches to Mr Mason, for which, late the night before, I had got the Secretary's signature. They were to go at ten that morning to Wilmington, by the Navy Department's special messenger. I had taken them to ensure care and certainty. I had worked on them till midnight, and they had not been signed till near one o'clock. Heavens and earth, and here it was five o'clock! The man must be half-way to Wilmington by this time. I sent the doctor for Lafarge, my clerk. Lafarge did his prettiest in rushing to the telegraph. But no! A freshet on the Chowan River, or a raid by Foster, or something, or nothing, had smashed the telegraph wire for that night. And before that despatch ever reached Wilmington the navy agent was in the offing in the *Sea Maid*.

'But perhaps the duplicate got through?' No, breathless reader, the duplicate did not get through. The duplicate was taken by Faucon, in the *Ino*. I saw it last week in Dr Lieber's hands, in Washington. Well, all I know is, that if the duplicate had got through, the Confederate government would have had in March a chance at eighty-three thousand two hundred and eleven muskets, which, as it was, never left Belgium. So much for my treading into that blessed piece of wire on the shelf of the cedar closet, up stairs.

'What was the bit of wire?'

Well, it was not telegraph wire. If it had been, it would have broken when it was not wanted to. Don't you know what it was? Go up in your own cedar closet, and step about in the dark, and see what brings up round your ankles. Julia, poor child, cried her eyes out about it. When I got well enough to sit up, and as soon as I could talk and plan with her, she brought down seven of these old things, antiquated Belmontes and Simplex Elliptics, and horrors without a name, and she made a pile of them in the bedroom, and asked me in the most penitent way what she should do with them.

'You can't burn them,' said she; 'fire won't touch them. If you bury them in the garden, they come up at the second raking. If you give them to the servants, they say, "Thank-e, missus," and throw them in the back passage. If you give them to the poor, they throw them into the street in front, and do not say, "Thank-e." Sarah sent seventeen over to the sword factory, and the foreman swore at the boy, and told him he would flog him within an inch of his life if he brought any more of his sauce there; and so – and so,' sobbed the poor child, 'I just rolled up these wretched things, and laid them in the cedar closet, hoping, you know, that someday the government would want something, and would advertise for them. You know what a good thing I made out of the bottle corks.'

In fact, she had sold our bottle corks for four thousand two hundred and sixteen dollars of the first issue. We afterward bought two umbrellas and a corkscrew with the money.

Well, I did not scold Julia. It was certainly no fault of hers that I was walking on the lower shelf of her cedar closet. I told her to make a parcel of the things, and the first time we went to drive I hove the whole shapeless heap into the river, without saying mass for them.

But let no man think, or no woman, that this was the end of troubles. As I look back on that winter, and on the spring of 1865 (I do not mean the steel spring), it seems to me only the beginning. I got out on crutches at last; I had the office transferred to my house, so that Lafarge and Hepburn could work there nights, and communicate with me when I could not go out; but mornings I hobbled up to the Department, and sat with the Chief, and took his orders. Ah me! shall I soon forget that damp winter morning, when we all had such hope at the office. One or two of the army fellows looked in at the window as they ran by, and we knew that they felt well; and though I would not ask Old Wick, as we had nicknamed the Chief, what was in the wind, I knew the time had come, and that the lion meant to break the net this time. I made an excuse to go home earlier than usual; rode down to the house in the Major's ambulance, I remember; and hopped in, to surprise Julia with the good news, only to find that the whole house was in that quiet uproar which shows that something bad has happened of a sudden.

'What is it, Chloe?' said I, as the old wench rushed by me with a bucket of water.

'Poor Mr George, I 'fraid he's dead, sah!'

And there he really was – dear handsome, bright George Schaff – the delight of all the nicest girls of Richmond; he lay there on Aunt Eunice's bed on the ground floor, where they had brought him in. He was not dead – and he did not die. He is making cotton in Texas now. But he looked mighty near it then. 'The deep cut in his head' was the worst I then had ever seen, and the blow confused everything. When McGregor got round, he said it was not hopeless; but we were all turned out of the room, and with one thing and another he got the boy out of the swoon, and somehow it proved his head was not broken.

No, but poor George swears to this day it were better it had been, if it could only have been broken the right way and on the right field. For that evening we heard that everything had gone wrong in the surprise. There we had been waiting for one of those early fogs, and at last the fog had come. And Jubal Early had, that morning, pushed out every man he had, that could stand; and they lay hid for three mortal hours, within I don't know how near the picket line at Fort Powhatan, only waiting for the shot which John Streight's party were to fire at Wilson's Wharf, as soon as somebody on our left centre advanced in force on the enemy's line above Turkey Island stretching across to Nansemond. I am not in the War Department, and I forget whether he was to advance *en barbette* or by *échelon* of infantry. But he was to advance somehow, and he knew how; and when he advanced, you see, that other man lower down was to rush in, and as soon as Early heard him he was to surprise Powhatan, you see; and then, if you have understood me, Grant and Butler and the whole rig of them would have been cut off from their supplies, would have had to fight a battle for which they were not prepared, with their right made into a new left, and their old left unexpectedly advanced at an oblique angle from their centre, and would not that have been the end of them?

Well, that never happened. And the reason it never happened was, that poor George Schaff, with the last fatal order for this man whose name I forget (the same who was afterward killed the day before High Bridge), undertook to save time by cutting across behind my house, from Franklin to Green Streets. You know how much time he saved – they waited all day for that order. George told me afterwards that the last thing he remembered was kissing his hand to Julia, who sat at her bedroom window. He said he thought she might be the last woman he ever saw this side of heaven. Just after that, it must have been – his horse – that white Messenger colt old Williams bred – went over like a log, and poor George was pitched fifteen feet head-foremost against a stake there was in that lot. Julia saw the whole. She rushed out with all the women, and had just brought him in when I got home. And that was the reason that the great promised combination of December 1864, never came off at all.

I walked out in the lot, after McGregor turned me out of the chamber, to see what they had done with the horse. There he lay, as dead as old Messenger himself. His neck was broken. And do you think, I looked to see what had tripped him. I supposed it was one of the boys' bandy holes. It was no such thing. The poor wretch had tangled his hind legs in one of those infernal hoop-wires that Chloe had thrown out in the piece when I gave her her new ones. Though I did not know it then, those fatal scraps of rusty steel had broken the neck that day of Robert Lee's army.

That time I made a row about it. I felt too badly to go into a passion. But before the women went to bed – they were all in the sitting-room together – I talked to them like a father. I did not swear. I had got over that for a while, in that six weeks on my back. But I did say the old wires were infernal things, and that the house and premises must be made rid of them. The aunts laughed – though I was so serious – and tipped a wink to the girls. The girls wanted to laugh but were afraid to. And then it came out that the aunts had sold their old hoops, tied as tight as they could tie them, in a great mass of rags. They had made a fortune by the sale – I am sorry to say it was in other rags, but the rags they got were new instead of old – it was a real Aladdin bargain. The new rags had blue backs, and were numbered, some as high as fifty dollars. The rag-man had been in a hurry, and had not known what made the things so heavy. I frowned at the swindle, but they said all was fair with a pedlar – and I own I was glad the things were well out of Richmond. But when I said I thought it was a mean trick, Lizzie and Sarah looked demure, and asked what in the world I would have them do with the old things. Did I expect them to walk down to the bridge themselves with great parcels to throw into the river, as I had done by Julia's? Of course it ended, as such things always do, by my taking the work on my own shoulders. I told them to tie up all they had in as small a parcel as they could, and bring them to me.

Accordingly, the next day, I found a handsome brown paper parcel, not so very large, considering, and strangely square, considering; which the minxes had put together and left on my office table. They had a great frolic over it. They had not spared red tape nor red wax. Very official it looked, indeed, and on the left-hand corner, in Sarah's boldest and most contorted hand, was written, 'Secret service'. We had a great laugh over their success. And, indeed, I should have taken it with me the next time I went down to the Tredegar, but that I happened to dine one evening with young Norton of our gallant little navy, and a very curious thing he told us.

We were talking about the disappointment of the combined land attack. I did not tell what upset poor Schaff's horse; indeed, I do not think those navy men knew the details of the disappointment. O'Brien had told me, in confidence, what I have written down probably for the first time now. But we were speaking, in a general way, of the disappointment. Norton finished his cigar rather thoughtfully, and then said – 'Well, fellows, it is not worth while to put in the newspapers, but what do you suppose upset our grand naval attack, the day the Yankee gunboats skittled down the river so handsomely?'

'Why,' said Allen, who is Norton's best-beloved friend, 'they say that you ran away from them as fast as they did from you.'

'Do they?' said Norton, grimly. 'If you say that, I'll break your head for you. Seriously, men,' continued he, 'that was a most extraordinary thing. You know I was on the ram. But why she stopped when she stopped I knew as little as this wineglass does; and Callender himself knew no more than I. We had not been hit. We were all right as a trivet for all we knew, when, skree! she began blowing off steam, and we stopped dead, and began to drift down under those batteries. Callender had to telegraph to the little *Mosquito*, or whatever Walter called his boat, and the spunky little thing ran down and got us out of the scrape. Walter did it right well; if he had had a monitor under him he could not have done better. Of course we all rushed to the engine-room. What in thunder were they at there? All they knew was they could get no water into her boiler.

'Now, fellows, this is the end of the story. As soon as the boilers cooled off they worked all right on those supply pumps. May I be hanged if they had not sucked in, somehow, a long string of yarn, and cloth, and, if you will believe me, a wire of some woman's crinoline. And that French folly of a sham *Empress* cut short that day the victory of the Confederate navy, and old Davis himself can't tell when we shall have such a chance again!'

Some of the men thought Norton lied. But I never was with him when he did not tell the truth. I did not mention, however, what I had thrown into the water the last time I had gone over to Manchester. And I changed my mind about Sarah's 'secret-service' parcel. It remained on my table.

That was the last dinner our old club had at the Spotswood, I believe. The spring came on, and the plot thickened. We did our work in the office as well as we could; I can speak for mine, and if other people – but no matter for that! The 3 April came, and the fire, and the right wing of Grant's army. I remember I was glad then that I had moved the office down to the house, for we were out of the way there. Everybody had run away from the Department; and so, when the powers that be took possession, my little sub-bureau was unmolested for some days. I improved those days as well as I could – burning carefully what was to be burned, and hiding fully what was to be hidden. One thing that happened then belongs to this story. As I was at work on the private bureau – it was really a bureau, as it happened, one I had made Aunt Eunice give up when I broke my leg – I came, to my horror, on a neat parcel of coast-survey maps of Georgia, Alabama, and Florida. They were not the same Maury stole when he left the National Observatory, but they were like them. Now I was perfectly sure that on that fatal Sunday of the flight I had sent Lafarge for these, that the President might use them, if necessary, in his escape. When I found them, I hopped out and called for Julia, and asked her if she did not remember his coming for them. 'Certainly,' she said, 'it was the first I knew of the danger. Lafarge came, asked for the key of the office, told me all was up, walked in, and in a moment was gone.'

And here, on the file of 3 April was Lafarge's line to me –

'I got the secret-service parcel myself, and have put it in the President's own hands. I marked it, "Gulf coast," as you bade me.'

What could Lafarge have given to the President? Not the soundings of Hatteras Bar. Not the working-drawings of the first monitor. I had all these under my hand. Could it be – 'Julia, what did we do with that stuff of Sarah's that she marked *secret service?*'

As I live, we had sent the girls' old hoops to the President in his flight.

And when the next day we read how he used them, and how Pritchard arrested him, we thought if he had only had the right parcel he would have found the way to Florida.

That is really the end of this memoir. But I should not have written it, but for something that happened just now on the piazza. You must know, some of us wrecks are up here at the Berkeley baths. My uncle has a place near here. Here came today John Sisson, whom I have not seen since Memminger ran and took the clerks with him. Here we had before, both the Richards brothers, the great paper men, you know, who started the Edgerly Works in Prince George's County, just after the war began. After dinner, Sisson and they met on the piazza. Queerly enough, they had never seen each other before, though they had used reams of Richards's paper in correspondence with each other, and the treasury had used tons of it in the printing of bonds and bank-bills. Of course we all fell to talking of old times – old they seem now, though it is not a year ago. 'Richards,' said Sisson at last, 'what became of that last order of ours for water-lined, pure linen governmentcallendered paper of *sureté*? We never got it, and I never knew why.'

'Did you think Kilpatrick got it?' said Richards, rather gruffly.

'None of your chaff, Richards. Just tell where the paper went, for in the loss of that lot of paper, as it proved, the bottom dropped out of the Treasury tub. On that paper was to have been printed our new issue of ten per cent, convertible, you know, and secured on that up-country cotton, which Kirby Smith had above the Big Raft. I had the printers ready for near a month waiting for that paper. The plates were really very handsome. I'll show you a proof when we go upstairs. Wholly new they were, made by some Frenchmen we got, who had worked for the Bank of France. I was so anxious to have the thing well done, that I waited three weeks for that paper, and, by Jove, I waited just too long. We never got one of the bonds off, and that was why we had no money in March.'

Richards threw his cigar away. I will not say he swore between his teeth, but he twirled his chair round, brought it down on all fours, both his elbows on his knees and his chin in both hands.

'Mr Sisson,' said he, 'if the Confederacy had lived, I would have died before I ever told what became of that order of yours. But now I have no secrets, I believe, and I care for nothing. I do not know now how it happened. We knew it was an extra nice job. And we had it on an elegant little new French Fourdrinier, which cost us more than we shall ever pay. The pretty thing ran like oil the day before. That day, I thought all the devils were in it The more power we put on the more the rollers screamed; and the less we put on, the more sulkily the jade stopped. I tried it myself everyway; back current, I tried; forward current; high feed; low feed, I tried it on old stock, I tried it on new; and, Mr Sisson, I would have made better paper in a coffee-mill! We drained off every drop of water. We washed the tubs free from size. Then my brother, there, worked all night with the machinists, taking down the frame and the rollers. You would not believe it, sir, but that little bit of wire – ' and he took out of his pocket a piece of this hateful steel, which poor I knew so well by this time – 'that little bit of wire had passed in from some hoop-skirt, passed the pickers, passed the screens, through all the troughs, up and down through what we call the lacerators, and had got itself wrought in, where, if you know a Fourdrinier machine, you may have noticed a brass ring riveted to the cross-bar, and there this cursed little knife – for you see it was a knife, by that time – had been cutting to pieces the endless wire web every time the machine was started. You lost your bonds, Mr Sisson, because some Yankee woman cheated one of my rag-men.'

On that story I came upstairs. Poor Aunt Eunice! She was the reason I got no salary on 1 April. I thought I would warn other women by writing down the story.

That fatal present of mine, in those harmless hour-glass parcels, was the ruin of the Confederate navy, army, ordnances and treasury; and it led to the capture of the poor President too.

But, Heaven be praised, no one shall say that my office did not do its duty!

Christmas Waits in Boston

FROM THE INGHAM PAPERS

When my friends of the Boston Daily Advertiser *asked me last year to contribute to their Christmas number, I was very glad to recall this scrap of Mr Ingham's memoirs.*

For in most modern Christmas stories I have observed that the rich wake up of a sudden to befriend the poor, and that the moral is educed from such compassion. The incidents in this story show, what all life shows, that the poor befriend the rich as truly as the rich the poor: that, in the Christian life, each needs all.

I have been asked a dozen times how far the story is true. Of course no such series of incidents has ever taken place in this order in four or five hours. But there is nothing told here which has not parallels perfectly fair in my experience or in that of any working minister.

I

I always give myself a Christmas present.

And on this particular year the present was a card party, which is about as good fun, all things consenting kindly, as a man can have.

Many things must consent, as will appear. First of all, there must be good sleighing; and second, a fine night for Christmas Eve. Ours are not the carollings of your poor shivering little East Angles or South Mercians, where they have to plod round afoot in countries which do not know what a sleigh-ride is.

I had asked Harry to have sixteen of the best voices in the chapel school to be trained to five or six good carols, without knowing why. We did not care to disappoint them if a February thaw setting in on 24 December should break up the spree before it began. Then I had told Howland that he must reserve for me a span of good horses, and a sleigh that I could pack sixteen small children into, tight-stowed. Howland is always good about such things, knew what the sleigh was for, having done the same in other years, and made the span four horses of his own accord, because the children would like it better, and 'it would be no difference to him'. Sunday night, as the weather nymphs ordered, the wind hauled round to the northwest and everything froze hard. Monday night, things moderated and the snow began to fall steadily – so steadily; and so Tuesday night the Metropolitan people gave up their unequal contest, all good men and angels rejoicing at their discomfiture, and only a few of the people in the very lowest *Bolgie* being ill-natured enough to grieve. And thus it was, that by Thursday evening was one hard compact roadway from Copp's Hill to the Bone-burner's Gehenna, fit for good men and angels to ride over, without jar, without noise, and without fatigue to horse or man. So it was that when I came down with Lycidas to the chapel at seven o'clock, I found Harry had gathered there his eight pretty girls and his eight jolly boys, and had them practising for the last time,

> Carol, carol, Christians,
> Carol joyfully;
> Carol for the coming
> Of Christ's nativity.

I think the children had got inkling of what was coming, or perhaps Harry had hinted it to their mothers. Certainly they were warmly dressed, and when, fifteen minutes afterwards, Howland came round himself with the sleigh, he had put in as many rugs and bear-skins as if he thought the children were to be taken new-born from their respective cradles. Great was the rejoicing as the bells of the horses rang beneath the chapel windows, and Harry did not get his last *da capo* for his last carol. Not much matter indeed, for they were perfect enough in it before midnight.

Lycidas and I tumbled in on the back seat, each with a child in his lap to keep us warm; I flanked by Sam Perry, and he by John Rich, both of the mercurial age, and therefore good to do errands. Harry was in front somewhere flanked in like wise, and the other children lay in miscellaneously between, like sardines when you have first opened the box. I had invited Lycidas, because, besides being my best friend, he is the best fellow in the world, and so deserves the best Christmas Eve can give him. Under the full moon, on the still white snow, with sixteen children at the happiest, and with the blessed memories of the best the world has ever had, there can be nothing better than two or three such hours.

'First, driver, out on Commonwealth Avenue. That will tone down the horses. Stop on the left after you have passed Fairfield Street.' So we dashed up to the front of Haliburton's palace, where he was keeping his first Christmastide. And the children, whom Harry had hushed down for a square or two, broke forth with good full voice under his strong lead in 'Shepherd of tender sheep', singing with all that unconscious pathos with which children do sing, and starting the tears in your eyes in the midst of your gladness. The instant the horses' bells stopped their voices began. In an instant more we saw Haliburton and Anna run to the window and pull up the shades, and in a minute more faces at all the windows. And so the children sang through Clement's old hymn. Little did Clement think of bells and snow, as he taught it in his Sunday school there in Alexandria. But perhaps today, as they pin up the laurels and the palm in the chapel at Alexandria, they are humming the words, not thinking of Clement more than he thought of us. As the children closed with 'Swell the triumphant song to Christ, our King', Haliburton came running out, and begged me to bring them in. But I told him, 'No', as soon as I could hush their shouts of 'Merry Christmas', that we had a long journey before us, and must not alight by the way. And the children broke out with 'Hail to the night, Hail to the day', rather a favourite – quicker and more to the childish taste perhaps than the other – and with another 'Merry Christmas' we were off again.

Off, the length of Commonwealth Avenue, to where it crosses the Brookline branch of the Mill Dam, dashing along with the gayest of the sleighing-parties as we came back into town, up Chestnut Street, through Louisburg Square; ran the sleigh into a bank on the slope of Pinckney Street in front of Walter's house; and, before they suspected there that anyone had come, the children were singing 'Carol, carol, Christians, Carol joyfully'.

Kisses flung from the window; kisses flung back from the street. 'Merry Christmas' again with a good will, and then one of the girls began, 'When Anna took the baby, And pressed his lips to hers', and all of them fell in so cheerily. O dear me! it is a scrap of old Ephrem the Syrian, if they did but know it! And when, after this, Harry would fain have driven on, because two carols at one house was the rule, how the little witches begged that they might sing just one song more there, because Mrs Alexander had been so kind to them, when she showed them about the German stitches. And then up the hill and over to the North End, and as far as we could get the horses up into Moon Court, that they might sing to the Italian image-man who gave Lucy the boy and dog in plaster, when she was sick in the spring. For the children had, you know, the choice of where they would go, and they select their best friends, and will be more apt to remember the Italian image-man than Chrysostom himself, though Chrysostom should have 'made a few remarks' to them seventeen times in the chapel. Then the Italian image-man heard for the first time in his life 'Now is the time of Christmas come', and 'Jesus in his babes abiding'.

And then we came up Hanover Street and stopped under Mr Gerry's chapel, where they were dressing the walls with their ever-greens, and gave them 'Hail to the night, Hail to the day'; and so down State Street and stopped at the *Advertiser* office, because, when the boys gave their 'Literary Entertainment', Mr Hale put in their advertisement for nothing, and up in the old attic there the composi-tors were relieved to hear 'Nor war nor battle sound', and 'The waiting world was still'; so that even the leading editor relaxed from his gravity, and the 'In General' man from his more serious views, and the *Daily* the next morning wished everybody a merry Christmas with even more unction, and resolved that in coming years it would have a supplement, large enough to contain all the good wishes. So away again to the houses of confectioners who had given the children candy – to Miss Simonds's house, because she had been so good to them in school – to the palaces of millionaires who had prayed for these children with tears if the children only knew it – to Dr Frothingham's in Summer Street, I remember, where we stopped because the Boston Association of Ministers met here – and out on Dover Street Bridge, that the poor chair-mender might hear our carols sung once more before he heard them better sung in another world where nothing needs mending.

'King of glory, king of peace!', 'Hear the song, and see the Star!', 'Welcome be thou, heavenly King!' and 'Was not Christ our Saviour?' and all the others, rang out with order or without order, breaking the hush directly as the horses' bells were stilled, thrown into the air with all the gladness of childhood, selected sometimes as Harry happened to think best for the hearers, but more often as the jubilant and uncon-trolled enthusiasm of the children bade them break out in the most joyous, least studied, and purely lyrical of all. O, we went to twenty places that night, I suppose! We went to the grandest places in Boston, and we went to the meanest. Everywhere they wished us a merry Christmas, and we them. Everywhere a little crowd gathered round us, and then we dashed away far enough to gather quite another crowd; and then back, perhaps, not sorry to double on our steps if need were, and leaving every crowd with a happy thought of 'The star, the manger, and the Child!'

At nine we brought up at my house, D Street, three doors from the corner, and the children picked their very best for Polly and my six little girls to hear, and then for the first time we let them jump out and run in. Polly had some hot oysters for them, so that the frolic was crowned with a treat. There was a Christmas cake cut into sixteen pieces, which they took home to dream upon; and then hoods and muffs on again, and by ten o'clock, or a little after, we had all the girls and all the little ones at their homes. Four of the big boys, our two flankers and Harry's right and left hand men, begged that they might stay till the last moment. They could walk back from the stable, and 'rather walk than not, indeed'. To which we assented, having gained parental permission, as we left younger sisters in their respective homes.

II

Lycidas and I both thought, as we went into these modest houses, to leave the children, to say they had been good and to wish a 'Merry Christmas' ourselves to fathers, mothers, and to guardian aunts, that the welcome of those homes was perhaps the best part of it all. Here was the great stout sailorboy whom we had not seen since he came back from sea. He was a mere child when he left our school years on years ago, for the East, on board Perry's vessel, and had been round the world. Here was brave Mrs Masury. I had not seen her since her mother died. 'Indeed, Mr Ingham, I got so used to watching then, that I cannot sleep well yet o' nights; I wish you knew some poor creature that wanted me tonight, if it were only in memory of Bethlehem.' 'You take a deal of trouble for the children,' said Campbell, as he crushed my hand in his; 'but you know they love you, and you know I would do as much for you and yours,' – which I knew was true. 'What can I send to your children?' said Dalton, who was finishing sword-blades. (Ill wind was Fort Sumter, but it blew good to poor Dalton, whom it set up in the world with his sword-factory.) 'Here's an old-fashioned tape-measure for the girl, and a Sheffield wimble for the boy. What, there is no boy? Let one of the girls have it then; it will count one more present for her.' And so he pressed his brown-paper parcel into my hand. From every house, though it were the humblest, a word of love, as sweet, in truth, as if we could have heard the voice of angels singing in the sky.

I bade Harry good-night; took Lycidas to his lodgings, and gave his wife my Christmas wishes and good-night; and, coming down to the sleigh again, gave way to the feeling which I think you will all understand, that this was not the time to stop, but just the time to begin. For the streets were stiller now, and the moon brighter than ever, if possible, and the blessings of these simple people and of the grand people, and of the very angels in heaven, who are not bound to the misery of using words when they have anything worth saying – all these wishes and blessings were round me, all the purity of the still winter night, and I didn't want to lose it all by going to bed to sleep. So I put the boys all together, where they could chatter, took one more brisk turn on the two avenues, and then, passing through Charles Street, I believe I was even thinking of Cambridge, I noticed the lights in Woodhull's house, and, seeing they were up, thought I would make Fanny a midnight call. She came to the door herself. I asked if she were waiting for Santa Claus, but saw in a moment that I must not joke with her. She said she had hoped I was her husband. In a minute was one of those contrasts which make life, life. God puts us into the world that we may try them and be tried by them. Poor Fanny's mother had been blocked up on the Springfield train as she was coming on to Christmas. The old lady had been chilled through, and was here in bed now with pneumonia. Both Fanny's children had been ailing when she came, and this morning the doctor had pronounced it scarlet fever. Fanny had not undressed herself since Monday, nor slept, I thought, in the same time. So while we had been singing carols and wishing merry Christmas, the poor child had been waiting, and hoping that her husband or Edward, both of whom were on the tramp, would find for her and bring to her the model nurse, who had not yet appeared. But at midnight this unknown sister had not arrived, nor had either of the men returned. When I rang, Fanny had hoped I was one of them. Professional paragons, dear reader, are shy of scarlet fever. I told the poor child that it was better as it was. I wrote a line for Sam Perry to take to his aunt, Mrs Masury, in which I simply said – 'Dear mamma, I have found the poor creature who wants you tonight. Come back in this carriage.' I bade him take a hack at Gates's, where they were all up waiting for the assembly to be done at Papanti's. I sent him over to Albany Street; and really as I sat there trying to soothe Fanny, it seemed to me less time than it has taken to dictate this little story about her, before Mrs Masury rang gently, and I left them, having made Fanny promise that she would consecrate the day, which at that moment was born, by trusting God, by going to bed and going to sleep, knowing that her children were in much better hands than hers. As I passed out of the hall, the gas-light fell on a print of Correggio's *Adoration*, where Woodhull had himself written years before,

Ut appareat iis qui in tenebris et umbra mortis positi sunt.

'Darkness and the shadow of death' indeed, and what light like the light and comfort such a woman as my Mary Masury brings!

And so, but for one of the accidents, as we call them, I should have dropped the boys at the corner of Dover Street, and gone home with my Christmas lesson.

But it happened, as we irreverently say – it happened as we crossed Park Square, so called from its being an irregular pentagon of which one of the sides has been taken away, that I recognised a tall man, plodding across in the snow, head down, round-shouldered, stooping forward in walking, with his right shoulder higher than his left; and by these tokens I knew Tom Coram, prince among Boston princes. Not Thomas Coram that built the Foundling Hospital, though he was of Boston too; but he was longer ago. You must look for him in Addison's contribution to a supplement to the *Spectator* – the old *Spectator*, I mean, not the Thursday *Spectator*, which is more recent. Not Thomas Coram, I say, but Tom Coram, who would build a hospital tomorrow, if you showed him the need, without waiting to die first, and always helps forward, as a prince should, whatever is princely, be it a statue at home, a school in Richmond, a newspaper in Florida, a church in Exeter, a steam-line to Liverpool, or a widow who wants a hundred dollars. I wished him a merry Christmas, and Mr Howland, by a fine instinct, drew up the horses as I spoke. Coram shook hands; and, as it seldom happens that I have an empty carriage while he is on foot, I asked him if I might not see him home. He was glad to get in. We wrapped him up with spoils of the bear, the fox, and the bison, turned the horses' heads again – five hours now since they started on this entangled errand of theirs – and gave him his ride. 'I was thinking of you at the moment,' said Coram – 'thinking of old college times, of the mystery of language as unfolded by the Abbé Faria to Edmond Dantes in the depths of the Chateau d'If. I was wondering if you could teach me Japanese, if I asked you to a Christmas dinner.' I laughed. Japan was really a novelty then, and I asked him since when he had been in correspondence with the sealed country. It seemed that their house at Shanghai had just sent across there their agents for establishing the first house in Edomo, in Japan, under the new treaty. Everything looked promising, and the beginnings were made for the branch which has since become Dot and Trevilyan there. Of this he had the first tidings in his letters by the mail of that afternoon. John Coram, his brother, had written to him, and had said that he enclosed for his amusement the Japanese bill of particulars, as it had been drawn out, on which they had founded their orders for the first assorted cargo ever to be sent from America to Edomo. Bill of particulars there was, stretching down the long tissue-paper in exquisite chirography. But by some freak of the 'total depravity of things', the translated order for the assorted cargo was not there. John Coram, in his care to fold up the Japanese writing nicely, had left on his own desk at Shanghai the more intelligible English. 'And so I must wait,' said Tom philosophically, 'till the next East India mail for my orders, certain that seven English houses have had less enthusiastic and philological correspondents than my brother.'

I said I did not see that. That I could not teach him to speak the Taghalian dialects so well that he could read them with facility before Saturday. But I could do a good deal better. Did he remember writing a note to old Jack Percival for me five years ago? No, he remembered no such thing; he knew Jack Percival, but never wrote a note to him in his life. Did he remember giving me fifty dollars, because I had taken a delicate boy, whom I was going to send to sea, and I was not quite satisfied with the government outfit? No, he did not remember that, which was not strange, for that was a thing he was doing everyday. 'Well, I don't care how much you remember, but the boy about whom you wrote to Jack Percival, for whose mother's ease of mind you provided the half-hundred, is back again – strong, straight, and well; what is more to the point, he had the whole charge of Perry's commissariat on shore at Yokohama, was honourably discharged out there, reads Japanese better than you read English; and if it will help you at all, he shall be here at your house at breakfast.' For as I spoke we stopped at Coram's door. 'Ingham,' said Coram, 'if you were not a parson, I should say you were romancing.' 'My child,' said I, 'I sometimes write a parable for the *Atlantic*; but the words of my lips are verity, as all those of the Sandemanians. Go to bed; do not even dream of the Taghalian dialects; be sure that the Japanese interpreter will breakfast with you, and the next time you are in a scrape send for the nearest minister. George, tell your brother Ezra that Mr Coram wishes him to breakfast here tomorrow morning at eight o'clock; don't forget the number, Pemberton Square, you know.' 'Yes, sir,' said George; and Thomas Coram laughed, said 'Merry Christmas'; and we parted.

It was time we were all in bed, especially these boys. But glad enough am I as I write these words that the meeting of Coram set us back that dropped-stitch in our night's journey. There was one more delay. We were sweeping by the Old State House, the boys singing again, 'Carol, carol, Christians', as we dashed along the still streets, when I caught sight of Adams Todd, and he recognised me. He had heard us singing when we were at the *Advertiser* office. Todd is an old fellow-apprentice of mine – and he is now, or rather was that night, chief pressman in the *Argus* office. I like the *Argus* people – it was there that I was South American Editor, now many years ago – and they befriend me to this hour. Todd hailed me, and once more I stopped. 'What sent you out from your warm steam-boiler?' 'Steam-boiler, indeed,' said Todd. 'Two rivets loose – steam-room full of steam – police frightened – neighbourhood in a row – and we had to put out the fire. She would have run a week without hurting a fly – only a little puff in the street sometimes. But there we are, Ingham. We shall lose the early mail as it stands. Seventy-eight tokens to be worked now.' They always talked largely of their edition at the *Argus*. Saw it with many eyes, perhaps; but this time, I am sure, Todd spoke true. I caught his idea at once. In younger and more muscular times, Todd and I had worked the Adams press by that fly-wheel for full five minutes at a time, as a test of strength; and in my mind's eye, I saw that he was printing his paper at this moment with relays of grinding stevedores. He said it was so. 'But think of it tonight,' said he. 'It is Christmas Eve, and not an Irishman to be hired, though one paid him ingots. Not a man can stand the grind ten minutes.' I knew that very well from old experience, and I thanked him inwardly for not saying 'the demnition grind', with Mantilini. 'We cannot run the press half the time,' said he; 'and the men we have are giving out now. We shall lose all our carrier delivery.' 'Todd,' said I, 'is this a night to be talking of ingots, or hiring, or losing, or gaining? When will you learn that Love rules the court, the camp, and the *Argus* office. And I wrote on the back of a letter to Campbell – 'Come to the *Argus* office, No. 2 Dassett's Alley, with seven men not afraid to work;' and I gave it to John and Sam, bade Howland take the boys to Campbell's house – walked down with Todd to his office – challenged him to take five minutes at the wheel, in memory of old times – made the tired relays laugh as they saw us take hold; and then – when I had cooled off, and put on my cardigan – met Campbell, with his seven sons of Anak, tumbling down the stairs, wondering what round of mercy the parson had found for them this time. I started home, knowing I should now have my *Argus* with my coffee.

III

And so I walked home. Better so, perhaps, after all, than in the lively sleigh, with the tinkling bells.

> It was a calm and silent night! –
>   Seven hundred years and fifty-three
> Had Rome been growing up to might,
>   And now was queen of land and sea!
> No sound was heard of clashing wars –
>   Peace brooded o'er the hushed domain;
> Apollo, Pallas, Jove, and Mars
>   Held undisturbed their ancient reign
>   In the solemn midnight,
>   Centuries ago!

What an eternity it seemed since I started with those children singing carols. Bethlehem, Nazareth, Calvary, Rome, Roman senators, Tiberius, Paul, Nero, Clement, Ephrem, Ambrose, and all the singers – Vincent de Paul, and all the loving wonder-workers, Milton and Herbert and all the carol-writers, Luther and Knox and all the prophets – what a world of people had been keeping Christmas with Sam Perry and Lycidas and Harry and me; and here were Yokohama and the Japanese, the *Daily Argus* and its ten million tokens and their readers – poor Fanny Woodhull and her sick mother there, keeping Christmas too! For a finite world, these are a good many 'waits' to be singing in one poor fellow's ears on one Christmastide.

> 'T was in the calm and silent night! –
>   The senator of haughty Rome,
> Impatient urged his chariot's flight,
>   From lordly revel, rolling home.
> Triumphal arches gleaming swell
>   His breast, with thoughts of boundless sway.
> What recked the *Roman* what befell
>   A paltry province far away,
>   In the solemn midnight,
>   Centuries ago!

Within that province far away
    Went plodding home a weary boor;
A streak of light before him lay,
    Fallen through a half-shut stable door
Across his path. He passed – for naught
    Told *what was going on within*;
How keen the stars, his only thought,
    The air how calm and cold and thin,
        In the solemn midnight,
            Centuries ago!'

'Streak of light' – Is there a light in Lycidas's room? They not in bed! That is making a night of it! Well, there are few hours of the day or night when I have not been in Lycidas's room, so I let myself in by the night-key he gave me, ran up the stairs – it is a horrid seven-storied, first-class lodging-house. For my part, I had as lief live in a steeple. Two flights I ran up, two steps at a time – I was younger then than I am now – pushed open the door which was ajar, and saw such a scene of confusion as I never saw in Mary's over-nice parlour before. Queer! I remember the first thing that I saw was wrong was a great ball of white German worsted on the floor. Her basket was upset. A great Christmas-tree lay across the rug, quite too high for the room; a large sharp-pointed Spanish clasp-knife was by it, with which they had been lopping it; there were two immense baskets of white papered presents, both upset; but what frightened me most was the centre-table. Three or four handkerchiefs on it – towels, napkins, I know not what – all brown and red and almost black with blood! I turned, heart-sick, to look into the bedroom – and I really had a sense of relief when I saw somebody. Bad enough it was, however. Lycidas, but just now so strong and well, lay pale and exhausted on the bloody bed, with the clothing removed from his right thigh and leg, while over him bent Mary and Morton. I learned afterwards that poor Lycidas, while trimming the Christmas-tree, and talking merrily with Mary and Morton – who, by good luck, had brought round his presents late, and was staying to tie on glass balls and apples – had given himself a deep and dangerous wound with the point of the unlucky knife, and had lost a great deal of blood before the haemorrhage could be controlled. Just before I entered, the stick tourniquet which Morton had improvised had slipped in poor Mary's unpractised hand, at the moment he was about to secure the bleeding artery, and the blood followed in such a gush as compelled him to give his whole attention to stopping its flow.

He only knew my entrance by the 'Ah, Mr Ingham' of the frightened Irish girl, who stood useless behind the head of the bed.

'O Fred,' said Morton, without looking up, 'I am glad you are here.'

'And what can I do for you?'

'Some whiskey – first of all.'

'There are two bottles,' said Mary, who was holding the candle – 'in the cupboard behind his dressing-glass.'

I took Bridget with me, struck a light in the dressing-room (how she blundered about the match), and found the cupboard door locked! Key doubtless in Mary's pocket – probably in pocket of 'another dress.' I did not ask. Took my own bunch, willed tremendously that my account-book drawer key should govern the lock, and it did. If it had not, I should have put my fist through the panels. Bottle of bed-bug poison; bottle marked 'Bay rum'; another bottle with no mark; two bottles of Saratoga water. 'Set them all on the floor, Bridget.' A tall bottle of Cologne. Bottle marked in MS. What in the world is it? 'Bring that candle, Bridget. "*Eau destillée*. Marron, Montreal".' What in the world did Lycidas bring distilled water from Montreal for? And then Morton's clear voice in the other room, 'As quick as you can, Fred.' 'Yes! in one moment. Put all these on the floor, Bridget.' Here they are at last. ' "Bourbon whiskey". Corkscrew, Bridget.'

'Indade, sir, and where is it?' 'Where? don't know. Run down as quick as you can, and bring it. His wife cannot leave him.' So Bridget ran, and the first I heard was the rattle as she pitched down the last six stairs of the first flight headlong. Let us hope she has not broken her leg. I meanwhile am driving a silver pronged fork into the Bourbon corks, and the blade of my own penknife on the other side.

'Now, Fred,' from George within. (We all call Morton 'George'.) 'Yes, in one moment,' I replied. Penknife blade breaks off, fork pulls right out, two crumbs of cork come with it. Will that girl never come?

I turned round; I found a goblet on the washstand; I took Lycidas's heavy clothesbrush, and knocked off the neck of the bottle. Did you ever do it, reader, with one of those pressed glass bottles they make now? It smashed like a Prince Rupert's drop in my hand, crumbled into seventy pieces – a nasty smell of whiskey on the floor – and I, holding just the hard bottom of the thing with two large spikes running worthless up into the air. But I seized the goblet, poured into it what was left in the bottom, and carried it in to Morton as quietly as I could. He bade me give Lycidas as much as he could swallow; then showed me how to substitute my thumb for his, and compress the great artery. When he was satisfied that he could trust me, he began his work again, silently; just speaking what must be said to that brave Mary, who seemed to have three hands because he needed them. When all was secure, he glanced at the ghastly white face, with beads of perspiration on the forehead and upper lip, laid his finger on the pulse, and said – 'We will have a little more whiskey. No, Mary, you are overdone already; let Fred bring it.' The truth was that poor Mary was almost as white as Lycidas. She would not faint – that was the only reason she did not – and at the moment I wondered that she did not fall. I believe George and I were both expecting it, now the excitement was over. He called her Mary and me Fred, because we were all together everyday of our lives. Bridget, you see, was still nowhere.

So I retired for my whiskey again – to attack that other bottle. George whispered quickly as I went, 'Bring enough – bring the bottle.' Did he want the bottle corked? Would that Kelt ever come upstairs? I passed the bell-rope as I went into the dressing-room, and rang as hard as I could ring. I took the other bottle, and bit steadily with my teeth at the cork, only, of course, to wrench the end of it off. George called me, and I stepped back. 'No,' said he, 'bring your whiskey.'

Mary had just rolled gently back on the floor. I went again in despair. But I heard Bridget's step this time. First flight, first passage; second flight, second passage. She ran in in triumph at length, with a *screwdriver!*

'No!' I whispered – 'no. The crooked thing you draw corks with,' and I showed her the bottle again. 'Find one somewhere and don't come back without it.' So she vanished for the second time.

'Frederic!' said Morton. I think he never called me so before. Should I risk the clothesbrush again? I opened Lycidas's own drawers – papers, boxes, everything in order – not a sign of a tool.

'Frederic!' 'Yes,' I said. But why did I say 'Yes'? 'Father of Mercy, tell me what to do.'

And my mazed eyes, dim with tears – did you ever shed tears from excitement? – fell on an old razor-strop of those days of shaving, made by C. Whittaker, Sheffield. The 'Sheffield' stood in black letters out from the rest like a vision. They make corkscrews in Sheffield too. If this Whittaker had only made a corkscrew and what is a 'Sheffield wimble'?

Hand in my pocket – brown paper parcel.

'Where are you, Frederic?' 'Yes,' said I, for the last time. Twine off! brown paper off. And I learned that the 'Sheffield wimble' was one of those things whose name you never heard before, which people sell you in Thames Tunnel, where a hoof-cleaner, a gimlet, a screwdriver, and a *corkscrew* fold into one handle.

'Yes,' said I, again. 'Pop,' said the cork. 'Bubble, bubble, bubble,' said the whiskey. Bottle in one hand, full tumbler in the other, I walked in. George poured half a tumblerful down Lycidas's throat that time. Nor do I dare say how much he poured down afterwards. I found that there was need of it, from what he said of the pulse, when it was all over. I guess Mary had some, too.

This was the turning-point. He was exceedingly weak, and we sat by him in turn through the night, giving, at short intervals, stimulants and such food as he could swallow easily; for I remember Morton was very particular not to raise his head more than we could help. But there was no real danger after this.

As we turned away from the house on Christmas morning – I to preach and he to visit his patients – he said to me, 'Did you make that whiskey?'

'No,' said I, 'but poor Dod Dalton had to furnish the corkscrew.'

And I went down to the chapel to preach. The sermon had been lying ready at home on my desk – and Polly had brought it round to me – for there had been no time for me to go from Lycidas's home to D Street and to return. There was the text, all as it was the day before –

> They helped everyone his neighbour, and everyone said to his brother, 'Be of good courage.' So the carpenter encouraged the goldsmith, and he that smootheth with the hammer him that smote the anvil.

And there were the pat illustrations, as I had finished them yesterday; of the comfort Mary Magdalen gave Joanna, the court lady; and the comfort the court lady gave Mary Magdalen, after the mediator of a new covenant had mediated between them; how Simon the Cyrenian, and Joseph of Arimathea, and the beggar Bartimeus comforted each other, gave each other strength, common force, *com-fort*, when the One Life flowed in all their veins; how on board the ship the Tent-Maker proved to be Captain, and the Centurion learned his duty from his Prisoner, and how they '*All* came safe to shore', because the New Life was there. But as I preached, I caught Frye's eye. Frye is always critical; and I said to myself, 'Frye would not take his illustrations from eighteen hundred years ago.' And I saw dear old Dod Dalton trying to keep awake, and Campbell hard asleep after trying, and Jane Masury looking round to see if her mother did not come in; and Ezra Sheppard, looking, not so much at me, as at the window beside me, as if his thoughts were the other side of the world. And I said to them all, 'O, if I could tell you, my friends, what every twelve hours of my life tells me – of the way in which woman helps woman, and man helps man, when only the ice is broken – how we are all rich so soon as we find out that we are all brothers, and how we are all in want, unless we can call at any moment for a brother's hand – then I could make you understand something, in the lives you lead everyday, of what the New Covenant, the New Commonwealth, the New Kingdom is to be.'

But I did not dare tell Dod Dalton what Campbell had been doing for Todd, nor did I dare tell Campbell by what unconscious arts old Dod had been helping Lycidas. Perhaps the sermon would have been better had I done so.

But, when we had our tree in the evening at home, I did tell all this story to Polly and the bairns, and I gave Alice her measuring-tape – precious with a spot of Lycidas's blood – and Bertha her Sheffield wimble. 'Papa,' said old Clara, who is the next child, 'all the people gave presents, did not they, as they did in the picture in your study?'

'Yes,' said I, 'though they did not all know they were giving them.'

'Why do they not give such presents every day?' said Clara.

'O child,' I said, 'it is only for thirty-six hours of the three hundred and sixty-five days, that all people remember that they are all brothers and sisters, and those are the hours that we call, therefore, Christmas Eve and Christmas Day.'

'And when they always remember it,' said Bertha, 'it will be Christmas all the time! What fun!'

'What fun, to be sure; but Clara, what is in the picture?'

'Why, an old woman has brought eggs to the baby in the manger, and an old man has brought a sheep. I suppose they all brought what they had.'

'I suppose those who came from Sharon brought roses,' said Bertha. And Alice, who is eleven, and goes to the Lincoln School, and therefore knows everything, said, 'Yes, and the Damascus people brought Damascus wimbles.'

'This is certain,' said Polly, 'that nobody tried to give a straw, but the straw if he really gave it, carried a blessing.'

Wordsworth American Library

IRVING BACHELLER
Eben Holden

AMBROSE BIERCE
Can Such Things Be?

KATE CHOPIN
The Awakening

JAMES FENIMORE COOPER
The Deerslayer

STEPHEN CRANE
The Red Badge of Courage
Maggie: A Girl of the Streets

RICHARD HENRY DANA JR
Two Years Before the Mast

FREDERICK DOUGLASS
The Life and Times of
Frederick Douglas

THEODORE DREISER
Sister Carrie

BENJAMIN FRANKLIN
Autobiography of
Benjamin Franklin

ZANE GREY
Riders of the Purple Sage

EDWARD E. HALE
The Man Without a Country

NATHANIEL HAWTHORNE
The House of the Seven Gables
The Scarlet Letter

HENRY JAMES
Washington Square
The Awkward Age

JACK LONDON
The Iron Heel
Call of the Wild/White Fang

HERMAN MELVILLE
Moby Dick

HARRIET BEECHER STOWE
Uncle Tom's Cabin

MARK TWAIN
The Man That
Corrupted Hadleyburg
The Tragedy of Pudd'nhead
Wilson

HENRY DAVID THOREAU
Walden

EDITH WHARTON
Ethan Frome
The House of Mirth

OWEN WISTER
The Virginian

WORDSWORTH DISTRIBUTION

Great Britain and Ireland
Wordsworth Editions Limited
Cumberland House, Crib Street
Ware, Hertfordshire SG12 9ET
Telephone 01920 465 167
Fax 01920 462 267

USA, Canada and Mexico
Universal Sales & Marketing Inc
230 Fifth Avenue, Suite 1212
New York, NY 10001, USA
Telephone 212-481-3500
Fax 212-481-3534

South Africa
Struik Book
Distributors (Pty) Ltd
Graph Avenue,
Montague Gardens
7441 P O Box 193 Maitland 7405
South Africa
Telephone 021-551-5900
Fax 021-551-1124

Italy
Magis Books SRL
Via Raffaello 31c
Zona ind Mancasale
42100 Reggio Emilia, Italy
Telephone 0522-920999
Fax 0522-920666

Germany, Austria and Switzerland
Swan Buch-Marketing GmbH
Goldscheuerstrabe 16
D-7640 Kehl am Rhein, Germany

Portugal
International Publishing
Services Limited
Rua da Cruz da Carreira, 4B
1100 Lisboa
Telephone 01-570051
Fax 01-352-2066

Spain
Ribera Libros S L
Poligono Martiartu, Calle 1, no 6
48480 Arrigorriaga, Vizcaya
Telephone
34-4-671-3607 (Almacen)
34-4-441-8787 (Libreria)
Fax
34-4-671-3608 (Almacen)
34-4-4418029 (Libreria)

India
Om Book Services
1690 First Floor, Nai Sarak
Delhi 110006
Telephone 327 9823– 326-5303
Fax 327-8091